BUDDIES

ALSO BY ETHAN MORDDEN

Nonfiction

Better Foot Forward: The Story of America's Musical
    Theatre
That Jazz!: An Idiosyncratic Social History of the
    American Twenties
Opera in the Twentieth Century: Sacred, Profane,
    Godot
A Guide to Orchestral Music
The Splendid Art of Opera
The American Theatre
The Hollywood Musical
Movie Star: A Look at the Women Who Made
    Hollywood
Broadway Babies: The People Who Made the
    American Musical
Smarts: The Cultural I.Q. Test
Demented: The World of the Opera Diva
Pooh's Workout Book
Opera Anecdotes

Fiction

I've a Feeling We're Not in Kansas Anymore
One Last Waltz

BUDDIES

Ethan Mordden

St. Martin's Press
New York

BUDDIES. Copyright © 1982, 1983, 1984, 1985, and 1986 by Ethan Mordden. All rights reserved. Printed in the United States of America. No part of this book may be used or reproduced in any manner whatsoever without written permission except in the case of brief quotations embodied in critical articles or reviews. For information, address St. Martin's Press, 175 Fifth Avenue, New York, N.Y. 10010.

Typeset by Fisher Composition Inc.

Library of Congress Cataloging-in-Publication Data

Mordden, Ethan
    Buddies.
    I. Title.
QS3563.07717B8   1986   813'.54   86-13788
ISBN 0-312-10686-6

First Edition

10 9 8 7 6 5 4 3 2 1

To

Chuck Ortleb

Contents

Acknowledgments

The author wishes to acknowledge the guidance and stimulation of his editor and friend, Michael Denneny, who has committed a substantial portion of his career to the nurturing of a literature for the age of Stonewall. Some years hence, when the chronicles are written, his entry in the indices will be rich.

Introduction

The French tend to write about manners, the Germans about knowledge, the English about sex. Americans write about families, gay Americans particularly. The gay writer's unique contribution to literature, the *Bildungsroman* of gathering self-awareness and coming out, is essentially a family novel; and our secondary invention, the New York camp-surreal romance, is notable for its desperate flight from the family, its attempt to reconstruct an existence without any relations but those we choose ourselves. Yet our family haunts us, like it or not, in allusions rapt and rueful. At times, all gay fiction, even (perhaps especially) porn, seems fascinated by father and brother figures, masked and idealized as passing strangers, companions, lovers.

The human need for romance, for erotic affection, is basic to storytelling. Most narrative art, from *Ulysses* to *Carousel*, from *The Sheik* to *Love's Labour's Lost*, celebrates it; and it is everywhere about us in our daily lives, in the touch of strolling couples, in scandals and wedding announcements in the newspapers, in acceptance speeches on awards nights. This is why the younger and less worldly gays are surprised when straights express irritation at the slightest public show of gay romance. Gays think there's room for everyone; most straights are willing to make room for gays on the condition that gays pretend they don't exist. Thanking one's wife for support is a convention; thanking one's male lover is a subversive act.

Yet, despite straights' lack of comprehension and outright intolerance, gays inevitably comprehend straights, because, whatever our sexuality, we all grow up within the straight culture as participators. You can be homosexual from birth, but you can't be gay unless you voluntarily enter the gay world, a culture all its own. Gays understand straights; but straights don't understand gays any more than whites understand blacks or Christians understand Jews, however good their intentions. Gay is a unique minority: strictly elective. If, called to the colors, you resist, no one may ever know who you really are.

This may be why *The New York Times* is so fanatic about terming gays "homosexuals." It's like calling blacks "niggers," calling Jews "kikes." It demotes them, questions their right to a culture. But black and Jewish separateness is inevitable; visual, aural, historical. Gays don't *have* to be gay. Denying their right to be is the act of a repressive father trying to herd errant sons back into the heritage, into the life's roles assigned them: back into the family.

So if the gay and straight worlds touch, it is only in the experiential sensibility of gays. Yet the two share one important element, a need for friendship, for nonerotic affection: for buddies. It is an American obsession, from *Moby-Dick* through *Of Mice and Men* to *The Sting*; and American gay life, in what I believe is its most compelling iconoclasm, has bettered the straight world in combining romance and friendship. One's lover is one's buddy—and who knows if the father- or brother-lover is not meant as much to eroticize one's only lifelong relationships as to soothe the less permanent relationships of one's love life: to accommodate the fierce and the tender, rivalry and alliance, at once?

This book is about these unique friendships, mostly gay ones but also some straight ones and even a few between gays and straights. Here, too, are fathers and brothers and recountings of family legends, of men in their youth, when rivalry often develops more naturally than alliance. In an earlier story collection, *I've a Feeling We're Not in Kansas Anymore,* I tried to show how gay life behaves; this time, I want to show how it feels, how it pursues its self-discovery. This book is different also on the technical level, structurally, for these are more pieces than stories, counting character studies, nostalgic recollections, and essayistic analyses as well as outright tales.

As before, my setting is New York, where gay has most thoroughly, most variously, come out. If the first will of Boston is work, the first will of San Francisco is sex, and the first will of Los Angeles is money, New York cannot choose. It needs all three at once, and so do my characters. But they need one other thing, perhaps above all: comradeship. I have known men whose need drove them to a multiplicity of sexual adventures with partners they knew as slightly as possible, and men who could communicate sexually only through a personal intensity. Men who would do anything but kiss, and men who did little else. Men who would Go With Anything and men who could only touch themselves. Yet all traveled the Circuit, treated the metropolis as their private lonely-hearts club. Sometimes I think they seek someone better than they are; sometimes I think no, they seek themselves. And sometimes the two searches are one. This is what makes our times interesting.

BUDDIES

On the Care and Training of Parents and Siblings

An introduction to the whole, in which our boy propounds his rules for growing up and coming out.

My two younger brothers have driven up from Los Angeles to visit my folks in Sacramento; I call in from the metropolis, New York. Brother Andrew is on the phone, and in the background the dogs and Mother are barking. "No, you can't make pizza!" she cries. "Get out of the refrigerator! Where did you find that revolting shirt? Your socks don't match! Wash your hair! Who left these dishes in the sink? Don't you *dare* touch that cheese—I said you cannot make pizza! The kitchen is closed! And stop that belching; I'm not one of your contemporaries, you know!"

"Guess who hasn't mellowed?" says Andrew.

Actually, she has. My dad, as a character in my childhood, was as peaceful as a Rodin, ensconced in his chair, dreaming deep in a book (whereupon we kids would hit him for advances on our allowance— by my fourteenth birthday I was overdrawn through 1997). But Mother was a series of interrogations, moralistic harangues, and grouchings. She would even attempt making corporal correction upon us (we would simply head for the dining room and run around the table until she wore out or caught my littlest brother Tony). Two less alike parents there never were. Yet they agreed on the basics: love them, give them culture, and treat them for life as if they were permanently stuck at the age of eight.

1

Parents are tyrants, even the nice ones. I recommend taking the offensive as surely and early as possible, never letting up—and my system works, for I had a reasonably cute childhood, an amusing adolescence, and a profitable teenage career. My oldest brother Ned, a vaguely Fitzgeraldian figure, made a stab at defining a code for us kids, but it wasn't a *conquering* code. It reflected too much, stuttered, yearned. A code should confront. Ned was more afraid of taking power than of suffering engulfment. Through trial and error, I trimmed his romantically elaborated novel of wistful resistance into a terse handbook whose name was *Defiance*:

Rule One: Don't try to love Them; just get along with Them. Love in families only makes for ghastly scenes that will haunt you for life.

Rule Two: Obeying Their rules only encourages Them to create new ones. *Disobey* as often as possible: for gain, for sport, for the art of it.

Corollary: Pursue the rebellion by being perversely nonconformist in all things—try, in fact, to act as if you're committing an enormity even when what you are doing is technically permissible. For instance, on the day report cards come out, you—having achieved straight A's—arrive home with your face alternating looks of shame and dread. They will pounce on your card, gloating and drooling as they dream up new and terrible punishments. Then They'll see the honorable grades, perhaps Teacher's enthusiastic commentary (". . . though he does insist on organizing chic brunches during blanket hour"), and They'll begin to blush, stutter, babble. Don't grin at Them, revealing the art of the stunt: look innocent and ever so slightly wounded. They'll avoid you in fear for days.

More quotidian possibilities include eating corn on the cob with a fork (the kernels come off in sedate little rows, which for some reason exasperates all the males at the table) and developing ersatz but noisy phobias about bridges, escalators, and religious activities of any kind.

Rule Three: Never lie. Childlike honesty throws Them completely off. Moreover, as parents are virtually made of lies (e.g., "Don't be afraid of bullies; stand up to Them and they'll run away," "If you stop crying and wait till we get home, I'll make you an apple pancake," "We have no favorites; we love you all equally"), your speaking truth undermines Their ethical position. Furthermore, lying is a sophisticated art generally beyond even the most gifted youngster. Almost any effort is doomed. And, remember: your failure is Their success. It is essential to avoid any error that will invigorate Their sense of power, and Their joy in that power. The sight of a small boy pathetically trying to worm his way out of a spanking enchants Them even more than administering the spanking itself. If you must be spanked, despoil it of all savor. Be cold and adult about it, like George Will at the dentist. Or try to look embarrassed for Them, as if you had spotted Them committing some atrocious peccadillo in a secret spot. Advanced students may want to Do the Manly Thing and insist on taking it bare-bottom. With all but the most diehard parents, this will force Them to retreat, perhaps even apologize.

Rule Four: Abjure reason and justice; only strength counts. As the tenant of a house owned by grown-ups, you are not the inhabitant of a moral universe: you live in a world populated exclusively by winners and losers. Show me a good loser, and I'll show you a loser.

Rule Five: Choose the major battles very carefully. Go to the mat over bedtime, food, and presents, major issues that will color your existence for nearly two decades. Don't overextend yourself fighting over the small things—and of course it's useful every so often to give in and let Them think They're in charge.

This was where Ned went wrong. He let Mother set policy on such vital issues as whether or not he would stay up late on Saturday nights to watch *The Gale Storm Show*, or precisely what comprised an acceptable vegetable plate, but would fall into a Gatsbyian gloom over the shade of brown in his new shoes. Romanticism is impedient in childhood; it turns one inward, toward poetry perhaps but away from power.

One must be Nietzschean. One must exercise power to gain power; and be prepared for violence. Isn't liberty worth it? True, I blush now when we all get together for viewings of our ancient home movies, when reel after reel reveals tantrums and riot: devastated birthday parties wherein I smash boxes of insulting gifts to the keening of wounded aunts; peaceful afternoons in the backyard worried by the sight of some crazed adult chasing me through the trees after a revolutionary act; festive recreation around some neighbor's pool suddenly humiliated as I push deck chairs, a chaise longue, and the local poodle into the water because the hosts were serving an inferior brand of candy bar. So: there is no glamour in power. Yet it is worth taking; one ought to win; the winner lives.

My classic seizure of power in the house was The War of the Antiques; but I hesitate to set it before my readers, for fear they might turn from me in disdain and contempt—as, indeed, many have done at our celebrated metropolitan brunches, or at predisco cocktail stations, even at one Thanksgiving I spent with my *Pooh* editor Jerrett and her friends, grown-up children of the sixties, of the Great American Generational Rebellion, and surely thus receptive to a saga of youthful insurgence. Shock of shocks, when I told my tale, the Thanksgiving guests sat silent in suppressed fury, the men brandishing their fists, knuckles white, and the women shaking their heads in dire sympathy for the enemy, Mother.

The antiques, yclept Mary Gregory, were vases, flagons, bowls, and utility pieces of every imaginable kind, made of colored glass and marked by silhouettes of children painted in white bas-relief. Mother conceived a fascination and began to collect, filling the house with Mary Gregory, floor to ceiling in every public room, or here or there, especially vulnerable, on little marble tables. After some years, Mother had cornered the market, for each piece was one of a kind, hand-crafted, the only version of itself there would ever be. Mother even became Known For Her Collection, an exciting suburban event. Impressively hefty magazines you couldn't purchase in Wilkes-Barre bore her name, our name, my name; one even sent a photographer to the house, where we all posed before a particularly bulging breakfront, never knowing that I was shortly to engage a very pungent history with Mary Gregory. A true enthusiast, Mother assembled subsidiary processions of Mary Gregory's imitators, easy to unmask, with their uncomely colors and uncouth silhouetting. It was about this time that I undertook application of Rule Five, and it seemed to me that threatening to smash whole rows of antiques might enable me to defy oppressive edicts.

Do you dare? you ask, boys and girls? I scarcely thought about it as a dare. I saw it as a dash to freedom. Remember, reader: it's winners and losers.

I don't recall the issue that sparked my first sortie, but it turned into a "No, I won't!" "Yes, you will!" contest, broken only when I moved to the nearest breakfront, placed my hand at the end of a long shelf, and proposed to shatter two bud vases, a pillbox, three cigarette holders, a stationery chestlet, a mail caddy, six barony cups, a mirror case, a matchbook trunk, and an animal bank (Mother said it was a napping cow, but it looked like a deranged yak taking a whizz) if I didn't have my way.

Mother refused to give in and made a grab at me; foolish Mother—she knew me better than that. The ensuing crashes brought the entire family in, and the thunder was fierce. Yet I was already at another shelf, threatening, threatening. There were a few such episodes, but at length Mother had to surrender, for if I needed to I would gamely have raged through the entire Collection, and she knew it. Oddly, one piece I had had my eye on for some time ultimately eluded me: Grandpa busted that one (by accident, but then everything grandparents do is by accident). This piece was a gigantis egg, silhouetted to death and revealing, when opened, a miniature decanter and eight tiny toasting glasses. It was so spectacular—Mother said that Mary Gregory aficionados considered it the climax of the line—that we had never used it. Yet, with a sweep of his hand, inveighing in some political context, her father dashed it to the floor. The egg was so complex an architecture that the breaking noises went on for some little time, and serially, like the minuet movement in a twelve-tone suite. First, the egg itself went *crash*. Then the decanter and a glass went *floink, dizzle, kinkle*. Then the bracings gave and the egg's outer surfaces diminished into crystal sneezes. At last the remaining glasses gave up, each with its own *kmlip*. Mother was holding me in despair: for only I, of all, knew what she was giving up.

I believe it's that last aperçu, of the two hostiles pledging sorrowful complicity, that sets everyone off. Oh, it's *too* much! Why was I not punished, beaten down, chained, imprisoned? We just didn't have that kind of family. And look on the bright side: by partitioning the collection I at least drove the price up on all Mary Gregory, thereby heavily reendowing the surviving pieces.

Naturally, such exploits are designed for large families like mine, wherein the sizable cast of characters crowds the days with incident. It helps especially if one's brothers get into trouble by themselves; this deflects attention from one's own eccentricities. Andrew, for instance, was always losing things—hats, lunchboxes, pencil cases, a galosh. Once he came home on a rainy day missing the hood of his slicker, and it wasn't even detachable. Mother raged. "*Why* did you lose your hood?" she kept asking. "I want to know *why*!"

Years later, he and I reviewed the event, and he pointed out how senseless these questions were. "It was an accident," he insisted. "There is no 'why.' It just happened."

"It doesn't just happen that you lose a raincoat hood that doesn't come off," I told him. "That's like losing a leg of your pants. You *did* something to it."

"Well, what about the other times? 'Why did you lose your hat? Why did you lose your gloves?' That's like asking 'Why did you get cancer?'"

The foolish boy; one must interpret. "She didn't mean 'Why did you lose your hat?'" I explain. "She meant, 'Stop losing things, you sordid fool.'"

Actually, Andrew sometimes got into scrapes that made my antique wars look like a scuffle over dominoes. A favorite example in the family is the Celebrated Pizza Incident, the most notable event of the year we spent in Venice. In the square dominated by La Fenice, the opera house, there was a trattoria with outdoor tables that served the most exquisite little pizzas to order, and, as Piazza la Fenice stood on our walk home from the Danieli boat that took us, that summer, from the Lido back to town, we became familiars of the place—Andrew in particular. He is, without question, an outstanding amateur of proletarian junk food. He would babble in his sleep, and—aside from an occasional romantic confession—the burden of his nocturnal text was "Pizza and hamburgers," repeated over and over, sometimes for an hour. Naturally, he became the most intent of us all on afternoon pizza breaks. Sometimes Mother would agree, sometimes not. One certain day, Andrew demanded, and Mother resisted. Tomorrow, she said.

But tomorrow she was too tired. The next day.

The next day she had a headache. Another time.

No. Andrew would not budge, and the rest of us stopped to wait. There were rules about such things, at any rate a custom. One remained neutral, no more than a witness. (This suggests a corollary to Rule Five: Don't take on your siblings' battles. You have enough to do winning your own.)

"You said *today*," Andrew insisted, his head bucking as if for attack.

"I have a *headache* today," said Mother, rather dangerously.

Ned shot me a look reading, "This is not suave"—his fiercest condemnation. But Jim shot me a look reading, "Let's see how it comes out"—for nothing failed to amuse him.

This is how it came out: Mother solemnly promised that we would have pizza tomorrow, no matter what. Not today, but—*absolutely*—tomorrow. Andrew accepted this and home we went, over the Accademia Bridge and around the corners to 127 Rio Terra dei Catecumeni. But on the way, I told Jim I was a touch worried about the grade of commitment in Mother's promise. He said, "So what? It's not about us, is it?" This is the converse of the corollary to Rule Five: Don't count siblings as allies.

Anyway, the next day, when the moment came, Mother decided it was too late, too hot, and too nervous for pizza; perhaps she resented being boxed in by a promise. Or who knows what was happening?—

but Andrew had her by the contract and would not yield. "You promised," he kept saying. "You *promised*." As we others stood around, the two of them debated it, Andrew (about ten years old then), staunch and stony, shaking with righteousness. She had put him off for days. She had left her promise. He *must* collect.

"All *right!*" Mother roared, leading us to a table. "I'll show you! Yes! Yes! I'll show you promise! Yes, *promise!*"

We ordered in an atmosphere laden with airs of betrayal and counterbetrayal. But the pizzas came, hot as hell, and Andrew, forking his in a hell-for-leather escapism, accidentally flipped it up into the air and down onto his lap.

"*So!*" Mother cried. "*Now* you see! *Now* you'll learn! When I say *no*, it's *no*. But you insist, do you? *So!* God hears us. God *sees!* And God will make punishment! *Yes!*"

The hot cheese was eating right through Andrew's shorts; in fact, steam was rising in their color, and he looked as if he were in shock. Ned was regarding the façade of La Fenice as if moved to poeticize, and Tony had begun to eat his pizza. Jim simply got up, smacked the food off of Andrew's lap with a napkin, pulled his pants off, and tossed our cold drinks at his flesh.

Andrew lived. But he glowers, even rages, when this classic tale is retold. Brothers were born to glower. You can make peace with parents eventually, but only somewhat with brothers. Actually, if possible it's best to keep sibling combat to a minimum. Why spend energy on your fellow oppressed when the true war impends with the authorities? Besides, one should maintain diplomatic relations with one's brothers for later years, when they come in handy for lending money, showing up at Christmas so you won't have to, and serving as models for villains in one's fiction.

I must admit I slipped here. Fighting with my brothers was irresistible, as stimulating as a Crusade. Unfortunately, as the middle child, I had the natural military advantage only over my two younger brothers; and one's more instructive battles tend upward, in audacity: against older ones. Actually, Ned ignored me—he ignored the entire family and finally ran off to Europe without saying "May I?" and became a reporter for the Paris *Herald-Tribune*. But Jim and I were born to battle. He was only a year older than I, counting in years, but had a good decade on me in smarts. Some of his wisdom he passed along to me in an alternative handbook, *On the Care and Training of the Entire World*, with such rules as "Never let anyone know what you're thinking, but make sure they hear what you say." He was a cool number, distantly polite when my folks were around, by turns contemptuous or confidential with his siblings, slow to move but fast as the devil when he pounced: an enigma that looked you in the eye. I suppose that, given our respective natures, Jim and I could not have avoided confrontation. He liked a peaceful house, running smoothly on the theory that you verbally gave in to your parents in anything they they wanted; then unobtrusively, off the record, did as you liked.

Under public scrutiny, he was a David Copperfield, perhaps a reformed Huckleberry Finn; back on the third floor, where we kids lived, he was John Dillinger. My rebellion irritated him; smashing antiques and making provocative statements, he warned me, would "bring heat down on the whole compound." But I could not submit to his two-faced system. I liked the clarity of honest insurrection. My way to freedom had a Tolstoyan éclat; Jim's reptilian accommodations seemed very downtown, mean-streets, like the little white lies working-class men tell their wives when they come home late. He was pragmatic, I symbolistic. So he stepped in, to pacify me and relieve the agitation, and I found myself fighting something of a two-front war.

At least all this violence prepared me for life in New York. Long before I heard about mugging, I experienced it, in The Attack of the Moon Mice, a ritual of seek-and-destroy that Andrew and Tony concocted under the influence of horror movies, psychodrama, and Saturday morning cartoon shows. Starting in the bedroom they shared, they would crawl through the house, gnawing the ankles of any human who happened by and chanting their louche anthem, which ran, in its entirety, "*We* are the *moon* mice/We *grunch* all your *stuff*!"

Reaching my room, they would crash in, snapping their jaws and trashing everything they could get ahold of before I could repel them and institute Draconian retribution. Of course they would go right for the Oz books, the records, and everything else I most valued. Worse yet, the moon mice would attack even when I wasn't around to defend my treasures.

Once I came home late from soccer practice, exhausted and exasperated. (I know soccer is in nowadays, but in my day it was the fag sport. However, Friends Academy had no gym class. Everybody had to be on some team or other, and the only alternative, football, seemed lurid and bogus.) As I dropped my books on the kitchen table and sank into a chair I heard, in the remote distance, cries of "Grunch his puppet theatre! Grunch his theatre posters!", the unmistakable noises of a moon mice raid. Roaring "I'll murder you alive!", I hurtled through the house to my room. It was a shambles, but deserted. Had they fled? Were they hiding? I sensed a presence . . . the closet! Fools, you have trapped yourselves. Gloating at the thought of chopping them into messes, I grabbed for the closet door. It held fast. I pulled, I tugged, I turned. No! They had locked themselves in from the inside. Damn, these crazy old houses.

"Come out of there, you cretins, and take your deserts!" I shouted.

Silence.

"I know you're in there."

Nothing.

"I'm going to get you if I have to rip that door off with my bare hands."

Whispers.

"If you don't come out by the count of three—"

The closet exploded in a hail of coats, headgear, shoes, games, and books, and out poured the moon mice in full cry. "Grunch his room!" they caroled, as I struggled to catch them. "Grunch his desk! Pull out the drawers!" Andrew exulted. "Pee in his bed," advised Tony. The things they think of.

I don't remember how this episode finished; there were so many of them. Did I punish them for six days and six nights when I was twelve, or for twelve days and twelve nights when I was six? Was I harsh? Mother says I became a writer solely to sentimentalize a vicious past, to cast myself as an innocent trying to get along. Yet consider what I was up against. It was not only moon mice raids and the battles over bedtime, never finally won—for, like evil Sauron of Middle Earth, parents may at times retreat but will never give in. It was the totalitarian climate of the American family in general, the tenderness applied as blackmail, the mischievousness expressed as "concern." It was the simple day-to-day madness of intimate strangers experimenting on one another. By day Andrew might be Tony's ally; after dark he would join up with me in the kitchen, where Tony, the world's foremost aficionado of presweetened breakfast cereals, would in advance of the morning have laid out a bowl, filled it with Sugar Jets or such, and arranged the box at an angle conducive to breakfast reading. Andrew and I would look upon this egregious decadence holding our noses, then, with delicacy, would each drop a dollop of spit into the bowl.

Don't look away, reader; for a wise man, asked what were the three most powerful forces in the world, answered, "the revenge of fathers, the suffering of mothers, and the guilt of brothers." To which I would add a fourth, the memorable vehemence of a mother whose kitchen has been violated. Eager to free herself of having to make lunches for her little men, Mother taught us all how to make bacon and eggs. On the other hand, our pottering around in the kitchen—anywhere in the house, really—made her nervous. She was only content when we were asleep or away. One day, I was fixing myself lunch while the maid, Mildred, sat to a cup of coffee, muttering gospel to herself. Confidently juggling the toast, the pans, the bowl, and so on, I poured the boiling bacon fat into the great American coffee tin with one hand while I broke the eggs open with the other. Too confidently. Fastening the plastic lid on the tin, I lost my grip and plunged my hand into the fat, yanking it out to see layer after layer of skin calmly peeling away. The pain was so terrible I couldn't say anything, just stood there hypnotized. You could die in a kitchen, I thought. Mildred screamed and Mother came raging in. In silent horror, I showed her my wound. The damn thing was actually smoking.

"He burned his hand in the bacon fat!" Mildred wailed.

Mother looked at it in cold fury. "And who," she asked, "told you to make bacon?"

The suffering of mothers! To this day, when I hear the word "bacon" I can smell my hand cooking—and, as with Andrew and the Celebrated Pizza Incident, I fail to smile when someone reminisces in this territory.

The pressure did not let up as the years went on. On the contrary, as I neared the end of my high-school period, I was expected to take up the duties of man's estate—to wit, a summer job. The only jobs available in summers on Long Island, whither we had moved, were bagging groceries and pumping gas. Of course I refused. I had just got my driver's license and a motorcycle, and looked forward to idling away the days with my school chums. What was the point of belonging to the upper middle class if you had to waste a vacation laboring tediously for a minimum wage? Here we see Rule Five in its most practical application: this was a major battle.

How to proceed? The devil in me longed for an all-out offensive, but wisdom advised me to whittle them down, bargain, stall. We skirmished. "Next week," I assured them, then the week after that. "Now," they said—or no allowance. Fine. My comrades had wheels, so they picked me up and we passed the time at each other's houses. Who needed money? Anyway, I had a huge collection of rare opera scores, and could always sell off the duller ones, or those irreparably grunched by the moon mice, to used music dealers. It was delicious seeing my parents fume, frustrated by their own law; nothing incenses them more than a cure that doesn't take.

Finally they pulled out their ace, never before played in our lifelong game: "Get a job or move out."

I moved out. No forwarding address, no farewell, nothing. My father went into a panic, my older brothers shrugged, Andrew and Tony danced a jig and, as the moon mice, held solemn festival in my room. But Mother stormed through the house inveighing against my mutinous wickedness. "No more breakfast in bed for *him*! It's a new regime!" This was her theme song whenever one of us was in trouble, though we had never had, or wanted, breakfast in bed. The very notion appalls me—toast crumbs everywhere and jam all over the sheets. That Mother would make a mantra out of a notion that didn't even apply to the local scene reveals another convention of the parent, the stock retort. (Others in the repertory: "We nurtured you!," "Because I said so, that's why!," and, my personal favorite, "Every day is children's day.")

Naturally I reestablished myself in the family in due course. But I exacted heavy peace terms, including an immediate cash settlement and the promise that this nonsense about a summer job would be decked for life. Mother, when she heard, went into turbulent despair, like the melodrama character who cries out "Foiled again!" And I never did tell them where I had gone, nor ever will. But something interesting happened to me while I was away, and this much I will tell.

I had gone to Manhattan on a lark, yet for a purpose. This was the mid-1960s, before gay had asserted its style, and there were intriguing mysteries in the air, enigmatic looks from strangers as they passed, the sensation of belonging to a club so secret it hadn't yet held its first meeting. I had the feeling that to explode this mystery would be a major rite of passage in my life, the next thing to do now that I was on the edge of leaving home for college and the great world. My day trip to Manhattan, then, was by way of sifting and watching. I sold off a few scores, strolled here and there, and paid a visit to one of my choice haunts, a huge store on the west side of Sixth Avenue in the low forties, now long vanished, that sold old magazines of every kind. It was a grand place, where one could browse for hours as if in a library, and where two dollars netted one a week's elite reading. That these "back-date" parlors were in fact the early equivalent of the porno shop never entered my mind. They were stocked mainly with *Theatre Arts, Popular Mechanics, Life, The New Republic,* and the like; and I thought these were their intended ware. Actually, the respectable titles were simply a front for the skin magazines, which—in a time when *Playboy* was still considered daring—I ignored.

But while paging through an old *Opera News,* I found hidden inside it another magazine, called *Physique Pictorial* and filled with the opulent beefcake drawings that I later learned to be the work of that arbiter of classic gay type, Tom of Finland: men in cowboy hats lounging by the corral, men in (and promptly out of) leather, lumberjacks, lifeguards, hitchhikers, hustlers. I feasted my eyes. I had heard of this, or imagined it, but had never been there.

"So you've found Griselda's secret file. She loves to look, but she's afraid to be seen. Isn't she silly?"

I looked up, and there was this tall, thin, fortyish, effeminate man, arms folded and fingers twitching. I think he worked in the store.

"We call him Griselda," he went on. "His real name's probably Joe, and he thinks he's fooling the world, reading trash behind the cover of *Opera News.*" He peered over my shoulder at the drawings. "Oo, look at that one. Do you know Griselda?"

I shook my head.

"He comes in all the time. Poor thing. She's quite talkative, too. Tells me all about his wife and his little girl. I hope you're shocked. *I* am. Poor Griselda's such a mess—everything happens to her. Her car breaks down, her little girl wears braces, her transvestite balls keep getting raided. She's all upset now because she has to have a colostomy operation—and she's afraid she won't be able to find shoes to match the bag!"

He bustled away, and I noticed a pleasant-looking fellow about my age across the table from me, who had been looking through *The Illustrated London News.* He seemed as bemused as I was by what had just happened. Suddenly, we both smiled.

"What was in that magazine?" he asked.

I held up the secret.

He nodded. "Griselda," he said, savoring it.

"I hear his real name's probably Joe."

He laughed. "What's your real name?"

"Dorinda," said the effeminate man, dancing by us. "Am I right?"

Now I laughed.

"And you're Samantha," he told the *London News*. "You know you must have a name that your lover can whisper to you like music. You *know*."

"Frank," said the *London News* to me, with a smile.

"Bud," I said, as we shook hands.

"Frank! Bud!" the effeminate man cried. "Oh, my goodness gracious, it's the Garden City Little League!" Nevertheless, the first meeting of my chapter of the club had come to order. For till that moment I had thought of gay life as a choice of Griselda or *Physique Pictorial* cowboys. It was neither—these are the fantasies of gay. Gay naturalism was Little Leaguers with real names and good manners. Gay was . . . possible, legitimate, a reflection of oneself. Returning to the family nest, I sadly realized that the war would be winding down at home, its great issues dwindled into a nostalgia, into quaint farces flickering through the home-movie projector. Now I reckoned the final entry in the handbook, Rule Six: Self-knowledge is the final power. And I came home ready to leave it.

I have always figured that my family was more or less like others, but the looks of horror my associates give off when we trade childhood anecdotes suggests otherwise. "You did *what* into your little brother's cereal bowl?" they howl. Replying, "Of course, didn't you?" makes it worse. First they're repulsed, then they're insulted. But, mark me, all of them now maintain extremely conflicted relationships with their folks, while my parents and I get on famously. Even my two younger brothers and I, after all that scrapping, get along. (I haven't crossed paths with the two older ones in quite some time now; I believe that trying to accept one's older brothers after adolescence is psychologically unsound, perhaps masochistic, not unlike keeping one's cast-off lovers in spare bedrooms.)

Younger brothers are vastly easier to handle than older, though they do grow up and shed their vulnerability. Tony is now in computers and Andrew took up weight lifting, went into business, and became generally impossible to push around, even arrogant. I think I liked him better as a moon mouse. Nor does he approve of my cataloguing our past in these pages. After reading one, he said, "You should be locked up!"—I wonder if he knows why. Mother thinks these pieces would read better if I didn't keep trying to slip touching incidents into them. Ours was a crisp family, no sentiment, except for my dad. His idea of family is like a TV Christmas special, in which six or seven grown-up, married offspring congregate at the manse with recriminations, wonder, outcry, two dozen grandchildren, and, at the fade, embraces and joy.

But our real-live Christmases are like "The People's Court": strict, neat, plain, at times grimly rowdy, and always somebody not getting what he wants. Mother set the tone for the household, but Mother lost all the wars. She dreamed of children tucked into their beds by nightfall, but, came the wee hours, there I was before the TV, taking in Ann Sothern in *Lady in the Dark*, or Rosalind Russell in *Wonderful Town*, or some other unmissable proposition for which I was willing to die. The *Mommie Dearest* movie stirred Mother: *there* was a parent who knew how to express authority. Mother didn't like the business with the hangers—it was sloppy, uncrisp—but the scene in which little Christine refuses to eat a blood-red steak and is not released from the table till she does eat it thrilled Mother. She talked of it for days, and I could see her thinking how different her life might have been if she had instituted such procedures early enough.

I was ready for it long before it came. "I wish," she said at last, "that you had had Joan Crawford for your mother."

"I did," I answered.

She laughed. She's a good sport.

Hardhats

In which we start with an impressionistic study and end with a story.

As the son of a builder I spent high-school spring vacations on various construction sites in and around New York. It was my first experience of absolutely impenetrable men, not only tough but emotionally invulnerable. Ironworkers—the men who lay a building's steel skeleton—are a class unto themselves. Passing someone while carrying a load of material, they don't say, "Excuse me," but "Get the fuck out of my way"—yet they say it in the tone Edmund White would use for "Excuse me." Challenged by their own kind, they can be vivacious; challenged by an alien, they are fast and lethal.

It's an intolerant class, racist, sexist, fascistic yet patriotic about a democracy; almost the only place to see the flag these days, besides outside federal agencies, is on the trucks serving construction sites. (They also mount a flag atop each building as the last girder is placed, as if they had climbed rather than built a mountain.) Ironworkers are not merely proletarians; they are proletarians without the barest internal contradictions, without ambition, pull, or PR. They are the cowboys of the city, skilled workers who are also vagabonds with nothing to lose. They have one of the toughest jobs in America: exhausting, permanently subject to layoff, and extremely dangerous. The raising of office towers routinely claims a life or two. At least bridgework is worse. The Whitestone Bridge was regarded as a life-sparing marvel because only thirty-five men were lost on it.

There is one major contradiction in the ironworker, his endless enthusiasm for street courtship. What other set of Don Juans ever went out so unromantically styled?—casually groomed, tactlessly dressed, unimaginatively verbal? "Got a cookie for me, honey?" they will utter as a woman strolls by. Of course she ignores them; it wouldn't get you far in the Ramrod, either. Sometimes a group of them will clap and whistle for a ten, and I've seen women with a sporty sense of humor wave in acknowledgment. But there the rapport ends.

So why do they keep at it? Has one of them ever—in the entire history of architecture from Stonehenge to the present—made a single woman on the street? There are the occasional groupies, true: a few days ago I saw a young woman with an intense air of the bimbo about her waiting outside the site next to my apartment building just before quitting time with a camera in her hands. But this is the kind of woman these men have access to anyway, not least in the neigh-borhood bars where they cruise for a "hit." The ladies of fashion who freeze out these lunch-break inquiries are a race of person these men will never contact. After all, women like being met, not picked up, especially not on the street.

One of the workers next door eats his lunch sitting on the sidewalk in front of my building. Men he discounts or glares at; women he violates in a grin. The pretty ones get a hello. I was heading home from the grocery when I saw a smashing Bloomingdale's type treat his greeting to a look of such dread scorn that, flashed in Ty's, it would have sent the entire bar into the hospital with rejection breakdowns. But the ironworker keeps grinning as she storms on; "Have a nice day!" he urges. Emotionally invulnerable, I tell you. Yet are they really trying to pick these women up—sitting on the ground in a kind of visual metaphor of the plebeian, chomping on a sandwich while ladling out ten or twelve obscenities per sentence? This ironworker at my building is young, handsome, and clean-cut; still, he's riffraff. Sex is class.

When I started working on my dad's sites, I saw these men not as a social entity but as ethnicities and professions. There were Italians, Poles, Portuguese, and the Irish, each with a signature accent. There were carpenters, electricians, cement people, and the ironworkers themselves, the center of the business, either setters (who guide the girders into their moorings) or bolters (who fasten them). They were quiet around my brothers and me, not respectful but not unpleasant, either. We were, as they term beginners, "punks." Still, we were the boss' punks.

My older brother Jim fit in easily with them and my younger brother Andrew somewhat admired them; I found them unnervingly unpredictable. They were forever dropping their pants or socking each other. They'd ignore you all day from a distance of two feet, then suddenly come over and bellow a chorus of "Tie a Yellow Ribbon Round the Old Oak Tree" about two inches from your nose. Surpassingly uncultured, they were nimble conversationalists, each with his unique idioms, jokes, passwords. One might almost call them sociable but for their ferocious sense of kind, of belonging to something that by its very nature had to—but also by its simple willfulness wanted to—exclude everyone who wasn't of the brotherhood. Their sense of loyalty was astonishing—loyalty to their work, their friends, their people. Offend that loyalty and you confronted Major War.

Most of them were huge, the mesomorph physiques expanding with the labor over the years so that even fat wrecks sported gigantic muscles under the flab. Strangely, ironworkers don't throw their weight around, don't try to characterize themselves the way gay Attitude Hunks so often do. Ironworkers don't care whether you're impressed with them or not: they are what they are. *They're* impressed. And just when you think you've figured them out, they'll pull a twist on you. My dad built the Louisiana pavilion at the 1962 World's Fair, an evocation of "Bourbon Street," and one of the setting crew, a tall, silent Irish guy who drank literally from start to finish of every day, impressed me as being the meanest bastard on the site. "Hey, you," he said to me, on my first hour on the job, "what the *fuck* are you *doing*?" I had been sorting material so bizarre I don't think it has a name, and I said as much. He stared at my mouth for a moment, then said, "Fuck *you* and fuck your *college*." I avoided him as much as was possible. And it happened that one day, some weeks later, the wind blew a speck of dirt into my eye while I was on the roof, and before I could do anything about it, he had come over, pulled out the bandanna they all carry, and was cleaning out my eye with the most amazing tenderness. "Okay?" he asked. It was, now. "Thanks," I said. He nodded, went back to what he was doing, and never spoke to me again.

The younger ironworkers had a certain flash and drove dashing cars, but my dad warned us not to take them as role models; they spent their evenings getting drunk and came home to beat their wives when they came home at all.

"Is that what you want to be?" he asked us grimly.

"Yeah," said Andrew.

The superintendents on these various jobs were supposed to keep an eye on us lest we get into trouble, but they seemed to delight in posing us atrocious tasks, such as climbing rickety, forty-foot ladders on wild-goose chases. Sometimes they'd give us a lift home, whereupon we'd be treated to an analysis of the social contours of the business: "Doze Italians, now, all dey wanna do is make fires. De niggers are lazy good-for-nothings." And so on. Once, on lunch break, Andrew told my dad about this. "That idiot," was my dad's comment. "Look," said Andrew, pointing to a group of Italians who had just made a pointless little fire so they could watch it go out.

Unlike the rest of us, Jim stayed with it. After a year of Rutgers he abandoned college forever and joined the ironworkers' union, an unthinkable act for a building contractor's son, virtually a patricidal betrayal of class. Yet I doubt he could have gotten his union book without my dad's assistance; the building trade is harder to get into than a child-proof aspirin bottle. By the time I reached New York he was living in Manhattan. We ended up a few blocks from each other in the east fifties, and tentatively reconvened the relationship. My dad's "Is that what you want to be?" ran through my head when I first visited Jim's apartment, nothing you'd expect from a birthright member of the middle class. It was somehow blank and gaudy at once, rather like a pussy wagon with walls. Mae West, reincarnated as a blind lesbian, might have lived there. No, I'm giving it too much texture. It was the house of a man whose image of sensuality was a nude photograph of himself, his torso turned to the side to display a tattoo of two crossed swords. The photograph hung on his wall, and when I saw it I said, "If that thing on your arm is real, you'd better not let Mother see it." He pulled off his shirt, smiling. It was real.

"Girls like a breezy man, sport," he told me. No one else in my family talks like him.

I don't understand this craze for tattoos among working-class men. Permanently disfiguring oneself falls in with that hopeless flirting with inaccessible women and other self-delusory acts of the reckless straight. At least Jim's tattoo was high up on the arm, easily hidden even in a T-shirt; his pal Gene Caputo had a tattoo on each biceps, forearm, and thigh. Colored ones, no less—snakes and eagles and murder and paranoia. Socially, Gene had one topic, "layfuck." For the first three beers and two joints, he would expound on the attracting of "my woman." Four beers and another joint along, he would outline the various methods of layfucking them. By the eighteenth beer, he'd get into how to dispose of them. Then he'd pass out wherever he happened to be.

Plenty of ironworkers are happily familied, jovial, and intelligent. I even knew one who was—on the quiet—a Dickens buff. But it is not a settled life: the work wanders, the schedule is erratic, the weather can freeze you, boil you. It's not for anyone who has the chance to do something better. So ironworkers tend to be roughnecks—and in this Gene was the essential ironworker. He was a fabulously uninhibited slob. He was also one of the largest men I've known. The flow of beer bloated him a bit, but he had something like six shoulders and a chest that could cross the street. A good man to have on your side, if you've got to be in the war.

He was hard company, the sort who expresses his *joie de vivre* by putting headlocks on you. He also laced his endearments with threats of sexual attack, a typical ironworker anarchism. When I asked him to stop mauling me, or do it more gently, he said, "I could screw your butt. Would that be gentle enough for you?" Of course, one doesn't take any of this literally. They like to shake up the taboos. Jim would say, "I don't know why I'm so exhausted," and Gene would reply, "Because I was fucking you all night and now your fucking asshole's all sore." Imperturbable Jim would observe, "Yeah, that might be it," and they'd proceed to other matters. After a number of these outbursts, I began to wonder if something genuine might be pouring out of Gene.

He was often at Jim's when I was, elaborating his theory of layfucking, and, out of loyalty to Jim, would attempt to draw me into his philosophy. Or perhaps it was just because I was there; perhaps he would have polled Eleanor Roosevelt for the dos and don'ts of layfuck had she had been in the room. He would be deep in depiction of a pickup, acting out the parts, even filling in for passersby who, he once said, were "huffy and out of date." Then, he told us, tensing, showing us how it felt, "My woman spots this briefcase dude and she is traveling. She is traveling away." Now he showed us Rodin's *The Thinker*. "But what she don't know is, see, those guys in suits don't spend money on my woman like an ironworker does! Am I wrong or what?"

"You're right, my man Gene," says Jim; and I'm trying to figure out where all this lingo comes from.

"What about you?" says Gene, to me.

"What about *what* me?" I respond, trying to look about six foot eight.

"What do you think of my woman dodging me like so?"

I took up my beer can, swirled the liquor thoughtfully, and offered,

"I read that as an uncanny act on the part of my woman." Had I made it, passed? Jim was nodding, but Gene was just looking at me. I looked back.

His face a puzzle, Gene asked me, "So like tell us why you didn't join the union like Jimbo here."

"Jim already knows," I said, backpedaling.

"So me."

"The punk's a writer," Jim put in.

"What kind?" asked Gene, his brow clouding. "Novels, fiction, stories?"

"All of the above," I answered, for they already *were* all of the above.

Gene looked dire.

"Fuck me and fuck my college," I said. "Right?"

"How come you could have joined the union and instead you're being a writer?"

"Well," I said, "every family has its black sheep."

Gene looked over at Jim, digesting this comic flattery, and I believed I had scored the point. But there was one more test.

"So tell us," said Gene, "some of your unique procedures in the enticing of my woman."

Jim smiled. I hadn't told him I was gay, but brothers always know. Sometimes they care; not Jim. Gay neither irritated nor interested him. It was like water polo or raising sheep: someone else's fucking problem.

As it happens, I am bent toward the analytic. I love codes, theories, lists. So, despite our differences, I easily fell in with Gene's taxonomy, following—and sometimes leading—him into theoretical situations calling for the most finely honed expertise in layfucking. And I laid one concept in particular on him that struck vastly home: the wearing of shirts with a college insigne, I had noticed, encourages people to talk to you. "It's a mark of class," I concluded. "Especially if it's a snappy college."

Gene thought it over. "Girls like college, don't they?"

"They admire a college man."

"Yeah," said Gene, slowly. "I could be the fucking football hero."

Well, rougher men than Gene have attended school on jock scholarships. Jim remembered a Rutgers sweatshirt in some closet at my folks', and I retrieved it the next weekend. It was early spring, a nice wind up—excellent sweatshirt weather, and apparently Gene did score a social coup in his new accessory, though he had had to cut it up to fit into it. He didn't win any women over to a date, but a few actually replied to his addresses; according to Jim the most popular remark was, "Did you *really* go to Rutgers?"

From then on, I was Gene's main man, after Jim, and he took to dropping in on me for confidence and advice. He called me "little brother." I put up with him, at first because I was trying to straighten out my standing in the family at that time and I thought it politic to tolerate Gene as a favor to Jim. After a while, however, I began to like Gene himself, for under the perversely insensitive behavior he had a rather touching sweetness, a Dostoyefskyan idiocy, maybe. Too, there was that amazing ironworker loyalty, something I've never encountered in members of the leadership classes, gay or straight. There was this as well: though his days were filled up with labor and his evenings with pub talk, he was a very lonely man. Jim and I were his only friends; the women he took to bed, I gathered, were whores of small quality. He disposed of them not because he was heartless but because there was nothing between him and them but a hit. One summer night he turned up at my place in his Rutgers shirt, drunk and sorrowful and inarticulate, but clearly heading toward something. The subject was love.

"When you got a buddy, man," he said. "Then you can show him how you feel about him, right? It's *radical*. Because when you really like a guy, and he trusts you, you *know* him . . . you know him right down to his cock, know him like a man. You get a buddy like that, you can do anything with him. *Anything*. You could ask him to lie down on his stomach because you're going to lock him up and ream his cherry out for him, and he'll do it. That's what love is. Loving your buddy." He gazed at me as if measuring my ability to understand what he was saying. "You hear me, little brother?"

I nodded.

"Now, your brother is really solid. That is a fucking solid guy, and there aren't many. You better know that. Right?"

"Right."

"Sure. Because if you don't know it I'll kick your butt in. Shit, he's solid. But he doesn't like to let a guy show him how he fucking feels. Know what I mean?"

"You're hurting my arm."

"I'll be good, little brother," he said, releasing me. "Because listen. This fucking city is filled with buddies. And they trust each other. Sure they do. But there comes a moment when you got to show your fucking buddy how you feel about him. You got to. There's no words. A guy just looks at his buddy, and he loves him. He *loves* him. Not just as a friend but as a man. He's got to show him, don't he? Put his arms around him, show his buddy. Am I wrong or what?"

"You're right."

"Say my name, too."

"Gene."

"Okay. I like to hear it. So, like all this time there's buddies together, and there's this one fucking moment, and they both feel it. They know it's true. It's fucking true. So one guy just takes his buddy and shows him how he fucking feels, whatever it fucking takes. That's how they know they're buddies." Finally he slowed down, took a deep breath, and shook his head. "I can't do that with Jimbo, little brother. Do you know what he's like?"

"I grew up with him."

"A rubber band. You can stretch it *just so far*, and then . . ." He pantomimed an explosion that almost blew me off the couch. "I just wish there was a place you could go and find a buddy. You know?"

A thought hit me.

"There is one, Gene."

"A buddy club, like."

"Listen, there is one!"

I had been going to the Eagle, and it occurred to me that what Gene needed and couldn't quite name was a man to take home. Or was I making the mistake of taking him literally?

"What is it?" he asked. "A gin mill?" Their term for a pub.

"Sort of. Potential buddies stand around and try to meet."

"Then what happens?"

"They go somewhere and show how they feel about each other." That didn't sound right. "No, they . . . they try to like each other."

"How?"

"That's hard to say." Then I added, "It doesn't always work." The greatest understatement in Stonewall.

He took a last swig of his drink. "I don't fucking care anymore. Let's go."

Thirty seconds after we entered the bar, I decided I had made a mistake. The Eagle, then in its heyday, was the showcase for tough men, and I knew Gene would never have taken it for a gay bar. It looked, in fact, like what he had asked for: a buddy club. Still, Gene may have been too authentic a buddy for this gang. There was always a lot of leather and muscle, and bar discounts for shirtless men encouraged a trashy savor. But that impenetrable invulnerability set Gene off from the others, and the tattoos, when he pulled off the sweatshirt, were a shock. After all, this was the place where I once saw two incredibly ruthless-looking hombres intently conversing in low tones, and innocently sidled over to eavesdrop. One of them might say, "So we stripped the kid and secured him and then . . ." The other might say, "Belts are kid stuff, just makes them giggle. You have to whip those butts." Lo, this is not what I overheard, boys and girls. One was saying, "Barbara Cook could play Sally and Angela could play Phyllis," and the other replied, "What about Liza?"

In fact, I couldn't have blundered worse if I had set up Ozma of Oz on a blind date with Leo Tolstoy. This was a place of sculpted hunks; Gene was lewd. They were practiced; Gene was improvisational. And they had polish; Gene was basic. He'd find no buddy here. A partner for the night, maybe: but he would have been repelled by the idea. A man has one-night stands with women, not men. Anyway, Gene didn't want a sex partner. He wanted a buddy he could like so badly he would be bound, almost incidentally, to fuck him. That particular stylistic riddle he could only solve among his own people, where tattoos are not exotica but a convention, and where loyalties fiercely combine. Sex is class.

Dimly, through the liquor, Gene realized this. He said he liked the place, and energetically approached a few men, yet nothing panned out. "Let's blow," he said; once we got outside, he didn't want to go: "Let's just talk." We leaned against a car on the corner and watched the others saunter back and forth between the Eagle and the Spike. We didn't say much, and, after a long silence, Gene put his arm around me. I looked up to cheer him with a joke and saw that he was crying.

We stood frozen like that for a long while, till he put his arm down and said, "I don't think those guys liked me."

"Maybe I should have—"

"I couldn't fucking understand half the things they were saying. And one of them called me a fucking *Bulgarian*! I never even been there! I never been out of this country!"

Hell, I thought, if Gene is a vulgarian, whoever called him that, *you're* a Firbankian!

"I want to deck somebody. Anyone here you don't like? Point him out."

"Let me call Jim."

"Huh?"

"He's your best buddy, right?"

"Yeah, but . . . look, does he ever come here?"

"No. But let's see what we can arrange."

Jim, roused from sleep, was annoyed till I explained the delicacy of the case.

"Shit, the fucker's on a crying drunk, that's all," said Jim. "Everyone does that now and again. He can stay with me tonight."

"Jim's coming to get you," I told Gene.

He mauled me in relief.

The Eagle–Spike parade had picked up notably—but for all the lingering stares, no one actually dared to cruise Gene. Is it possible that there's a man too authentic to be hot?

Gene was still crying when Jim's cab pulled up—it is, as they say, a jag. I thought, Everyone likes my brother except his family, as Gene threw himself at the door. Suddenly he turned back.

"Gotta thank little brother," he said, and, staggering back to me, he planted a huge wet kiss right on my mouth.

"The fucking meter's running, man," said Jim.

After they left I noticed that Gene had left his Rutgers shirt on the car with me.

Later, when I told friends of this incident, they invariably turned against me, one of their favorite activities. How did I dare bring one of those violent homophobes to a gay bar? What if he had wrecked the place? Or me?

Rubbish. I was protected by ironworker loyalty: your buddy's brother is *your* brother. As for ironworker homophobia, Gene would never have taken the Eagle for a gay bar, because ironworkers don't believe in gay. Males are men or faggots; men are solid and faggots are weak. A husky leather dude who beds his own sex is even so a man. A little *New Republic* nerd who proudly bangs his wife and sneers at gays is still a faggot. This is why ironworkers casually throw around what we regard as gay references, and why they can climb into the sack with a buddy without regarding it as a sexual assertion.

No doubt all Gene got out of Jim was the chance to sprawl in his arms all night. There are buddies you fuck and there are buddies you only love; and I think Gene loved Jim. And I also think there are ironworkers and there is everyone else, because in looks, world view, and behavior they are unique. I have been wrong about one thing: they are not invulnerable. When I pass a file of them, I look for

Gene, but he is probably working some other part of the country now; they move around a lot.

However, they never change, whether in their habits, dress, loyalties, or patriotism, though their fix on love of country is at times comprehensively ignorant. Just a few days ago, as I walked by our local gang lounging out the lunch break, I heard one of them casually call out, "Hey, traita!" Accustomed as I am to New Yorkers' public speaking, I paid no notice. About a block later, I began to wonder what the heckler had seen to inspire the epithet. Jane Fonda? La Pasionaria? There were only a few shoppers and businesswomen walking with me.

Then I realized that he had been speaking to me. I was wearing my Yale sweatshirt, and ironworkers regard the big eastern schools as hotbeds of Stalin-loving treachery. Inadvertently, I had challenged an ironworker's loyalty to his kind, and probably baited his sense of class as well.

Anyway, it proves my contention that college-logo sportswear encourages people to talk to you.

Confessions of
a Theatregoer

*Or: how to be precocious, single-minded, and
"pseudo" whether the world likes it or not.*

A housewife in Sheboygan writes, "Why is it that gay men always seem so much more interesting than straight men? Many of them are cute as the dickens, I have noticed, and they are always fun to be around. When my husband Ivan comes home from work he just drinks beer and grouches till he falls asleep halfway through *Cagney and Lacey*. Whereas my gay nephew Lester comes home from the K-Mart and just locks himself right in his bedroom to primp with the stereo going. And though I must say he goes out in some pixilated getups, as far as he is concerned the night is young and he is ready to party."

I don't agree that all gays are fun to be around, but our culture does surely bring out one's vivacity just as straight culture tends to dim it—as witness the fact that gays tend to look up to people like Oscar Wilde, Gertrude Stein, and Madame while straights claim Theodore Dreiser, Midge Decter, and George Will. Ask yourself which set of people you'd rather brunch with.

Where does the gay spirit come from? I think, possibly, from the theatre; and the spirit runs toward theatre, too: toward its romanticizing fantasy as well as its cathartic grotesquerie. The gay mind, too, raised on impersonation (of the straight style), comes out by rebelling against that fascism with impersonations of antistraight in the drag queen's camp, the hoofer's bizarrely debonair tap, the juvenile's passionate love song. Rebellion. Defiance. Offensive alchemical caricature mixed of too much knowledge of them and too much spoof of us—and it works the other way as well. Notice that it was drag queens who launched Stonewall, in true war. I expect the queen as archetype will last as long as homophobia, for he/she is our reply. Straights think the queen mocks them: no, they disgust her. She *loathes* them. All of show biz is useful in this rebellion, but the musical is especially, for it is most subversive: apparently straight to straights but, as young gays learn, secretly and profoundly gay.

The musical was my key to the culture, for Mother was messianic in the Finer Things. She got us to Europe at an age when the availability of Special K was a crucial issue, favored series titles in books in hopes that we'd plow through a library of them, made everyone play an instrument (respectively violin, trumpet, piano, drums, and utility reed—it sounds like the Brandenburgs in the Busch version), and hit us with recordings of Classics for Kiddies. I remember a Decca 78 of the *Nutcracker* with Fred Waring's Pennsylvanians singing descriptive fantasy travelogue—I could echo it verbatim before I knew what half the words meant. And there was an adaptation of the *Iliad* set to the music from Prokofyef's *The Love for Three Oranges*, with the famous March treating the scene in which the Trojans pull the Horse into the citadel. The music was threateningly satiric and so caught my ear more than Sousa might have, and I listened more closely, and imagined. There was something rich here, some telling music for the tales. I asked for more, and Mother made the leap. For my third birthday, in late January 1952, she took me to Broadway to see *The King and I*.

I remember little of it. One moment stands out, when the king, about to beat Tuptim, meets Mrs. Anna's imperialistic gaze and runs off in humiliation. The psychology was too dense for me and I asked Mother what had happened.

"No talking during the show," she whispered.

I was taken aback. "Are you still my mother?" I asked, and she went, *"Shh!"* Still, it was a momentous afternoon: that day my life took on its format.

I could not have said why at the time, of course. But I knew that I was suddenly mad wild for theatre. Sundays, fine or bitter, I would study Section Two of *The New York Times* for the theatre ads and articles. (We called it "Section Two." New Yorkers refer to it as "Arts and Leisure," and today when I mention "Section Two" everybody goes "What?") Annually, I had one birthday show and one in the summer to grow on, so I had to choose carefully. It was never difficult: something in a logo, the ring of the names involved, the charisma of adaptational source—these were my map. I picked *The Pajama Game*, for instance, because Peter Arno designed the logo, and Arno was a *New Yorker* artist. I figured the more exposure I had to *New Yorker* types, the faster I'd grow up. Then, too, I would devour the playbills my parents brought back, especially the song listings, where a title like "My Home's a Highway" or "I Feel Like I'm Going to Live Forever" would tease my imagination.

Most telling of all, of course, were the show recordings. My parents were record-oriented, and bought nearly everything, some several times over—there must have been six or seven *Carousels* floating around the house at one point. Here was a vocabulary, and a catalog of ideas. What did it mean when Julie Jordan liked "to watch the river meet the sea"? What were "vittles"? "Gullets"? Why, in "June Is Bustin' Out All Over," has April "cried" and why was May "pretty"? Here, also, was a lesson in stagecraft, in how composition is made vivid, pure, just. To see a musical after having memorized its score is a rare pleasure, for you get not only the device of the entertainment, but the aplomb of verification. To see the dream become fact is to stoke the imagination for more and bigger dreams.

With all this homework to do before selecting a subject for the matinee, I couldn't hope to catch a flop. Only hits stayed open long enough for me to consider, sample, and clear them with the authorities. I caught the major statistics of the day: *Can-Can; Fanny*, perhaps my introduction to opera in its expansive vocalism; *Damn Yankees; Plain and Fancy*, which touched on the Amish folk and underlined the notion of a culture within a culture; *My Fair Lady*, to which I was more assigned than devoted, because I sensed that popular things were less interesting than recondite things; *The Most Happy Fella*, more opera; *Li'l Abner*, with its enlightening novelty of musclemen *en cabriole; Happy Hunting*, confronting a legend in Ethel Merman; *New Girl in Town*, more legends in Eugene O'Neill and, yet in the making, Gwen Verdon; *Goldilocks*, more terrain covered in the silent-movie setting and, once the allusions were explained, D. W. Griffith and Mary Pickford. I didn't realize it then, but I was learning history, genre, personality, taste. Friends, I was being activated. Of them all, one stood out experientially, partly on sheer size, partly for its spectacular voices and orchestration, but mainly because it played to the utmost that intent, deluded fantasy about romance that all Americans, straight and gay, long to believe in and find best articulated in operetta: *Kismet*. It blew me away.

I was as up for that show as Columbus was for new world, but when Mother and I got to the Ziegfeld Theatre and I made my habitual investigation of the streetfront photographs, I was somewhat unnerved to see that Alfred Drake had suddenly grown a beard. In the *Oklahoma!* and *Kiss Me, Kate* pictures he was clean-shaven; that's how I liked him; and everyone else. I was just turning six and beards were strangely threatening to me. I suggested that I wait outside, but Mother, who, like some of my friends, sometimes sounds like Bette Davis, wasn't having any. "The nerf!" she cried, propelling me indoors. "We nurtured him, and now he's afrit of a beart!"

That *Kismet* afternoon stayed with me long after *Promises, Promises* and *Two by Two* faded into nothing. The overture, always a crucial element in my theatregoing as the unalterably novel first moment of contact, was bigger, broader, and grander than any I had yet heard,

filled with Arabian cymbals and bells and gongs, and ecstatic in the
"Stranger in Paradise" section, with *lots* of piano. (Much later I
learned the show biz term for this, "concerto style.") *Kismet* didn't
have a show curtain to flash during the overture. *The King and I*
didn't, either. *Can-Can* had one, a dazzling aerial view of Paris, and I
eventually realized that operettas and the more serious types of musical play did without show curtains almost as a rule. An embellished
curtain was a promise of guiltless fun, and a sober show meant to
enlighten. I learned to distinguish lampoon from myth.

I suppose the Ziegfeld Theatre's interior was a show curtain in itself, but I only have pictures to go by, as I don't recall looking up. I
was too intent on the stage, even covered, even dark, even waiting.
Though curtained, the stage appeared to glow once the overture began—and, to my delighted horror, the overture didn't end. It grew
quiet. The curtain rose on a dark street scene in Bagdad. A tenor
wandered through singing "Sands of Time." As he reached the last
note—"All that there is to know, only lovers *know*"—the gong
erupted, the scrim rose, and the stage awoke as grotesquely high
voices way up in the balcony imitated the cries of the faithful in the
minarets of Mohammed. I gasped and trembled; Mother, who had
already seen *Kismet*, assured me in a whisper, "This is only the beginning." "No noises during the show," I countered; I try to seize the
revolutionary moment.

She was right, however. By the time the show had ended I was so
enthralled I didn't want to leave the theatre. I wasn't alone, either. All
around us were kids with parents, all the kids begging to be allowed to
stay to see it again. We were entranced by expert show-shop marketing, yes, by the American musical's typical jumble of fun—jokes
about sex, picture-book tableaux, steamy choreography, and in general a surprising amount of hotcha for a show thought to be one of the
last of the old-time operettas. But at the heart of all this, unmistakable
even to my tender youth, was a profound commitment to the fantasy
of romance. Most musicals take the love plot for granted: comedy

is about courtship. But *Kismet* was about the *intoxication* of romance: "And This Is My Beloved," "Night of My Nights," "Stranger in Paradise." The tender are impressionable; and I left the theatre in a daze.

It was not long before I was gathering such afternoons, Section Two, *Theatre Arts* magazine, cast albums, and playbills into a cult. It is at this point, I believe, that many gay men begin to share a profile, a quest, a sequence of discoveries. When I meet someone who tells me he never saw shows in his youth, I am staggered. "Where are you from?" I want to ask. Tucson? Lodz? The Sargasso Sea? Going to the theatre is *getting to the city*: sighting the place of the independence to come—for gay culture is city culture. It thrives on the sophistication and vitally needs the tolerance that cities develop. So being taken to the theatre is not the passive act it may seem. One invites it, wills it, *chooses* the event—or would a show choose you, put its name on your through an enchanting poster design, a startling song title, a performer of note?

A show was elite and you had to go. *Candide* was like that for me, from my first view of the logo illustration in Section Two, a parade of urbane-looking people bearing the credits on kites; from the charisma in the name Voltaire; from reverberations that Leonard Bernstein, Dorothy Parker, and Tyrone Guthrie gave off in jazz-classical crossover, in New York wit, in British stagecraft. Look, you want to be urbane? Go for it; it's never too soon.

This one, I knew, I must have. *Candide!* I remember reading Brooks Atkinson's review in *The New York Times*, which opened with some reference to the Flying Dutchman—so would the vaults of imagination swing open! My friends only knew Captain Video and Sky King. I had always sensed that I was destined to know more than anyone around me, and somehow I comprehended that the theatre was going to be my education. *The King and I* and *Kismet* had not quite

connected me to anything; they were autotelic pleasures. But *Candide*
was interdisciplinarily instructive.

This would be my eighth-birthday visit and luckily the faltering run
lasted just long enough for me to get there, quiet as a postulant
throughout the interminable ride to the Martin Beck Theatre. Divin-
ing that this was a momentous occasion, my dad had nabbed us front-
row seats; and all the grown-ups around us thought it was so cute that
this little boy was blissing out at sitting close. It's cute at age eight,
perhaps; but it would seem less cute than suspicious later on when I
counted the amenities of theatregoing more heavily than those of
making the team. Real men don't care where they sit at a musical.
Real men don't watch spellbound, taking in every move that Barbara
Cook and Irra Petina make, memorizing the show like a camera. I
wonder if I sensed, even then, that a lot of things real men don't do
were the most stimulating things done.

By this time my parents had begun to realize that they had called
up a monster in me. My older brothers played touch football and
my little brothers played Candyland; I played show albums. Who
were their heroes? Mickey Mantle and Rocky Jones, Space Ranger.
Mine was Alistair Cooke. My mother took to calling me "The
Changeling." Perhaps I was too sophisticated, or too self-important
in my sophistication. When our maid Sarah Lee Patterson purloined
my *Mr. Wonderful* souvenir book, I fired her. I was nine years
old.

My brothers were flabbergasted; my mother, for once, speechless.
But Sarah Lee had been generally screwy, using the carpet sweeper on
the lawn, eating TV dinners frozen, right out of the box, and
spending her days in her room writing a movie script decorated with
colored stick-on stars and stolen from *Raintree County*, with Sarah
Lee all set to replace Elizabeth Taylor. Sarah Lee knew I had the
goods on her, and went quietly. And lo, when the smoke cleared, it
turned out that she had been systematically looting the house of treasures great and small. "Bud fired the maid" became a catchphrase in

the family, admiration and horror at once. Real men don't fire maids at the age of nine. Real men have no relationships with maids whatsoever.

Theatre governed my existence to the extent that I can chart my *Bildung* through the titles: *Peter Pan*, my first chance to see the magic worked upon someone younger than myself—my brother Andrew, who crowed at Mary Martin. *New Girl in Town*, my first *musical noir*. *Auntie Mame*, my first nonmusical. *Redhead*, my first inkling that not everyone loves musicals to death, when my dad abruptly got up after ten minutes of—I must admit—infantile nonsense, told me he'd meet me in the lobby at five o'clock, and left. *Salad Days* (in London), an experience in culture shock: the playbill cost money, Britishers tend to cluster in the middle of the house (leaving me alone in the first row, cowering under the souvenir program), and the level of production was far below what Broadway took for granted. *Flower Drum Song*, the first show I saw twice, first with Mother and then in one of those dynastic theatre parties in which every living relative takes part, serried along an entire row of seats. My littlest brother Tony, who was so excited by *The Music Man* that he couldn't sit down once the curtain went up, did not take to the solemnity of Rodgers and Hammerstein, and wandered in and out of the house in search of the men's room, the candy counter, and other arcana, to my digust. Worse yet, my dad happily sang along with the orchestra during the overture—and I mean aloud, improvising lyrics when memory failed. "No talking during the show!" I explained. He just tousled my hair and went right into "Grant Avenue." You can't get anywhere with someone like that.

Not many real men get into musicals. My dad and Oscar Hammerstein II are the only two I know of. The rest of us do almost as a matter of course. Why? One possibility is what I call the *Candide* theory: musicals make you smart. I got more out of that one show— in lit, music, and social history—than some people got out of four years of college. Its overture taught me what a rondo and a Rossini

crescendo were before I knew the terms. The auto-da-fé scene introduced me to McCarthyism. (My father caught the parallel and explained it to me during the intermission.) From Voltaire I leaped to
Diderot, Leibniz and the Enlightenment, from Tyrone Guthrie to
Olivier, Gielgud, the Old Vic, and the Kembles, from Dorothy Parker
to the New York wits, from the word "satire" to the notion of irony. If
I followed *Candide*'s allusions and implications to their ends, I would
know everything.

Of course, gays have to. At any rate, we have to know more than
the straights know: have to understand what we are as well as what
they are—have to find *our* unique place in *their* culture. For some of
us, isolated in the straight system, the stage gave off one's first whiff of
the gay tang. Certain clues led one to postulate the existence of another system, a secret one. One saw signs in the behavior of the male
gypsies and gratuitous torso bearings, in questionably quaint rhymes
and sly jokes, even in Daniel Blum's emphasis on male body shots in
his *Theatre World* annuals. I remember looking up *Kismet* in one of
these volumes and being surprised by a photograph of Steve Reeves,
that icon of pre-Stonewall calculus. The photo caught an insignificant
moment of the show and was clumsily cropped; it didn't belong in a
book. Why was it there? Because Reeves in Arabian pajamas was too
toothsome not to be included? Obviously Blum thought so; his
*Theatre World*s were like certain New York parties: always room for
the beautiful. This is an exclusively gay notion, and coming upon it
through my cult told me I wasn't alone.

Overtly, I pretended membership in the straight club; this was the
1950s. Yet we cultists found our way around it: for taking up theatre
as a hobby was not unlike coming out in code, reserving a place in a
possible gay future without having to challenge the hypocrisy of the
social contract. Kids always want to be like each other, have what they
all have and fashion clubs of belonging; to have something different
and join one's own club was to practice for later, when the system was
no longer secret. Thus, liking musicals was like a legalized coming

out. The connection made sense: what other profession is as gay-identified as theatre?

Indeed, an ancient queen who has been everywhere and known everyone once told me that gay was invented in a theatre, in 1956. Yes, there were the Greeks, but all their secrets were lost. Petronius? Fragments, dreams. Ronald Firbank was a fluke and Nöel Coward was an abundance of suave, not a sexuality. No, the queen tells, gay came about at the City Center revival of *A Streetcar Named Desire* in which Tallulah Bankhead played Blanche DuBois. Everyone who attended that production was instantly struck gay, the old queen says, including the usherettes, the candy sellers, the stage crew, and—on Tallulah's good nights—even those who were passing outside the theatre. This must be gospel. What else is common to this scattered, unwieldy, and inherently contradictory condition we term the "gay community" but a bent for the stage? We all go; we all look upon those who don't as unintellectual, uncultured, gross. True, we don't all want the same thing from it. Some want a poetry of life, some a keen comix, some a colorful immortality. But I notice that *A Streetcar Named Desire* has all of these, as well as the two basic gay characters, the stud and the queen.

If attending theatre educates, putting it on stimulates, which is why most of the men who write, produce, stage, perform, or even drum hype for the theatre are gay, with emphasis on musicals. Why musicals? Because gays love boas and sequins? Or because they have been attracted by a unique form of music theatre that sophisticates all arts so deftly and—on occasion—profoundly that it sweeps other pastimes and enlightenments to the side? Musicals aren't a fetish, then: they are the stimulation of the cultivated.

This is why many of us get into playwriting in youth, laying down versions of our favorite shows, adapting novels and plays, even attempting originals. When I was scarcely old enough to stand I was herding my parents into my living room for cameo pageants, written, scored, and acted by our boy. This may be why I never liked little off-Broadway musicals, with their simplistic composition and undecorated staging style—mine were no smaller and no more terrible. Off Broadway was tyke theatre. It was the racy wisdom of grown-up Broadway that I prized—not the glamour, but the self-knowledge.

Yet, years later, as we graduates of this eccentric college congregated and met in the metropolis, I learned that some of them did not have any perspective on themselves at all. The theatre had instructed them, but never let them go to learn about other things. Socially, professionally, even sexually, they were unversed and unmotivated. They were overgrown precocious kids, using their love of theatre to protect them from all the other loves they could not collect. Disreputably dressed, showing up everywhere bearing bags containing the day's haul of records, books, or memorabilia, sporting the breath of a dragon, and blaring idiotic trivia about record matrix numbers, they put something of a punk on the image of the buff. And, of course, they were always gay.

Why of course?

Yet I wonder what they would have had if they didn't have the theatre. Musical comedy doesn't ruin them: it saves them, gives them a topic and a confraternity, even if, at times, that brotherhood consists of a body of strangers enchanted in a darkened auditorium. Their first love became a lifetime obsession; but if it set them strictly apart, it did set them somewhere. How much worse to have nothing to believe in, to be, like many people I have met over the years, utterly devoid of interests. Work detains them. Companionship eludes them. Only the bodily appetites impel them: food, sleep, sex. Absurd as it is to see Gene Caputo the ironworker as an aficionado—once I mentioned Liza Minnelli and he said, "Who's that? Some bimbo?"—if Gene had had the ability to be enlightened, redeemed, perhaps merely diverted by entertainers, he might not have been so lonely, a homosexual straight who couldn't touch men and didn't appreciate women, a truly single man.

This fraternity aspect of the musical comedy life is significant: types tend to cluster. When my father's hurtling success, my brother's implacable rivalry, and my own ornate precocity suggested something (respectively) fancy, remote, and advanced in the way of my education, my folks sent me off to Friends Academy in Locust Valley, Long Island. Friends no longer accepted boarding students, so I stayed, through some occult arrangement, with a family that turned out to be shockingly informal; had I been Ralph Bellamy, it would have been a screwball comedy. Their huge house stood a short walk from the Glen Cove railroad station, and I found to my delight that Mrs. Pratt saw nothing objectionable in my spending Saturday afternoons in the metropolis, lunching at the big Automat (now vanished) on Broadway at Forty-sixth Street, catching a matinee of just about anything, and generally nosing around. Here was when my coming of age really began, when theatre trips evolved into trips into city life, into the notion that a people as chosen as gays are must erect a ghetto not so much for segregation as for concentration: to learn what gay is.

True, this side of me was not useful at Friends Academy, where most of the students were sheltered WASP kids of Brookville and Old Westbury who, for one reason or another, didn't go off to Choate or Deerfield. They were sheltered from notions of race and class and what might be called disopportunity; and from the notion of art as well. I felt like young Lord Greystoke, set down among not apes but talking macaroons. At the end of seventh grade, however, I somehow wangled the lead in the senior class show, *Seventeen*, and this gave me access to the group known as the "pseudos": short for pseudo-intellectual and meant as a put-down, but in fact describing all the creative people at Friends.

The pseudos were considered radical. In some ways they truly were—Michael Hadden spent his weekend evenings at the Apollo Theatre in Harlem, an unthinkably daring diversion for a birthright member of the white bourgeoisie, and one that perhaps corresponds to

my own metropolitan jaunts, for gosh knows the Apollo gave Michael
Hadden a feeling for the richness of American civilization he could
not have got in Locust Valley. I daresay he was one of the last whites
to feel comfortable in Harlem before its politicization (or before its
innate politicization became militant), and it certainly spunked
up the yearbook, amid the drearily facetious Likes and Dislikes everyone else listed, to see his references to Harlem and the Apollo. He
genuinely liked black music; that, for him, was an agent of what you
could call straight coming out, learning what there is and what else
you are.

But most pseudo-activity consisted of theatricals, assorted acts of
arrogance (Sylvia Dawkins marched into English class, told Miss
Blade she had set so much English homework Sylvia couldn't do her
geometry, and proceeded to do it, as Miss Blade cried out, "*Sylvia*
Dawkins! Sylvia *Dawkins*!), and turning up in bizarre outfits on slave
day. More typical of pseudo-style than Mike Hadden was Clodagh
Millham, perversely silent with whimsical eyes. On *her* yearbook
page, instead of the usual studio portrait and "personality candid" (a
jock staring at the field of war; a pre-deb modeling a prom frock in the
kitchen as the staff looks on in a bemused manner), Clodagh had
nothing—nothing bearing the legend, "Draw your own pictures of
Clodagh Millham here." Given Friends Academy's value system,
Clodagh's rejection of yearbook glamour was more shocking than
Mike Hadden's disdain for middle-class scruples. Mike Hadden wasn't
really a pseudo, anyway, for he was on the football team and led the
debating club, whereas the true pseudo didn't join things. Pseudos
were nonconformists as a rule, and by the time I reached my seniority
in this society and became a pseudo myself, I realized how much
Being Different had to do with being gay. Half of it is being marked,
being *made* different. The other half is acting marked, *accepting* the
difference. To be pseudo (straight for "phony") was to be creative (gay
for "vital"). That is: given a drab environment, you either rebel or
grow up drab.

Creative is often a euphemism for "neurotic." But, boys and girls, you can be neurotic without creating anything. And lots of creative people have *not* been neurotic. (Name three, you say? John Updike, Lilo, and Jack Pumpkinhead of Oz. You say some of those on my list are imaginary? Well, who isn't?) Anyway, I'd say that creativity is the route to travel, for all its awkward poignancy. It can be rough in childhood, but it gives one an intent sense of mission as an adult; and think of all the salons and brunches it makes available.

So, to the housewife in Sheboygan and others who ask why gay men have this vitality, I would say it's because we steal from and pay back to the intensity of show biz. We adopt its tart glitter, and then, experimenting, develop our opulence, whimsy, intelligibility.

My records, for instance. A pleasantly unsavory amusement arcade halfway on to Wilkes-Barre called Playland had a recording machine. For fifty cents you could make a 45, and I made plenty. If Bernstein and Hellman could dare Voltaire, should I not tackle *The Wizard of Oz, Treasure Island*? The sixty-second side duration limited my scope somewhat, but I was ace in short forms, including parodies of television variety shows. One time I took my younger brothers into the booth with me—Mother had forbidden them some promised trip as a result of the usual contretemps, so I cast them into my cult to cheer them up. They were to play announcer and delicious mystery guest in my show, though Andrew could not bring himself to announce anything but "Here comes Mr. Pickle!" (an arresting footnote in what turned out to be an insistently straight sex life) and mystery guest Tony, sullen with the humiliation of punishment, refused to say even a word. I liked to make multidisc sets, just like the 45 versions of show albums, and by the end of the third side Andrew and I were giggling and capering. Tony, however, remained obdurately silent, despite our prodding and hard looks. At length, he piped up, "I hate Mom." There the record ended.

But not the story. Years later, the three of us turned up for Christmas at the manse, and stayed up late to reminisce and get into trouble in the kitchen. My mother, who spent most of her parental life starting at the sound of an opening refrigerator door to scream, "Who's in the kitchen?" from the bedroom, screamed it now.

"Do you remember," Tony asked, "when that struck terror into our hearts?"

"We should wreck a dish or something," Andrew urged. "Let's make something vicious in the toaster-oven."

It was as if we had never grown up. They were still the moon mice, as capable of smashing up my room as of sharing a pizza; and I am still the theatre kid, throwing the word "satire" around and speaking of "Section Two." My folks were about to move to Sacramento, and in going through my old chest I found many a souvenir, including some of my old amateur 45s. I took them out now and played the Mr. Pickle show, running lampoon and myth together.

We were bemused, transported back to a time when losing a hat or catching cold was mortal sin. In the silence that followed, Mother came downstairs in her nightgown to expostulate and dither, and, suddenly wrenched by the horror of leaving friends and family for a strange culture, grew tearful. "There won't be a Fortunoff's," she explained. "They put tofu into the water supply." Tearful is bad enough, but now came nostalgic, not one of her characteristic modes. "I wish your father were here to see the three of you spending Christmas like brothers instead of fighting."

"He's just upstairs in bed," said Andrew. "Shall I get him?"

"Are you talking over old times?" she asked gently. I'd had enough of this. Consulting the phonograph, I replayed the last bit of the Mr. Pickle show:

"Well, Mr. Pickle, what's new on the Rialto?"
Silence.
("Say something, you spaz!")
Silence.

("Kick his knee.")

("No, let's give him noogies.")

"Mr. Pickle, won't you say hello at least?"

Long silence, then:

"I hate Mom."

Mother regarded us in fury. "You wretches! Who said that?"

I pointed at Tony, Tony pointed at Andrew, Andrew pointed at me. "He did," we chorused. Lampoon and myth.

Where did we learn our timing, you ask? Broadway taught us. Life is educational, if you know how to choose your college.

The Ideal Couple

After fraternities of siblings and of construction workers, we consider a third brotherhood, neither genetic nor professional but cultural.

Stonewall the event happened very unexpectedly, and Stonewall the culture developed, in response, almost overnight. All those men who had been living alone and quietly suddenly had boyfriends, Oscar parties, leather pants. The gay world took on its themes, conventions, and terms with a ferocious imagination—for these elements of our civilization were not revealed, brought out of hiding: they were invented on the spot. We were leaderless, but then gay had long been, like it or not, a somewhat freelance situation, a field of loners making do. And we began to find each other, trade observations, build up the folklore. Some rather essential items turned out to have been there all along—Fire Island, for instance. Some equally essential items came along a few years later—dancing, for one, officially launched at the Tenth Floor in the early-middle 1970s. Other essential items, however, were simply routined into place then and there. *The Advocate* appeared. Bars opened in revolutionarily central locations. Even the sex changed. As if to renounce the passive stance of the old trade-worshiping oral encounters, men began to insist on the more aggressive attack of all-night screwing. Staying over—especially if you had coffee the next morning and hugged at the door—became a political act.

Most important, trade virtually vanished. Not long before I came to

New York, homosexuals had no partners but hustlers. There would still be hustlers; but now most gays only knew of them from books like these. Hired help had become as useful as Victrolas: occult leverage raised by the lunatic fringe. Just as most record-playing people now relied on stereos, so did gays rely on . . . friendship. In fact, one of the first things you absolutely had to have in New York, fall of 1969, was a best friend.

With best friends, I believe: the older, the better. Long-term relationships weather idiosyncrasies more easily than new ones; and old investments are dearer. Perhaps it's a matter of simple arithmetic: after ten or twelve years, you've already fought about everything potentially available, and can settle back and just get along.

What of preferences, you ask? Who needs what kind of best friend? Boys and girls, there's no point in having preferences—even non-smokers can just hold their horses—because it was one of Stonewall's first rules that you can't choose your best friend: he chooses you. I got mine at the Met. It was that same Stonewall fall, and the opera season had begun; at the first intermission of a *Tales of Hoffmann* I ran into a vaguely familiar face at the bar, one of those you know well enough to start joking around with but not well enough to name. Finally I placed him. He and I had, so to say, cochaired a sit-down strike on the playing fields of—no, not Eton—the annual Valley Forge Boy Scout Jamboree. Small potatoes, you say. But how many men of your acquaintance ever led a sit-down strike *during* an all-American Capture the Flag? And called a scoutmaster a Nazi? (His assistant, an Eagle scout, was even worse, but he was also somewhat breathtaking, so we didn't call him anything.) Now it was ten years later, and my fellow rebel and I were men of the world, drinking champagne between the acts of a Met *Hoffmann* and comparing neighborhoods. I was living on the west side in a brownstone, he in the east fifties, in a doorman building with a fancy solarium on the roof. It sounded altogether metropolitan to me, and when some creep pushed my air conditioner in and robbed my apartment, I moved into my old friend's building. We had a lot in common and lived only two floors apart and thus became rather confidential. Also, we were the only two people we knew who had called a scoutmaster a Nazi and harbored ecstatic feelings for an Eagle scout. This will tend to draw men together. So we became best friends. His name was Dennis Savage, and still is.

Shocking to report, in those days you could live pretty much anywhere you wanted to just by moving in. Buildings were uncrowded and rents low. In such profusion, roommates were actually suspicious—except to gays. Our love lives were forming. Dennis Savage and I marveled as man after man buddied up and the crowd assembled the lists. The Five Most Colorful Couples. The Ten Most Passionate Couples. The Three Most Wonderful But Almost Certainly Temporary Couples. (There were a lot of those.) The Couple of the Month. Then I would say, "Couple of the Day would be more realistic," and of course everyone would get mad at me.

Part of Stonewall, I eventually realized, was not letting the side down, not admitting errors. But if straights are allowed to mess up their love lives, why can't we? Besides, as a storyteller I am bound for life to play a kind of devil's advocate about everything. I may not carry a notebook around, but I don't miss a move.

All of which is by way of introduction to the story of Greg and Calvin, because they were most frequently mentioned at list sessions as the Ideal Couple. Television was hesitantly taking up the gay scene, but no one was satisfied with the men the networks chose to interview. "Greg and Cal should be on the air," I was told. "*They* should speak for us, not those bitter political queens!" Another told me, "They're so handsome. So correct." Greg and Cal were a commercial for gays.

So it seemed. Greg was in his mid-twenties then, dark, quiet, slow-moving, and impressively solid. Calvin was a little older, fair, slight, mercurial. They mixed a notable chemistry, for while neither was astonishing on his own, together they were a compound of infinitely sympathetic currents, flowing between each other and outward to all around them. They were very social, very popular. They were always giving dinners, and because the guests were all, like Emma Wood-house, handsome, clever, and rich, you were flattered to have been asked. But there was something else going on, something clammy in the compound. You had only to let slip a faux pas—as I tend to, as a matter of course if not policy—and Greg would turn upon you the blackest, most intense eyes ever flashed. And once, when I was one of the last guests to leave, Cal pleaded with me to stay as if he feared to be alone with Greg. Fascinated, I took another scotch. But then Greg came out of the kitchen, sat down next to me, asked a few irrelevant questions, and ever so politely threw me out as Calvin stood against the wall like Saint Sebastian waiting for the arrows.

Calvin and I dated back to an East Side gym, now vanished, where two bodybuilders had a titanic fight over him in the weight room while he scrambled into his clothes in a panic and begged someone, anyone, to hide him out for a few hours. I spoke up. This was what we call a "mixed" gym (i.e., about fifteen percent straight and one hundred thirty percent gay), and the two bodybuilders—I had thought—were of the straight percentile. If Calvin actually had charm enough to draw strangers into the parish, he had to be quizzed, had to lend Stonewall his data. I took him to my place for coffee and sat entranced; he *was* that charming. Or was he rather a deftly tactful flatterer, the kind who makes you feel that you have somehow notched yourself up a rating or two and are about to have a wonderful life? I felt so elated when Calvin left that I had to go right up to Dennis Savage's apartment and stand to ten minutes of nonstop insults and grouching before I felt like me again.

Everyone called him Calvin then, in response to his whimsical dignity. Such a tidy bon vivant would bear no nicknames. *Calvin.* He was like one of James M. Barrie's lost boys who had found himself in one of the less onerous Professions. He wore high style without study. He was learned but he was funny. Anytime you ran into him—and you often did—he was on his way somewhere and took you along, to cocktails, surprise parties, screenings. He must have known a thousand doting people. And while you never quite caught the names, everyone present was lively and unique. You would hear the names again, when the times were ready. "Calvin," they would say, "tell us about it." And "Calvin, what did you do, *then?*" He never spoke of sex. He was the eternal kid, though he was getting on. And he did drink too much—this was something we of early Stonewall avoided almost politically, as reminiscent of the old have-not queer, dejected by hustlers and decaying with isolation.

Calvin and I lost track of each other after a while, as happens. I'd hear his name every so often, but we'd never meet. Then one day I ran into him: and suddenly he was Cal, not Calvin, and when he saw you he wouldn't blurt out some amusing confidence but tell you about people coming into inheritances. He knew a wholly different crowd, too; and Greg had entered the picture.

I disliked Greg at first sight, though I could understand why so many men liked to be around him. He was a hot preppy, and that's hard to pull off. He was so damn poised, so *ready* for everything. After a while, you began to feel that, every time you met him, he was reading from a script. And there was a new feeling of a collection at his and Calvin's dinners, as at that famous Bloomsbury jape at which all the guests had names ending in -bottom. Higginbottom. Pillbottom, Clambottom. The Calvin I had known never gave a thought to the luster of his cohorts. So I blamed Greg. He was the type who rated his associates on a scale.

Now I'll let Calvin speak for himself. We were having drinks at the Mayfair, and I told Calvin that he and Greg were the Ideal Couple, and he asked, "Says who?"

"Everyone but me."

He nodded. He was drunk. "We arranged it, you know. I'm sure you know. You know, don't you?"

"Look, Calvin—"

"It's Cal."

"*Calvin.* Don't give me secret dish. Or by the time I get off the phone tonight you'll be ruined."

"I hope so."

"Enough."

"No, *listen*. It's a hoax."

"What isn't?"

"We figured out what the championship would be and we scored it. We did, didn't we? We arranged it. Don't you see that? We aren't even friends. We're *partners*."

Why was he telling me this? I wondered. Isn't this sort of thing supposed to be a secret? Of course, you have to get people to reveal all sorts of privileged information if you want to understand the world, tell stories, be a writer. Stonewall had thrown up something like a hundred different words for what you can do in bed, but we still had only one name for love—that one. If Calvin and Greg were our Ideal Couple, I decided, we needed more words.

I thought that notion worth talking over with Dennis Savage. *He* thought it second-rate dish, but, like everyone, rather liked the picture Calvin and Greg made together. "If you were really smart," he told me, "you'd become a photo journalist and do a visual essay on those two. Catch them at the beach, in the park, on their terrace, in the workplace . . . Greg looks so amazing in those dark suits of his, and then he comes out in a sweater and jeans and you just think . . . what are you looking at?"

"What do you believe a photo essay would reveal about those two?" I said.

He was fumbling with a do-it-yourself framing kit he had bought to mount the *Follies* poster I had given him. "Why do they make these screws so tiny? Who has fingers small enough to—"

"Use a screwdriver."

"There's no screwdriver in the kit."

"Don't you just have one?" I asked. "Men are supposed to."

"Of course I have one!" he cried.

"Let's see it."

Without a word he marched over to the couch and folded up like old cardboard. He disgruntles easily. So I went downstairs, came back with my tool chest, and took over the framing.

"Actually," I said, "a photo essay on those two might disclose arresting aperçus about friendship."

"Poor Cal."

"Oh, suddenly it's poor Cal, huh?"

"Well, he *is* in over his head. Anybody would be with Greg." Dennis Savage and Greg went to college together. "He majored in intimidation."

"You got this wired all wrong," I said, readjusting the fastenings.

"He had this roommate he used to beat up all the time."

"Oh—"

"I was next door, wasn't I? I heard them."

"It was wrestling practice."

"Wrestling practice does not yield screams of 'Please, Greg, no! I promise! I promise!' Does it?"

"You surely did not hear—"

"I was there, you."

I silently drove the headbars into their slots.

"I was there," he repeated, coming over to watch the operation.

"'I promise'?"

"He promised."

Can I believe this? Dennis Savage is known to season his dish.

"The best thing," he tells me, "is once the roommate ran away from campus. Literally ran away."

"Why?"

"I suppose life in a small room with Megalon the Fire Monster made him nervous."

"What happened?"

"Well, it's hard to run away from Hamilton. There's almost nothing to take."

"So?"

"So Greg found him and brought him back."

"And it was hushed up."

"Hushed up? The spring mixer was entitled Runaway Roommates in their honor! Everyone knew about it."

"Did Greg get in trouble, at least?"

"The Gregs of the world never get in trouble," Dennis Savage opines. "The family's too powerful. Everything about Greg is right. His background, his address, his business, his looks. Think about it."

"And the lover? How right is he?"

"Come on, they make a marvelous couple."

"Calvin told me they aren't lovers. They aren't even friends, he said."

"What an odd thing to say. The two of them are inseparable."

"He says they arranged it."

"Well, if they did, they couldn't have arranged it better. No one person that I know of could afford that apartment, or attract quite that array of party guests, or just get that kind of respect."

"Manhattan's Ideal Couple," I said. "They won the contest. They arranged it."

"*They* didn't arrange anything," Dennis Savage laughed. "Greg arranges."

"And Calvin . . ."

". . . makes the promise." He shrugged. "Because we have to show the world what we're worth in our spotless white sweaters at our faultless dinners. Just wait. Ten years from now, when Hollywood makes a progressive film with a gay couple in it, that's what we'll look like. Greg and Calvin."

"Are you being ironic or do you believe that?" I asked.

"People respect a handsome picture above all," he said, surveying my handiwork. "Nice job."

"You know," I said after some thought. "I find it hard to visualize you at Hamilton. Or at any college."

He nodded. "And you're a pig."

Whenever friends would burst into a salute to monogamy, I would cite Greg and Calvin in a cautionary lecture on the terrorism of suitability in gay coupling. Of arranging and promising. True, plenty of men were showing up with the most unsuitable characters in tow— hot little tricks no better than hustlers, idiots whose very presence I took as a dire insult. Then I realized that I was falling into the Greg- and-Calvin camp, demanding that categories of education and bear- ing be satisfied before romance could commence, before admirable witnesses would form an admiring circle. Is this liberation? "I prom- ise" haunted me. What, precisely, is one required to promise?

I had the chance to find out when Dennis Savage called me and said, "You'd better get up here pronto. It's Cal and is he in a state!"

It's Calvin, I muttered in the elevator. It was Calvin before he promised, when he was himself.

Dennis Savage was right enough about Calvin's state. At first I thought he might be zonked on some new substance, so little aware was he. But after a while I got the impression that he was just scared. Carlo was there, half watching and half thinking of some pickup— Carlo, pure hunk, and our set's contact with Stonewall as absolute sex.

"Did you see the picture I framed?" I asked Carlo, explaining how Dennis Savage didn't have a screwdriver—or, for all we knew, a church key or a driver's license.

"Do you want to stay here tonight, Cal?" Dennis Savage was ask- ing. "Are you afraid to go home?"

Calvin's mouth worked, but little came out. "I . . . I'm sorry about all this. I . . . if only . . . I wished . . ."

"Has a story been structured?" I asked, plopping down next to Carlo.

"Not yet," said Dennis Savage, gently patting Calvin on the back.

"So what's the new thing?" I said to Carlo, who could always be counted on to report on some arcane sexual practice introduced in San Francisco, or some outrageously exclusive party he could get us into.

"Sure," Carlo said. He's a dazzling man; it's interesting to see how quiet new people get when they meet him. "Last night I fucked this beautiful kid, and then he got me to call his parents and say I was his teacher and I was keeping him after school."

"Okay," I said. "That's pretty damn new."

"Come here and do something," Dennis Savage told me. "Cheer him."

"Talk, Calvin."

"Could I have some more tea?" Calvin asked. He seemed ready to open up.

"Do you want to tell us what happened?" I asked. He sadly shook his head. "Was it . . . wrestling practice?"

"Wrestlers," said Carlo, warming to the subject. "Can you imagine what they might do to you in bed? They have all those holds and body locks."

"Why did you come here, Calvin?" I asked. "Are you afraid Greg will find you? Are you afraid he won't?"

"Don't listen to that waster," Dennis Savage told Calvin.

"He doesn't have a screwdriver," I told Carlo. "He can't put a frame together. Can you imagine?"

"He gives me yogurt," said Carlo, looking on the good side. "Blueberry. And he puts that healthy crinkle stuff on it."

"Wheat germ," Dennis Savage put in.

"So what's the deal, Calvin?" I said. "Do you want to break free? Huh? Are you afraid he won't let you? Is it time to stop trying to live life in the Movement's picture window?"

"Wheat germ is good for you?" said Carlo, enchanted by the oxymoron. "Wheat *germ*?"

"I'll tell you how easy it is to break free," I went on. "Make the relationship disreputable and Greg'll drop you like that. Let's try it. Let's see."

"You can't destroy a relationship on the moment," said Dennis Savage. "You don't—"

"A good paddling," Carlo put in, "could make an affair fresh. Especially when the guy who's going to be paddled is a little afraid of it."

"Greg goes for appearances, right?" I said.

Silence.

"Doesn't he?"

Still silence.

"He makes the arrangements, doesn't he?"

"It's really the threat of being paddled," Carlo went on, "not getting paddled in itself. Though some very sweet kids—"

"Sabotage the appearance," I offered, "and you're free. Ruin the arrangement. Break your promise."

"How can he do that?" asked Dennis Savage.

"What are Greg's values? Let's chart." I was a teacher once. "Greg's values are virility, money, correct taste, career success, and no passions, in something like that order. Make yourself useless to that system and he'll have to find another partner. Stroll through Tiffany's in a merry widow. Hang out in video arcades. Leave a Harold Robbins novel on your beach blanket. Wear purple. Get fired. Drool."

"Well, that's hopeless," Calvin said.

"Then go home and face the music."

Calvin sighed. "Would . . . would someone like to come with me? I wouldn't mind it if someone else was there."

"Mind what?" I asked.

"Stop being a bully," said Dennis Savage, "and take him home. Stay with him till Greg's under control." He helped Calvin into his Perry Ellis windbreaker.

"Then come back," said Carlo, "and tell us everything."

"You know what I think?" I said at the door. "I think someone or other made up that story about Greg and his college roommate and Calvin heard it somewhere and decided to boost the legend. And that's our picture. That's the respectable beauty of Stonewall. Because I don't believe there's anything in that apartment but a pompous lacrosse captain who's afraid he'll fart at a key moment of the awards banquet."

"Let's go then," said Calvin. "And you'll see."

"My, didn't you calm down," I noted. "You were quivering like a flan when I got here."

"Take him home, you beast!" Dennis Savage roared.

We walked. At the time, everyone I liked lived on the west side but everyone I knew lived in the east fifties. Greg came out of the bedroom as we walked in, pulling a tennis sweater over his jeans. Dennis Savage was right: he comes out and you just think. He was tousled and sleepy. He stood there, running his hand through his hair. We parked by the front door. Nobody said a word. I couldn't read either of their faces.

At length Greg spoke. "You know how I first hooked up with this guy? I raped him. He touched my arm and asked me to wait for another time. He promised to bring me beauties in his place. No one had ever had him, he said. He wept, but I held his hand and whispered to him. While I was stripping him, he leaned his head against my chest and pleaded with me. I told him if he didn't cooperate I would tie him to the bed and hurt him. I made him take his choice."

And he grinned.

Calvin turned to me, speechless, avid, his eyes wild. He was so turned on the air around us was crackling and falling to the floor in bits.

"What choice, Calvin?" I asked. "What choice did you make?"

Greg came up behind Calvin and put his arms around him. "Stick around for the drinks," Greg told me. "Quentin and Edward are coming. We'll probably go on to dinner." Calvin was smirking like a cowboy about to hang a rustler.

"So," I said. "The Ideal Couple. Continuous performances. All live acts. Come see the Celebrity Cocktail in the Dazzling Penthouse, where Best Friends Invent the Traditions of Stonewall. Starring the Big Scary Preppie Bear and his Christopher Robin."

"I'm not such a scary bear, am I?" Greg purred in Calvin's ear.

"Who says you're the bear?" I said.

"*Everyone* but you," Calvin replied. "I told you how it was with us."

"You told me something else." Was this the aim of Stonewall—to fill lavish apartments with the right sweater, the right brunch flowers, the right lover? Were we perhaps going to raise up a midtown suburb, a gay bourgeoisie voting Republican and muttering about interest rates? *Liars!* I thought, watching them. *Arrangers!* The puppet makes the promise and the stringmaster collects it. Then they put on the show. "*You* didn't make any promise, man," I told Calvin. "*Greg* did. Greg is your puppet, you lurid Bloomingdale's pimp!"

"What ever are you speaking of?" he asked, with a smile.

"So long, Cal."

And whenever I heard people call them the Ideal Couple, I said, "Oh, you mean Citizen Pain and the Battered Bride?" And of course everyone would get mad at me.

A Weekend with Straights

A trip to the island of fire—but, for once, to neither Pines nor Grove, and among Strangers.

I didn't mind being the only unattached male in the house, but it felt odd to be the sole person of either sex without a tattoo. My brother Jim and his pal Danny D., typical ironworkers, sported standard regalia on their upper arms. And Brenda, Jim's date, was of the downtown bimbo class: they'll do anything for attention. Even Norma, girlfriend to Danny D. and a strictly reared Italian from Bay Ridge, shyly revealed a tiny heart inked into her right instep—"so I can hide it from my parents," she told me. Thus all four representatives of the straight-couple class were decorated. And, of the freelancers, Laurie the tough-guy lesbian weighed in as well, with a death's head on her left shoulder. That left me as the only *tabula rasa* in the house.

This was Water Island on a July Fourth weekend in the early 1970s. I had just discovered Fire Island, just begun to sense how neatly it essentialized gay, made its complexes intelligible; and I never turned down an invitation. Water Island, the first colony east of The Pines, was where Norma and Laurie shared a four-bedroom house with two women who had gone off on vacation, and Norma, who knew Jim through Danny D., offered Jim and Brenda the third room and me the fourth. Perhaps because of her sweetheart upbringing, Norma liked wild men, and may have been disappointed by my mild manner. *This*, she must have been thinking, is Jim's brother? Don't they have something in a dangerous? "I'll bet you've got a *terrific* sense of humor," she told me as we shook hands, one of the most tactless salutes I've ever suffered. Besides, my sense of humor isn't terrific: it's occult.

Laurie, at least, seemed pleasantly jived at my appearance. Better a gay, her smile betokened, than another of these hardhat supermen. Her handshake was a vise, and I was amused to watch Jim take up the challenge and squeeze it out with her. He won. He's slim but deadly.

Brenda, an elated blonde, was my kind of person: she likes everybody. Danny D., too, was easy to get along with, provided you were not a Commie, a groveling cheat, or a faggot. He used the terms indiscriminately—Billy Martin he dubbed a Commie, Walter Cronkite a groveling cheat, and Norma a faggot the night she refused to accompany him to a Jets game. He had an engaging quirk whereby he would converse avidly with himself, usually to express what he feared to articulate directly. "What's this for?" he said at Jim's place once, handed a present. "It's because someone likes you," he answered himself, holding it. "Open it, you jerk." "No, I'm not ready now." "Everybody's watching you." "Well, maybe." "If you don't, I'll deck you busted." "Okay, okay." Jim grinned at me as Danny D. ripped off the wrappings, as if to say, See what fun ironworkers are?

Water Island let me down. A drab batch of broken-down houses too far from The Pines, it didn't even have a ferry stop, much less such amenities as a grocery or liquor store. You landed at The Pines, laid in supplies, took the last leg by water taxi, and waded into the bay to gain the blasted boardwalk. Nor was there much beach life, any coming and going. For that you had to walk to The Pines, and it was no mere hop and skip. Here I was hoping to jade myself on gay data, stuck in a straight version of Fire Island.

We had unpacked. Jim and Brenda into their room and Danny D. and Norma into theirs had retired for nookie; Laurie nodded toward the sea with a look of Let's go and I went. We sat topless in the late-afternoon sun and she said, "Tell me about it."

I told her about my family, about ironworkers, about writing, about New York, about those opposites nostalgia and ambition, about gay men, and about lesbians, though she was better informed than I. And I told her, who knows why, about the time we were all at the Jersey shore when I was ten and Jim eleven and I jumped him to give him a dunking and he threw me off and, his eyes on ice, told me that was the last time I'd sneak up on him. Then he held me under the water so long my lungs were about to burst when some stranger pulled us apart.

"One of those quaint family capers," I concluded, "that most people never mention."

"How did you two make that up?"

"We didn't. They sent me away to school, so we didn't see each other much after that. We're still trying to sort things out."

She nodded and we watched the water dance.

"Now you," I said.

"Guys like me have no past," she said. "What you see is the whole thing." She was right, in a way: real men don't go around lamenting their fearful kismet. But then, as Ernest Hemingway finally discovered, you can be a real man or a writer, not both.

"Does it hurt getting tattooed?" I asked.

"Tickles. Kind of funny having a brother out here. Mostly all we get is lovers and dates. Jim know about you?"

"I imagine so."

"Ironworkers are pretty homophobic. Doesn't that boil you?"

"Does it boil you?"

"They don't figure me for gay. They wouldn't even if I plowed Norma on the dining table. Women are beyond their typing rituals, see. We're exempt."

"Pardon me for busting into heartthrob city," said Norma over our shoulders. I had the feeling that she wasn't being ironic. "But cocktails are served."

"We'll get there," said Laurie.

"If you feel that way," said Norma, leaving.

"Doesn't she know," I asked, "that one doesn't launch dinner on Fire Island till nine o'clock at the earliest?"

"Jesus, you *are* gay."

I decided to try her patience. "If I got a tattoo, could I too pass as a man?"

She eyed me cannily for a bit, then chose to answer seriously. "Fact, they're a bargain. Cheap. Though all the artists want to stroke you up, doing it. Had to bust three guys before I got one would do his job and leave me be."

And she was not kidding, boys and girls.

"It's the loveboats!" Norma caroled when we joined the others on the deck. Brenda, in Jim's lap, held a goblet of wine. The men had bottles of Heinekens. Norma was doing revolting things to helpless slices of bread, salami, and cheese with a kit of molds and styli almost certainly Not Available in Stores. Laurie took a beer, and, though I wanted one, too, I asked for wine to avoid showing solidarity with a particular side.

"It takes a classy person," said Brenda, "to drink wine." She sipped hers, smirking at Jim. "Tongue me, big boy," she urged.

A curiosity of the house was a battered but working upright piano just inside the doors to the deck. I took my wine over and rattled into some Gershwin, though I find playing by memory difficult. Norma was thrilled to have live music to entrance her weekend commotion. Putting the thumbscrews to a hunk of munster, she carefully mimed Alert Sensitivity as I flailed through the release of "Nashville Nightingale," getting not a single note right.

"That sounded very tricky," she approved as I paused, defeated.

"That sounded like Arnold Schoenberg," I confessed.

"Hey, piano man," said Danny D. "Know any Scott Joplin?"

"Danny!" Norma cried. "Don't barge in with your B&T mentality! Maybe Jim's brother will favor us with Puccini."

Danny D. looked behind him. "She talking at you, Harry?" "Not me." "Who's she talking at?" "I don't know, but she better watch her step. She talks that way to *me* and pow! she'll be touring the far side of the moon."

"Well, naturally—" I began.

"Him, too," said Danny D., indicating me.

"The kid's okay," said Jim. "He's with me."

"Bud," said Norma sweetly, blinding an apple, "can you play Musetta's Valse Song?"

That one's a cinch. Partway through, Norma began to sing along, in one of those dowdy translations common around 1905:

> *And when I go out twirling on the boulevards*
> *The men all crane their necks to spy me . . .*

By the end she had opened up and was letting it rip right up to the climactic high B, for which she executed an antique coquette pose and accidentally upset some of her hors d'oeuvres.

"Hey Caruso," said Danny D., "you dropped your foodies."

Jim and Laurie exchanged a look, but Brenda clapped as Norma explained that she had trained as a singer and gave it up on parental suggestion.

"So who can blame them?" asked Danny D.

Actually, Norma was, like thousands who dally in that quarter, not good and not terrible: she fielded a sweet, tiny voice with neither authority nor musicianship. But now she felt encouraged, and the show was on. Norma produced a book of arias from the piano bench, and we ran through it till Danny D. came over and banged on the lower keys. "What is this?" he asked, "an opera house or the beach?"

Facing the bay as the sun sank away somewhere over Passaic, we dined uneventfully till one Sal, a neighbor, popped in. Now, The Pines is intent and Water Island zonked. So, if everything matters in The Pines, nothing matters in Water Island. Yet I got an intent feeling, in the laden comments passed and batted back, that Sal tended to drop in moochingly at mealtimes, that he and Norma had a small bit of a past she would gladly forget, and that Sal did not realize that forcing one's welcome on women was not the same thing as forcing it on men like Danny D.

Because Danny D. suddenly said, without the slightest provocation, "Look, can I tell you something? I don't want to see your fucking ugly face around here till I go, which is Monday night. So shove off, you Commie jerksucker."

Sal, a mite stunned, stared at him.

"And you got five," said Danny D.

"He means five seconds," said Laurie helpfully, "or else."

Sal waited out the five—more through confusion than defiance, I expect. But when Danny D. rose up, Sal sprang for the walk. At a safe distance, he turned to reply. Danny D. was still coming, and Sal vanished.

"That smart chick knows the code," said Danny D., of Laurie.

Now, what I wish to note here is that, in any other social group I have access to, such a scene would have considerably changed the complexion of the evening. Amongst trendy liberals, direly subtle commentary would have broken out, positions established. The literati would have prowled Danny D. for backstory and parts of him would filter into the *Paris Review* and *Grand Street*. A gay crowd might fashion it into dish, a condign scandal to do into tatters over tea. But this group went on as if nothing had happened. And, by their lights, nothing had: Danny D. didn't like an intruder and thus efficiently disposed of him.

There's a directness, an eagerness to confront, that sets certain kinds of people apart, at the beach or elsewhere, in trunks or a suit, out to boogie or looking for trouble. There's a look in the eye, a grab of the hands, and you're in over your head, drowning. If men tend to start fights and women tend to avoid them, it's interesting that gay men tend to avoid them, too. Spend an hour in an Irish bar with ten people present and you're sure to see men fight. Yet who has ever seen a fight in a gay bar, no matter how crowded? (Carlo dimly recalls one in the Eagle about twelve years ago.) Is this because gays are too busy confronting profound questions of male identity to spare energy for fighting? Or is it simply a cultural matter, another facet of the straight style?

Whatever its basis, it does put a certain quickness into the air. After dinner Norma asked me to institute some intellectual sport of a Manhattan savvy—no, not in those words—and in response I suggested we all try an old favorite in my family, the Question Game, in which the participants (five brothers can play) trade questions that must be answered truthfully.

"It's all the rage at those New York loft parties," Norma gushed; this was wishful thinking. "Now, Danny, do you love me for myself, or just for my physique?"—pronounced "*fi*-si-cyew."

Danny D. looked over at me and said, "What the hell kind of fucking stupid game is this?"

Imagine your ten closest friends in Danny D.'s position, thinking what he thinks, and consider what response they might make, as opposed to his: and you'll understand what I wish to note about confrontation.

The next day, after lunch, Norma cornered me with her aria book and expressed a life's dream to attempt "In questa reggia." I obliged. It sounded like Thumbelina singing the piccolo part of "The Stars and Stripes Forever," but, as we pulled into the finish, she clasped my shoulders and kissed my ear, her life's dream accomplished. And there, dripping wet from the shower, nude and irate, was Danny D.

"Look," he said, "I don't know what it is with this opera stuff, but Norma's my girl. Got it?"

Like Sal, I was too startled to react. Jim, out of nowhere, came up and said, "Hey, Danny D.!"

"Yo, Jimbo!" came the reply, familiar on many a building site.

"Take it easy," said Jim, touching Danny D.'s neck. "He's just playing piano for her. She's singing. End of bit, right?"

"What I see is she's a girl and he's a guy, huh?" He swung the flat of his hand through the air, meaning, "Cut!"

Danny D. went back inside to dress, Norma followed him, Brenda came up to Jim whispering, "Did I miss something, Honeycock?" and

Laurie again beckoned me to the beach, now with a jab of her thumb.

"Numbnuts," she began, as we settled on the sand just above the wetline. "Stop interfering with that romance. I thought gays were supposed to be sensitive."

"What did I do?"

"You assisted the world's champion cockbaiter in baiting her man's cock."

"Norma?"

"Don't you see how she makes Danny D. feel when she pulls out that opera jazz? It's supposed to be something *she* knows about, and *he* doesn't, so he's supposed to feel like a clod. Or didn't you know about these punk Italian *signorine*?"

"Who do you think I am, Errol Flynn?"

"Well, man, it turns out they're choice touch. But getting along with them is another thing. Because they bust ass and bite balls and torch cock." She imitated them: "'Buy me *that*! Where's my *ring*? It must be *catered* or my girlfriend Teresa won't be jealous!'"

I considered this.

"Your brother's a neat guy," she went on. "The way he covered for you with Danny D. You didn't know what the fuck was coming down. And he did. That's sensitive."

"Yeah, he was *so* sensitive on the beach some years ago, as I—"

"I'm talking now."

"Look how you defend a man like that. Haven't you heard the word chauvinist? Don't you know how he treats women? They're just packages of sexmeat to him."

"He was *there* for you, man!"

"Oh, come on! Any brother will defend you! That was to show you what a great guy he is."

She stared hard at the water, said, "I'm going to hit you because I want you to remember the next thing I'm going to say. Remember it for a long while." Then she grabbed me by the scruff of the neck and slapped my cheek harder than I've ever been slapped, harder than I thought I could be.

"Some brothers don't defend you," she said quietly, holding on to me. "Come *on*? Some brothers will stand by and watch their friends rape you. Listen, they'll do it themselves, brothers. You'll think maybe they'd look away at the time, lay a little shame on it, at least? Don't think that, mister. Don't think it. *Come on*? Listen. You got a brother to watch out for you, you be real glad of him." She released me and hugged herself, trying to calm the breathing. "Chauvinism. I hear it. That . . . logo word. How do you think *I* treat women, huh? Who am I, Tinker Bell? Jane Austen? I lay 'em and leave 'em! *I'm* Errol Flynn! And don't hand me that sisterhood shit! *Politics!* What the shit do I care who's king this year? They'll never be on my side, will they? Yours, either. Or your brother's. Know whose side the kings are on? Know who the kings *are*, for Christshit? Do you? *Rich! Straight! Males!*" She stood, walked into the bits of water at the end of the waves, and looked back at me. "Rich straight males," she repeated. "You're a subversive. And your brother's an exploitable prole. And I'm not on the chart."

After a few minutes, I said, "You know, you should have been an ironworker."

She laughed. Hell, she downright roared.

"I've got a nickname picked out for you," I added. "Stinger."

"Do they all have nicknames?"

"The hot ones do. What do you think 'Danny D.' is? His last name's O'Brien."

"Speaking of which," she said, glancing over my shoulder. Danny D. was heading over the dunes toward us, hopping daintily from one boiling footprint to the next in green nylon trunks that might have gone out of style in 1956.

"Yo hey," he said, plopping down next to me. "Going to apologize for blowing off steam like that there."

"Forget it."

"No. First it's that groveling cheat Sal, then that piano. You know, Norma, sometimes she leans on me with the music, sort of." He asked himself, "What do you mean leans on you?" "Leans on me, like suddenly she's too busy to play with me, or like it's this big put-down game. Like she's flirting with the songs, see?" "I see, man. So even though he's your pal's brother, you got to wonder what he's up to, right?" "Right."

"Danny D.," I said, "don't wonder. I'm gay."

"Gay who?"

"No, *gay*. As in Not Straight."

He turned questioningly to Laurie.

She said, "He means he's a faggot."

Danny D. gave me a searching look. "You shitting me?"

I shook my head.

"You mean gay like . . . boy meets *boy*? Boy gets *boy*?"

"Let's hope."

He thought this over, regarded me once more, leaped up with a whoop of joy, ran into the ocean, and ran right out again, shouting, "Cold water! Run for your lives!"

Her mind on other matters, Laurie asked me, "What's your brother's nickname?"

"Jimbo."

"You never call him that, do you?"

"I don't know Jimbo. I scarcely know Jim."

"You don't say it like a name," said Danny D. "You know that?"

"How does he say it?" Laurie asked.

"Like a . . . a secret."

I shrugged. "This has been being a holiday of secrets."

Danny D. was laughing again. "Wait'll I tell that bitchen Norma. Only thing is, how the fuck do I get back over that sand? Coming down, I almost burned my footsies off."

"Get your feet cold in the ocean," I suggested. "Then run like hell."

"Hey, you're a smart kid."

"Danny D., I'm older than you are."

"Yeah?" He got into the water to his knees. "You're still a kid." He faced the houses. "Okay," he began, "let's go," revving up. "It's *banzai time!*" And away he went.

Norma accepted my decision to curtail the operatic end of my repertory; she seemed to sense that the men had made one of their handshake pacts and, wise girl, bore it without reproach. I even managed to essay Joplin's "Peacherine Rag" (with the barest hint of Second Viennese School harmony) for Danny D., and he told Jim, "That's a swift kid, pal. You raised him right."

"He was hell at first," said Jim. "But he's cooling out nicely. Right, sport?"

"I'd rather die."

"Commie punk," said Danny D.

The usual nookie session followed dinner, and Laurie excused herself to, as she put it, "make a blonde." She probably did not mean by origami. Alone, then, alarmed and amused at spending a weekend at Fire Island without touching base at The Pines, I elected to put the time to use and got out notebook and pen and just started writing, as if by Ouija board, aim and tone wandering. What eventually came out was a story, an early version of this one, in fact. I had written plenty of stories, but till now they had been fantasies, or dialect romances, or urbane comedies about people I had never met. Now, suddenly, one was about someone's real life—rudely so, but a hard pen has no conscience. I wrote straight through, and, reaching a temporary lull in the tale, this lull, I stopped, stimulated and exhausted. It was well after midnight. I decided to walk down to the beach before turning in.

The Pines boardwalks can be tricky after dark, but Water Island's planks are fearsome, dilapidated and unmarked. It was worth any hazard, though, to reach that vast healing velvet of black sky trimmed by its knowing moon, a Pines moon. I searched westward for the lights of the gay citadel, just out of reach. Tomorrow, I resolved, I'll pay a call.

I heard whistling behind me and turned to find Jim in jeans and a ratty old yachting sweater.

"Thought you'd be out here," he said. "I saw your notebook on the table, sport. Fixing to write a story about something?"

"Did you read any of it?"

He swung a foot through the water. "Can't make out your handwriting. Thought I recognized some names, though."

"You want to play the Question Game?"

He laughed softly. "Uh-oh."

"One last time?"

"Okay, sport. One last time forever."

"You first."

He had it all ready. "What do they say about me now? Back home?"

"They . . . don't mention you at all."

He thought it over, nodded. He thinks that's fair. "Shoot."

"That time on the shore. Were you really trying to drown me?"

"Oh, that." He came up to me. "That time on the shore, right." He looked me in the eye; at close range, Fire Island moonlight permits excellent vision. "You blew it, sport. One last time forever. You know the answer to that question. The answer is yes. The question you should have asked is, *Why?*"

"I don't want to know that answer."

"Sure you do. You're going to be a writer, you've got to know everything." He took my arm. "Let's go back to the house. It's cold."

"I want to stay a bit more."

"That boardwalk's all busted up. It's dangerous alone."

"I got out here, didn't I?"

"Suit yourself." He started off, whistling.

"Jim." I guess it does sound like a secret. Telling, not keeping one. "Why . . . did you try to drown me?"

After a long while, he said, "Sport, some men just weren't meant to be brothers."

I watched him head back up the dunes in the moonlight, and I thought, Whatever happens, I can use it. I can observe, abstract, enhance it, distance myself from or embrace it. It was a great moment; years from now, white-haired, fêted and crabby, I may do a madeleine on this memory. I showed my fist to the virgin moon, to leave a picture for me to recall, and someone grabbed it and pulled me around: Jim, the brother I most resemble and am least like, more boyish than I would dare be and more man than I am permitted to use in my world of the *comme il faut* intelligentsia.

"Come on along," he said, annoyed at having to tell me twice.

One day they nearly drown you; the next, they want you on hand for social comedy. Oh, I'll come on along; the only things I don't resist are hard liquor and brute force. I'll come on and take a bead on all of you. I am eager to confront, now, and I'll get a story out of it, no matter what is done to me. From here on, I know everything and you got five.

Okay, sports?

I Am the Sleuth

A droll tale of sociosexual crossover, containing a treatise on sexuality thrown into the middle of the plot, for which the author makes no apology to his readers.

Well, there I am, as all too often, at my desk to scrimmage with the muse while everyone else in town is out on the streets having terse encounters. It's a Saturday afternoon in late fall, when the opinion-makers stroll Soho in awe of themselves, when fashionable people do the latest sweater along Madison or Second, when bagladies shop with such abandon that one finds overturned garbage cans all the way from Eighth Street to the Park. But I'm at my labor, painfully ooching through a piece I would knock off in two hours if only this were winter—if possible during a blizzard and with emergency rations of Johnnie Walker Red and Mars bars laid by in the pantry. Dragging along as the sunlight robustly streams down and the great world frolics only blocks away (am I missing a Major Brunch?), I seem to start this piece over again with each new sentence, making it something like a tiny encyclopedia. This proves, I ruefully reflect, that New York doesn't have more sex than other places, just more opinions.

So I was relieved when Dennis Savage came in, his eyes brightly furtive and his tread a fidgety sarabande.

"Well, well, well," I said. "Guess what you've been doing."

Smiling, he led me to the couch, sat me down, and prepared to launch his report.

"Anyone I know?" I asked.

"Shut up and listen and maybe you'll get a nice tale out of it."

"That's the story of my life."

"Last night I met this guy at the corner of Twenty-first and Eleventh. He was sitting on the curb because he had no place to go. He looked like he'd been on the streets for—"

"Whoa," I said, getting all set up. Basically we're best friends, but we have these verbal duels in which we try to pulverize each other. It keeps the relationship fresh. "What do you mean you *met* someone at Twenty-first and Eleventh, as if that were the lobby of the Algonquin or some prankish salon? Twenty-first and Eleventh is the Eagle. You don't just meet anyone there. You pick him up. You molest him. You pause to count the bugle beads on his art deco shorts and—"

"I knew you'd do this."

"What would you say if you handed a small child a lollipop and he unwrapped it and put it into his mouth to enjoy? 'I knew you'd do this'?"

"When calm sets in, I'll tell the interesting part."

I went to the piano and played "Getting to Know You," grinning at Dennis Savage. He let me get all the way through the chorus, then said, "The interesting part is, he's straight."

"Oh please, these banal gay daydreams. Mission ridiculous."

"I swear on your mother's life."

"I don't know," I temporized. "Didn't I read in the *Times* that there weren't any straights anymore, just electricians?"

"If you saw him—be good and you will—you'd change your tune."

"What does a straight do in bed?" I asked, bemused.

His eyes glowed again. "Everything," he breathed.

"But what would a straight be doing outside the Eagle?"

"He didn't know where he was. He was almost raving with hunger and fatigue."

"How come *you* got him?"

He shrugged happily. "I came out and there he was."

"Good career move."

"Oh, he's so nice," Dennis Savage told me. "To meet him is to . . . to—"

"To yearn to drill him, eh?"

"Will you clam up? To meet him is to understand him."

"Old news. Any gay can understand a straight because we all start out as insiders in straight culture. The headlines are due when a straight understands a gay, which will be never. And, excuse me for asking, but what's a straight doing in bed with the gayest man in New York?"

"Well . . ."

"Stop looking rapt and answer!"

"Oh, he was a mite shy at first. But you know how affectionate lost boys can be, when someone proposes to take care of them. Can I tell you what a pleasure it was to spend time with a man who wasn't scared by his mother when he was three?"

"Are you going to see this waif again?"

"I can't help but. He's sleeping upstairs right now."

"You left him alone in your apartment? Alone with your check-book, your plastic, and your complete collection—the world's only, I fear to say—of Alice Faye lobby cards?"

"*You're* the one who—"

"Did you at least hide your—"

"His name is Ray and he's as sweet as they make them. Do you want to come up and meet him or not?"

I was reminded of that scene in Tennessee Williams' play *The Milk Train Doesn't Stop Here Anymore*, wherein two beldames remark a splendid youth asleep in a bed, for Dennis Savage took me up to his place and there in the bedroom was his vagabond lover, one of those unruly innocents that delight at twenty-five, confuse at thirty, and irritate thereafter; but Ray was twenty-five. Curled up, clutching the pillow as if it were a teddy bear with a Mastercard, he looked trashily angelic, a little haunted and maybe a little intelligent. Maybe a lot intelligent: that's unusual in waifs.

Dennis Savage was beaming like Fafner over his hoard. Noting banter bubbling to my lips, he held up a ssh finger.

"Isn't he cute?" he whispered. "How jealous you must be."

"Not at all," I whispered back. "I'm happy for you."

"What are you, a saint?"

"I want all my friends content."

He regarded his treasure. "Please be jealous. I want you jealous."

"Why?"

"It's half the fun of being gay."

"I'll bet he squeaks when he's screwed."

"He doesn't do anything you'd expect. He even talks funny." He pulled me over to the window. "Last night, when we were dozing off, he farted and said, 'Guess a bedbug just bit me.'"

A guffaw yelped out of me and Ray was awake, eyes fluttering as he took us in. Interesting eyes. "I was oversleeping, fellas," he uttered.

"Ray," Dennis Savage blissed—no other usage quite captures the noise he made that moment.

Ray squirmed, lazily smiled, and kicked off the covers. Dennis Savage soared right on to introduce us, and Ray said, "A happy Saturdays to you."

"To someone, anyway," I replied. He pronounced it "Saterdies," which was charming enow. "Well," I added, edging out, "I'm off to farandole class."

"Wonder if I could get up eggs and buttered toast with fruit spread," Ray was saying, and I chuckled all the way home. Once again, another thrilling chapter in the gay chronicles—*True Love at Long Last*, for instance, or *Bad Hat Reformed by Influence of Nice New Friend*, or, as in this case, *Dennis Savage Makes Sexual Crossover*—boiled down to the usual participants making the usual pickup in the usual places. Not that true love, character reformation, and crossover were all that elusive; but they were secret, invisible, while cruising and tricking were all over the place and hard to miss. And Dennis Savage, in those plague-free days, before he hooked up permanently with Little Kiwi, did enjoy his pickups. I was a little startled to learn that he and Ray ran their morning after into the night of the following day (complete with periodic breathless reports from Dennis Savage on the wonders of bedding a straight). But then I've seen a lot of moving in and out on the part of the homeless—Carlo has spent half his life as a leaseless roommate, and a number of Brooklynites of my acquaintance routinely arrange their affairs around the securing of pieds-à-terre in more central locales. What was amusing was Dennis Savage's enthusiasm for the appeal of straight: the pure hot of A Real Man.

"He's so elemental!" Dennis Savage raved. "So true to life! At last I see it! All that old friends-of-Dorothy lore about waterfront bars and truck stops and dangerous men. That wasn't just because they didn't have preppie bars then. It was because they wanted to experience sexuality at its most masculine." He looked awed. He prepared his lecture. "Frustrated by their own giddy going-nowhere wit," he intoned, "by the covering-up, the apologizing, the hunger for peace, they fled their own kind and sought . . . what?"

"You know, that's about the most homophobic thing I've ever heard."

"Oh, great. If you can't be jealous, be political."

"They weren't fleeing anything," I insisted, "except the vicious credo of self-hatred laid upon them by everyone they knew all their lives. Society outlawed them so thoroughly they had to conceive their culture after-hours in secret places with murderous lunatics who have nothing to lose, and then society cried out in horror at 'the night world of the homosexual'! And when a dangerous man took them to a dark corner, lifted their wallet, and kicked them to death, with their last breath the contemptible faggots would sigh, 'Thank you, that was just.'"

His enthusiasm somewhat watted out, Dennis Savage regarded me resentfully. "I hardly think that boy upstairs is going to kick me to death."

"Why does he have to be straight, anyway?" I asked. "Would you enjoy him less if he—"

"He doesn't have to be. He is. Nothing embarrasses him. His world isn't a . . . a stage of drag shows and epigrammatic ripostes and all those delirious, skulking hungers."

"Oh, good."

"Shut up. His world is the world, and he's the center of it. I'm telling you, it's pure straight. As far as he's concerned, the universe exists to pleasure him."

"Sounds like an est instructor."

"It's more than the sex. It's like slipping through to the other side of the mirror. It's the difference between needing love and fucking love. Gays need love. Straights only need to fuck."

"According to Freud, then, gays are healthier than straights. Health is defined by the ability to love and work."

"I'm not looking for healthy just now," he fumed. "Do you mind?"

"Aren't we confusing issues, anyway? It's not a question of who's dangerous and who's nice. It's a question of who's emotionally available and who isn't. I would consider a man who is thus available to a gay man as gay. A man who is thus unavailable is straight—no matter whom he lies down with for what reason."

"Dick Hallbeck," he said suddenly, supporting my thesis. Dick Hallbeck is one of our favorite people, a man from Dennis Savage's hometown who turned up in the early days of gay cinema under a *nom de porn* screwing every man who chanced to come within camera range. Some porn actors are slithery hot, some less hot than hired, just there, minding the wrong business. Dick Hallbeck was hot. He outclassed men far more stunning than he and overwhelmed practiced veterans. Dark and forceful, he seemed on screen to offer a *summum bonum* of dead-on, take-no-prisoners promiscuity. He was the very energy of what Stonewall promised besides politics and art, virtually the protagonist of gay sex.

But he was straight. I don't mean latent. I don't mean bi. I don't mean avant-garde. I mean he was a straight who made his living fucking men. He appeared to be managing it lucratively. Ads offering stills, cinema, and even the kiss-and-tell journal of Jim Packer—Dick Hallbeck's public name—were everywhere one turned in those days, and the utterly humorless eyes that gave that ordinary face its show did not look like those of an exploitable man. There was no doubt that Dick Hallbeck held the major percentage on the marketing of Jim Packer.

Today Jim Packer is long forgotten and porn stars are in any case less prominent than they once were; we look to other heroes now. But in the first days of Stonewall, porn promised to be the most immediate source of gay independence, symbolically the unique defiance. Not every gay would revel in the emergence of a gay literature or monitor the airwaves for signs of "normalization" in the stereotype. But every gay responds to porn. Hell, what man doesn't, except George Will? Willing or no, there was no *Christopher Street* then, no Edmund White, no Gerry Studds. What there was was Jim Packer. To sit in the ruins of one of old Broadway's great relics—Henry Miller's Theatre as was, renamed the Park-Miller for purposes of porn exhibition—surrounded by hordes of hungry men, cruising, gasping, lurking, wandering, watching Jim Packer initiating applicants of many types in more positions than the *Kama Sutra* knows . . . well, to be there and to comprehend it, yet to hear Dennis Savage whisper that he had gone to high school with this man, and that he was as straight as our fathers are, was to realize that there might indeed be more things in heaven and earth than are dreamt of in my philosophy.

Naturally, I didn't believe this at first, partly because it was unbelievable and partly because I find it good policy not to believe anything Dennis Savage says, especially when he's in earnest. You have to understand that he was speaking of a man we had seen, over the course of an hour, plowing into a sizable fraction of the male porn population. And while I must admit that this man never cried out, "Hey, some fun!" or even smiled, still no one was holding a gun to his head.

I told Dennis Savage he was crazy, that the man was as gay as George Cukor (if different). Dennis Savage said that after all Dennis Savage's older brother was Dick's best friend, so he ought to know. But at the time all I could see—or all I could understand, and therefore all I *would* see—was that straight was one world and gay another, and that the two worlds were irremediably separate. I could believe that many a straight had lain with a man for personal, financial, or professional advancement. But would a straight so thrust himself into the gay scene that he could become its potent symbol?

The question fascinated both Dennis Savage and me, and his old friend's names became our buzz terms. "Dick Hallbeck" signified a straight of possibly expansive virtues. "Jim Packer" was gay, wildly appetitive, but somehow impersonal. These were fantasy figures, largely—but came the day, then, that we crossed paths with the two men ourselves. It was a spring afternoon; we were on a bench in one of the plazas the Sixth Avenue office towers use in order to frill up their bottoms, and a man left the passing crowd to examine Dennis Savage. His wrinkled shirt was open to the belt, his boots were busted, his scraggly beard looked like something a wrestler would wear to a cockfight, and he said, "How's Cliff doing?"

"He's in Seattle," said Dennis Savage. I think he was stunned.

"Who's this?" the man asked, about me, sitting next to us.

"Bud," said Dennis Savage, "this is . . ." Yes, who, or which, was he? "This is my brother's best friend from high school."

"Dick Hallbeck," he told me, as we shook hands.

That's one way of looking at it, I thought.

The meeting was short, merely a "What's new? encounter—Dennis Savage reporting on the family Cliff was raising in Seattle, Dick on the bar he was planning to open in New Jersey as soon as he had assembled his venture backing, along with a few idle aperçus. But we spoke long enough for me to realize that Dennis Savage had been right: Dick Hallbeck—even Jim Packer—was straight. Emotionally unavailable to gays, possibly to anyone. Some gays swear they can tell a fellow from an outsider within two minutes simply by his dress and eye movements and allusions; but these are blandishments. I can tell a comrade by a certain sensitivity, a sometimes determined and sometimes furtive awareness of place, of people, of the vibrations bashing through the ozone. Gays are never strangers, even when they're uncomfortable. Straights always hold something back. Dick Hallbeck did, too; and better, perhaps, than anyone I've met. He was focused entirely on us, never as much as glanced at the people storming by. Yet he gave nothing to us. There was no real transaction: because what he might have wanted, we could not supply. There was a barely perceptible gap between us, a hitch in delivery, as when one of the speakers in a conversation is not altogether fluent in the language. None of us was shy or brooding. We were lively, forthright, and we all spoke English. Yet we could not impress him. He could not touch us.

Dennis Savage, once he got over his surprise at seeing Jim Packer turn into Dick Hallbeck, became ebullient and began to flow with picturesque recollections of small-town life. Only in New York, I reminded myself—only in this absurd metropolis could you find yourself sitting between a schoolteacher and a porn star as they review a past of socials and canoeing. But once in this old-home convention did Dennis Savage tighten up, when Dick referred to "that time you guys bagged the Winky-Dink out by the sled hills." One of Dick's eyebrows jittered, as if he found this a questionable act, though his tone was noncommittal, and I made note to inquire into this matter as soon as was indecently possible.

It was Dick, anyway, who held my attention, for I always enjoy meeting proof that the riddles haven't all been solved—that some stories, after all, have yet to be told. What fascinated was not what Dick was, but what he *also* was, for Dick fielded the tough form of straight, based on the kind of self-reliance so brash it hardly needs to show itself. In fact, I began to understand—at that very moment, that chance meeting—that the straight-gay disparity was not a sexual but a *cultural* matter. Isn't it? I stopped listening to Dick and started watching him, and I got a picture of a man who cares only about withstanding assaults on his space, making women, filling his wallet, and satisfying a few secondary appetites. He cares about nothing else: he has no art, no representations, no themes. And that is pure straight. The exceptions are salesmen, unemployed actors, and hustlers, all of whom will go out of their way to engage you emotionally no matter how straight they may be. But then, of course, they want something from you; that gives them a theme.

"Who's the Winky-Dink?" I asked after Dick went on his way. "And why did you bag him?"

"Do you like me?" Dennis Savage countered.

"Uh . . ."

"Do you want to stay friends with me?"

"At least through next week."

"Leave it alone, okay? Just leave it, because it's a sacred, sad thing that no one should hear of."

"Okay," I said. Two beats, then: "Tell me or I'll make up something horrible and put it in a story."

"If I tell you, you're bound to put it in a story."

"Never."

"It already is horrible."

"I sensed that."

"I'd hoped to take it to my grave."

"None must know it."

"Exactly."

"Any who did would hate you."

"There you go."

"So tell me. Or else." I mimed a headline: "DENNIS SAVAGE MOLESTS MAYOR'S EIGHT-YEAR-OLD SON. 'HE BLEW ME APART,' CHILD REVEALS."

"Cut it out!"

"'IT HURT BUT IT'S FUN,' THE VICTIM WENT ON, AS HIS PARENTS SLAPPED HIM ABOUT—"

"I helped some homophobic straights beat up a helpless gay kid for a Halloween prank. We were so mean to him that whenever he saw us he quietly stood where he was and wept. Now, are you glad? And who made *you* head of the gay secret police, *huh*?"

He was angry and I was silent.

"Comes the revolution," he went on, "and you report me to the Committee, try to remember that the pressures to conform are tremendous in a small town. Tremendous, okay? And remember that many of us, in that last desperate surge of fake solidarity before we face up to what we are . . . what we need to be . . . pull one or two truly vicious stunts that hurt us for the rest of our lives."

"Imagine how the Winky-Dink feels."

He took a deep breath and silently counted to ten.

"Go joke," he said, in what may have been genuine melancholy. "Go ahead." He gestured feebly, like a dying insect. "Have one on me."

We were almost home by then; our encounter with Dick Hallbeck had made us long to get indoors, safe from chance meetings.

"What's bagging, anyway?" I asked. "Each time I hear it, it means something else. Carlo says it's where you pull off someone's pants in public. Lionel says that's debagging; plain bagging is dunking someone in water. The way you use it, it sounds like a mugging."

He just looked at me.

"You have to tell," I said. "I told you about Gary Lundquist making me play Strip Candyland in the attic."

"You never told me that."

"Didn't I?" I held the door for him; we had gone to my place. "Well, I will, one day. Right now, it's confess or else."

He nodded. "It was Halloween night," he began, speaking in a slow drag, as if showing me how repentant he was. "We were in tenth grade . . ."

"Pace! Pace!"

"All right," he said, and we began to sail. "His family called him Lance and their name was Winkler, but we called him the Winky-Dink, for the imaginable reasons. Total queer. He was eccentric, as you might expect, and he liked to go out trick-or-treating. Well, two jocks and I decided to jump him. You know, teach the faggot a lesson. I mean, here's a society in which tenth-grade males excel in sports and design racing cars and do ingenious things with cherry bombs. And here's this narrow-shouldered potzie named Lance who likes to dress up on Halloween and collect candy with the eight-year-olds. You have to admit that's pretty limp."

"I think it's pretty daring."

He shrugged. "Maybe it was the biggest night of his year—the one on which it was actually legal for him to go out in costume."

"So," I said, giving him unsweetened apple juice to steady his nerves. "What exactly happened?"

"We waited for him out by the sled hills, where there's this big empty space and no houses. And finally he came by, singing happily to himself, and we . . . well, okay, we bagged him."

"Such as what?"

"Oh, we harassed him and then we pulled him off the street into the shadows while he said, 'Please don't hurt me,' and 'I never did anything to you,' and all those unbelievably *stupid* things that have absolutely nothing to do with your relationship with implacable men. Is that what they say in a prison riot, as they're held down while someone trims their skull with an acetylene torch? 'I never did anything to you'?"

"More."

"More . . . We threw his candy all over the place and we punched him around a little, and then we stripped off his costume and ran off with it, laughing all the way. I know you love to humble me and rake me around, and here's your big chance. Let's get it over with."

"Did you really do that?"

He was still.

"No," I said. "I mean, *why* did you do that? How *could* you? I thought I knew you. 'I don't like his looks so let's bag him.'"

"On the contrary, he was very cute. Black hair and very dark skin. All the girls were crazy for him."

"I thought you hated violence."

He nodded. "Maybe this is why."

"And how," I pursued, "could you agree to go along with those two cretins? Why didn't you get sick or have to look after the house or something?"

"I didn't go along with them. I led them. It was my idea."

We drank our juice and contemplated the strange footnotes of the gay biography.

"The sled hills . . ." I said. "What's the derivation of that?"

"Oh, there was a series of interconnected slopes that were hell to walk on but great for sledding in the snow, which we always had a lot of. And there were no grown-ups around to . . . you know . . ."

"Bag you."

"We only went on them for sledding, so they were—"

"That's a great naturalistic detail. Authenticates the story."

"You mean I would have been safe if Dick hadn't mentioned that?" he asked. "You wouldn't have proposed to expose my shame?"

"No, I would have made something like that up. But it's more amusing when it's real." I noted down the term, and turned back to him, smiling.

"I'll never tell you anything again."

"I always thought teenage violence was a strictly straight phenomenon," I said. "Kind of like the physical interpretation of the state of being emotionally unavailable. You know, when I was a kid there was a Dairy Queen on the town road, and the parking lot was a meeting place for adolescents looking for a fight. I mean, literally. A violence market. The outlet closed at nine, and by ten there'd be kids hulking in the shadows, looking each other over, approaching, psyching up . . . What does it sound like?"

"A bar."

"Exactly. Jim used to hang out there and collect scalps. He'd invite me along now and then, but I got all the fighting I needed at home— with him, in fact—and besides, who in his sanity would lurk in a parking lot for the purpose of engaging in battle with another teenager for mere sport? Jim would come back and describe his adventures, and you know what I was thinking? Better he had this release for whatever's inside him, because if he didn't give it to them he'd probably give it to me."

"What did your parents say about this?"

"Are you kidding? They never knew."

"Interesting that your father never needed this outlet."

"Why should he? They had wars then. If you have the chance to

serve in the O.S.S. as liaison between Polish partisans and the Russian Army, who needs Dairy Queen parking lots?"

"Anyway, wasn't Jim the aberrant Mordden?"

"I always thought so. But then Andrew took it up in his time, too.
There's something in straight blood. Something in the mind."

"Maybe they intake a substance gays don't know about—Gatorade?
Sen-sen? Or effusions from polyester?"

"Incidentally, what costume did the Winkler boy go out in the
night you bagged him? I visualize a helter-skelter Liz Taylor, but
where would he have gotten the wig?"

"He went as a Mountie."

That took a moment to sink in. I said, "What?"

"You think every gay kid's idea of dressing up is drag?"

"You mean a Mountie like Sergeant Preston of the Yukon? Like
Dudley Do-Right?"

"I want more juice."

"Whatever happened to him? Winkler? I could really use a confrontation ten years on. He forgives you. Tearfully. Makes a nice
effect."

"You're really going to use this, aren't you?"

I refilled his glass. "If you don't want to be in a story, don't know a
writer."

"Anyway, I haven't heard of him in twenty years. I venture to guess
that he's in Rochester or Buffalo, has timidly joined some gay organi-
zation or other, and is alone and unhappy. He was cute, but he was
born to be pushed around and neglected."

"I wonder if that's a difference between gay and straight—that gays
are unhappy when they have no one to be emotionally available to."

"That sounds more like women."

"Anyway, what have we decided?" I asked. "Who hurts? Who
needs? Who gets? And what if the Lance Winklers come to New York
instead of the regional capital? Would that make a difference?"

"Do you know, every time I think of that Halloween I wish I were

Catholic so I could describe what I did to someone who doesn't hate me."

"The interesting thing about being a Protestant is you get to pay for your sins in this life."

"In that case, gays are the Protestants of the sexual revolution."

By all of which, boys and girls, I wish to put Dennis Savage's boyfriend Ray in context: as a willowy, charming fellow with hard skin and soft talk. He was far from the certifiably brusque remoteness of Dick Hallbeck, yet no Winky-Dink, either. He entered upon our scene in the early 1970s, at the height of our questing communications on the subject of the gay and straight identities, and so may well have seemed more attractive than he might have in some other season, as a kind of conversation piece.

He himself had little to say; and one was relieved, after hearing what little there was. Ask him a question and he'd say, "Huh? Lookit," before formulating a reply, and to the ponderous statements that we of the great world are prone to make, he'd offer, "Hey, that's for sure!" Then he'd smile at you as if patting you on the back after making a great save in the ninth inning against the other team's ace batter. He was the kind of fellow you introduced simply as "Ray"— only important people have last names—but he seemed content however he was treated. The official story told it out that he was staying with Dennis Savage till he could find work and a place of his own; and that was true in theory. But in fact Ray was around because Ray liked to take it easy and Dennis Savage liked company. So okay. And, unlike a lot of young men in his position, Ray did not horn in on the conversations of his betters with idiotic opinions. Nor did he scorn to do the marketing, the laundry, and other minor favors. Best (and rarest) of all, he did not quickly become less accommodating in bed. Ray was ideal for his role: there when you needed him and out of the way when you didn't. Moreover, he seemed completely honest, unlike most if not all hustlers, who feel they're missing something if they don't somehow sneak a little extra out of you one way or another. I still felt that there was something oddly intelligent about him, that he knew more than he let on. He would hear things, and be quiet, uninvolved; but you could tell he had heard. He reacted by not reacting.

When I caught him at this, I would smile wittingly, the cabaret detective; but his smile came back open and unknowing. Then I'd turn to Dennis Savage and he'd do one of his "What's going on here?" attitudes, like the cop in the movies who wants to be fair but gets a useful edge out of being tough first and fair later. Something *was* going on here, but I couldn't assimilate it yet.

"You think you're so smart," Dennis Savage would tell me.

"I just want to learn about straight from your friend," I reply. "I'm checking him for emotional unavailability."

"I can see you on the Ark. There's Noah and the family beaming at this amazing achievement. They've saved the world. And you come in and say, 'We forgot the unicorns.'"

"I'm looking out for him," I protested. "I'm afraid you'll find out he's gay after all and then you'll call him a funny name and take his candy and—"

"Of *all* the low tricks, *that's*—"

"Come to think of it, he already has a funny name."

"You should talk?"

"He pronounces it funny, too, doesn't he?"

Dennis Savage stopped grouching and looked at me, thinking about it. Listen: "Holgrave," he said, with the long *o* as in "hole" that most Americans would use.

"That's not how he says it," I told him. "He makes it sort of English. Hahl-grave. You know. The way they say 'hamaseksyual.'"

Dennis Savage shrugged.

"Ray Holgrave," I repeated. "It's a rather elaborate name for a rootless kid, isn't it? I mean, can you imagine a hustler named Holgrave?"

"You keep trying to turn him into some form of opportunist. Can't you believe that there are people with flexible taste? A straight who can enjoy something on the side?"

"This is simple market research. I'm trying to figure out what de-

fines a straight in terms of personality. What variables command an
individual's sexuality. Because it's undeniable that Ray isn't like us."

"Aha."

"Because he's *trying* not to be," I insisted.

"He isn't trying to be anything—that's his charm. He's a perfectly
styleless man." Dennis Savage seemed so glad to have reckoned it out
that I had to humor him with silence. But he went on, "Nothing has
been added to him and nothing taken away," and now I must speak.

"No one," I said, "is perfectly styleless. Whatever you do, that's
your style. Your diction and grammar, for instance. Are you telling
me the odd things he says don't feed into a style?"

"What odd things?"

"'Huh, lookit,'" I replied, in Ray's vapidly blithe manner.

"Everyone else thinks it's cute!"

"Yeah," I said. "Especially Ray."

It was rude of me, no doubt, to keep prodding in matters that were
none of my business, but The Case of the Questionable Straight
gripped me with its thousand riddles. The most arresting part of it all
was the defiance of the traditions of gay sexual crossover, which em-
phasize mystery and menace—those dangerous men, again, lying in
wait for the fluttery stone-age queers who covered the waterfront.
What were those men, really? Latent? Committed? Tolerant? Hostile?
Were they lovers who dared not speak their name, or reformers of the
underworld observing an informal purge technique? What would they
do? Lie back and let you go to town? Would they come along with
you? Take your money and follow you? Want you? Knife you? Here
was menace. But what was Ray? Innocuous, clean-cut. A sweetheart.
Dennis Savage had, it seemed, domesticated the crossover.

And yet. Time after time, at Dennis Savage's for dinner, or strolling with him and Ray through the Village of a Sunday, or in a cab
setting out for a West Side brunch, the detective in me would come
up for air and trouble. I would satirically test Ray with intellectual
call-outs—the Odessa Steps montage, *Zuleika Dobson*, June 16,

1904, Rosebud, the Mapleson cylinders. Ray's eyes—too big, too fully lashed, so pretty—would grow avid as he smiled at me. Was he aware that I was goading him to break cover or simply grateful for the attention?

"It's not good when you get like this," Carlo warned me over steaks at Clyde's. "You make it feel as if knowing things is all that matters."

"Come on, knowledge is power."

Carlo got intent applying mayonnaise to his steak, which is apparently traditional, or at least ordinary, in South Dakota, Carlo's point of origin and, to me, the most remote of all American provinces. Some states don't have opera houses; South Dakota doesn't even have Korean fruit markets.

"Origins," I said, having been thinking of them, "are very telling. You can tell a lot about a person if you know his origins—region, parentage, class . . . Did you know Dennis Savage and the porn star Jim Packer were in high school together? Dennis Savage says, and you won't believe this—"

"Jim Packer is a gringo?" Carlo's term for straights. "I know that."

"How?"

"I tried to take him home and he said no."

"That's proof enough for me," I said, not joking. "But don't you think a straight man in gay porn is a little pushy? I mean, we're not talking of someone in a jack-off scene, or getting tongued here and there. I've seen him. He does every activity in the checklist, and he does it with the opulence of an initiate."

"You don't know what he's thinking of, though."

"Carlo, he was a CIA agent or something in this movie, and he had a spy tied down on a bed and he was trying to get information out of him, yes? Think of it. The spy looked like the swimming champ of Walt Whitman High School or something, but let's move right on. And there's our boy, straight Jim Packer"—only it's not Jim Packer who's straight, it's Dick Hallbeck—"stroking the spy's tummy and pubic hairs and murmuring sweet nothings about 'the information,' and am I supposed to . . . I mean, let's face it, the spy's cock was so rigid you could have plugged the hole in the dike and saved Amsterdam. And the look on Jim Packer's face. I can't believe—"

"*Do you suppose* you could talk about something more suitable to decent public gatherings?" cried someone at the table behind me.

I turned around to find four men glaring at me.

"This is a restaurant," another of the four explained, "not a toilet!"

Carlo, who has done this a hundred times, got up and stood before them and said, with engaging mildness, "One of you come outside with me and settle it like a man or shut your mouths and mind your business. Because one more word out of any of you and I'll pick *you*"—he chooses the most vulnerable queen of the lot; it's always queens, by the way: clones don't start these scenes—"and drag you outside and kick your junk in." Then, paradoxically, he touches the arm of the man he addressed. "So keep your friends in line," he urges. It never fails.

When he sat down again, we began to eat in silence, thinking over the themes. Clones and brothers and fighting and love. Emotional availability. And that really is New York right there: someone's always got some idea to sell.

"Bud," he finally said, "you surely have to stop measuring people."

"I can't stop. It's my job."

"A lot of porn actors switch back and so. It's just work to them."

"What about Ray, Carlo? His current assignment—would you call that work or fun? Would you call Ray an actor? Or a true story?"

He ate, considering. "I will sincerely tell you what is true," he said after a bit, putting down his fork and leaning on the table. "Access," he said. "So you'd best include that, while you're scoring everybody up as gays or gringos."

"Access."

"Some people would call it chance. It isn't, because this is something people get to do without consciously willing it. They . . . they *contrive* it. That means they don't know what they want, but they know what they're afraid of. So they allow themselves to get into the position of being near the thing that threatens them the least."

He stopped, reached for his fork. I grabbed his hand. "No," I said. "Go on."

"Well. So, like." He's thinking; the talk comes out too fast in New York. Midwestern Carlo pauses to be sure of what he knows. "Why is it," he asks, "that so many men who can't deal with emotional involvements get into prison, where they either have to go without sex—which no one can do—or fuck men? Because when they get out, they go *on* fucking men, and they tell themselves it's because they got wrecked in jail, or because men are easier to get ahold of than women."

"Access . . ."

"But maybe it's because it's what they wanted in the first place. Not because they're gay, but because they want sex without affection."

"Emotionally unavailable . . ."

"They can always find a bimbo, I know. You know. Some women are as easy to take home as men are. But even those women scare them. They're different. Hard. Funny. Something."

He started to eat again, watching me, glancing out the window onto Bleecker Street, nodding, chewing. He's no literato, but there are more stories in him than in all the writers I know put together. Maybe that's why I like him so much.

"Carlo, you aren't saying that you've run into men like that. Convicts? In our bars?"

"They don't go to gay bars, boy. They wouldn't know where to find them." He grinned. "They go to other places."

"Working-class bars?"

He nodded.

"They actually go there to pick up men?" I asked, scandalized and incredulous.

Our very scion of the Circuit regarded me with forgiveness for, as usual, my lack of scope. "You think you can't take a man home from a Clancy's or a Blue Ribbon Bar and Grill, like with a Schaefer logo in the window? You think everyone there is guys and bimbos?"

How does he know so much? I was thinking, for we were all young then.

"It's a question of lifestyle, Bud. It's not hetero and homo. It's gringo and gay. It's . . ."

"Culture."

"Yes. It's how you learn to behave. People tend to stay in their culture. They avoid other cultures."

"So a homophobic hardhat," I posed, "is what?"

"A gringo."

"But if he secretly beds men?"

"He's still a gringo. Straight is how you act, not how you feel. You truly should know that by now. Do you *feel* gay? Or do you wear the uniforms and attend the dances and keep in touch with the politics? And feel like a man? Men is all it is. Men. Boys. Kids. All this. And you and Dennis Savage. Eric, Lionel, Scooter, Kenny. And Big Steve. Remember him? And the people you didn't see and the dancers at the Tenth Floor. All of us . . ."

"Carlo."

"We're all here."

"What do you—"

"Eat up, Bud."

"*Access.* Listen—"

"You have to stop. You're going to get yourself weird. The more you make rules, the farther you get from the truth. People aren't rules, Bud. People are exceptions."

"Ray is a gringo, right? But is he a hetero gringo? Could he be a gay gringo? Is there such a thing?"

Carlo speared the last of my broccoli and smiled.

"He's naive, I know," I said. "But is he clever naive? Or just naive? His eyes are . . ." Now Carlo was grinning. "What's so funny?"

"Are you going to spend the whole summer doing this?"

"I won't have to. Because nothing brings out the gay in the gringo like The Pines. Right?"

*   *   *

I was righter than I knew, but only by a fluke. As the summer began, Ray was still living with Dennis Savage, had found neither job nor apartment, and was going to serve as unofficial houseboy for Dennis Savage's gang. Ray was also still the coolest cat in our set *or* the most accomplished mimic alive, to the satisfaction of everyone but me. At his first tea, I carefully watched him noticing the girls who come over from Sayville to dance. He stayed in character, did not overplay. He saw them as one who knew what he thought they were for and would request an audition again one day, but for now had to abstain out of respect for the man who was paying his bills.

"Beautifully judged," I told him.

"Say what, now?"

"That, too."

He smiled, as he often did when I teased him, and gave the tiny shrug that meant, "I don't know what you're referring to, but I'll play along."

So I decided to press him a little. Maybe I was in a mean mood. "I'm on to you, Jack," I told him. "I'm looking and listening and you're going to slip, aren't you? I'll be there when you do."

"You don't ought to be so tough around me," he said. "I don't do nothing to you."

"If this were a movie, you'd be up for an Oscar."

"Lookit?"

"I wish Olivier were here for this. He'd want to worship at your feet."

He leaned over a touch, as if putting his ear closer to the words would render them intelligible.

"Oh, I love that one," I said. "Harry Langdon as Hamlet, right?"

He looked at me: bewildered but trusting.

"Instead of looking for a punk handyboy job," I went on, "why don't you become an acting coach? I mean, Robert de Niro's good, but you're better."

And did I see then, for a split second, a flicker of acknowledgment in those lovable eyes, a sign of the quick wit that knew the names, the notions I was throwing at him? But it fled so fast that Ray had squeezed my arm, said, "Catch ya later on here," and moved away before I could assess it all.

Carlo wasn't with Dennis Savage this summer. Some uptown gays had offered him a room in an oceanside palazzo rent-free, in order to improve the physical tone of their house. There I went after tea, to confess and be absolved of my vicious needling of Ray, to beg for advice in breaking the writer's congenital habit of sticking one's nose in. It was seven o'clock in the evening of the second Friday of the season, High Pines: yet the fabulous house seemed deserted, not only dark and silent but gloomy, as if Important People had seen unfashionable things inside and ordered it Closed. Could they all be having sex? I wondered, walking around to the back entrance at the dunes—rich gays made out like bandits in those preplague days. No, there was Carlo, standing in the middle of the deck, looking at the water.

He turned, saw me, and gazed at me wordlessly. He is the handsomest man in New York and, once you get to know him, the nicest; but when he gets moody nobody can do anything with him. A fierce wind was up; his clothes and hair were whipping around. I thought, If they ever make a commercial for The Pines, this is all they need, provided Carlo is willing to smile.

"I always forget to bring the right sweater at the beginning of the summer," he said. "Then I get cold."

"Why don't you borrow something from your housemates? Where is everyone, anyway?"

He shook his head. Not important. When he's like this—so beauty, too, is human, boys and girls—he concentrates on essentials.

"When I was growing up," he said, "if I was worried about something and I went to my father with it, he would give me a switching. If I went to my mom, she would make me a plate of Cream of Wheat with maple syrup."

"You must not have gone to your dad very often."

"Sometimes you have to."

He put his arms around me and we shivered together in the wind.
"Now this is a study," he said. "She prays for me. But I don't know if
it's working. I sincerely don't know. Sometimes I believe I can hear
her, halfway across the continent." He hummed a snatch of something. "Praying for me," he said.

"I was mean to Ray at tea."

He held me at arm's length. "You want Cream of Wheat or a
switching?"

"Maybe he is genuine and maybe he isn't, and it's absolutely none
of my business. I admit it. But I thought of something. *Why* would he
pretend to be a homeless, dumb kid if he isn't one? Why would a gay
play gringo *in* the gay world? A homosexual ditchdigger or carpenter
would have to play gringo because his culture runs on the gringo
code. But Ray's in the gay world. It makes no sense."

"You should tell him you're sorry. I do believe he's very sensitive."

"Straights have no feelings, Carlo."

"*Gringos* have no feelings. Straights are something else."

"Isn't Ray a gringo, after all?"

"No. Gringos are tough. Like John Wayne or . . ."

"Jim Packer?"

He nodded. "I never met a porn star who wasn't born tough."

"Then what is Ray?"

"Why don't you ask him?"

"Oh, come on."

"Do you want some Cream of Wheat with maple syrup?"

"Can you make that here? With real maple syrup?"

"Sure." He led me inside. "Their kitchen looks like the movie
Metropolis." As he got the fixings out of the cupboard, he said, "She's
probably praying for me right now. That's what drove me away from
them, back a while ago. And she knows that, but she prays all the
harder." He was almost murmuring. "I miss them," he added, a
highly accessible man.

The fluke that exploded Ray Holgrave's act occurred a few Sundays
after, on the beach at noon with the squad, gathered from our various

houses, in full congress. A number of things were happening at once. Carlo and Kenny Reeves had just come up from the ocean and were getting everyone wet, Lionel was reading aloud from *Valmouth*, two visitors from the Grove were grousing at a strange nosy dog, and a straight couple had come up to ask Ray if he was the Mr. Hamill who was the graduate assistant of Dr. Copelman's Hawthorne and Melville course at Bucknell two years before.

Ray said nothing, literally nothing. I couldn't see his face.

Well, was he? they repeated. It was clear they thought he was.

Ray shook his head. Everyone else was watching and listening.

"Are you sure?" said the woman, laughing at the absurdity of the question. "Because you gave me an A on my *Marble Faun* paper and a B- on my *Confidence Man* paper. I wouldn't forget the man who grades with that kind of enthusiasm."

Ray looked at Dennis Savage. From behind, I saw his shoulders slide up into that tiny shrug of his.

"*Perry* Hamill?" the woman went on. "Really you look just like him."

My eyes were boring into the back of Ray's neck, but he didn't turn. Nor would he yet speak, and the silence sounded rather loud.

"His name," Dennis Savage finally said, "is Ray."

"Well," the woman told him, beginning to sense, and surprised by, the tension she had created. "You've got a twin brother named Perry walking around somewhere."

I looked at Carlo, but he raised a hand, warding me off.

I looked at Dennis Savage, but he was looking exclusively at Ray.

I looked at everyone else, but they couldn't have cared less. Kenny Reeves put a wet hand on Lionel's neck and made him jump; the two Grove people were calling the strange nosy dog bad names in French; and the collegiate couple moved on down the beach.

I cleared my throat.

"In *The House of the Seven Gables*," I began, "there's a character named Maule who takes a pseudonym. Has anyone present read Hawthorne's *The House of the Seven Gables*? Anyway, would someone like to guess what pseudonym this guy named Maule takes in Hawthorne's *The House of the Seven Gables?*"

Ray turned around to see me, and it was the same ungrudging, mildly questioning gaze he invariably—almost invariably—presented.

I decided I must not go on, because I was being churlish and intrusive and boring; and what did it prove, anyway? Ray was Ray, as sure as Dick Hallbeck was Jim Packer—you see the problem? Ray was *not* Ray. Because gringo is *there* and gay is *here*, yet every other time I turn around, the two are trading slave bracelets. All right, it's not my business what Ray may have been in a former life. It's not, all right. Okay.

But, for the record, the pseudonym that Maule takes in Hawthorne's *The House of the Seven Gables* is Holgrave, and it's pronounced with an Anglo flip on the vowel: Hahlgrave, just the way Ray pronounced it.

Ray never did find an apartment, but he was offered a job by a straight couple who, legend told, had made an unholy fortune in cocaine dealing and owned one of the flashiest houses on the water. Ray moved out on Dennis Savage and into his new berth simply by ambling along the boardwalk.

"Just as well," said Dennis Savage. "I must admit, he did lack something in entertainment value."

As it was over, anyway, I told Dennis Savage about the Hawthorne correspondence. He was amused but unimpressed. "It's not conclusive," he said. "What it is is slightly arresting."

"You slept with him. You must know. Could he have been a teacher's assistant at Bucknell? Please. Just think about it. Just know what it is. Just tell me."

He considered. "Bucknell, maybe. But he couldn't have hacked it at Hamilton."

"Look, don't play rep audition with me. Is he or isn't he?"

"Is he what?"

"Jeepers," I said. "You *know* what."

"That's just it. I don't. And you don't. Only Ray knows."

"The story without end. We'll never find out."

"Why does it matter so much?"

"Because I believe culture is finite and taste is fixed. I've built life and art on those precepts. I have to know what is true in the world."

"Why?"

"Because I am the sleuth!"

He shook his head. "When you write it all down," he said, "I hope you make it clear to everyone just how irritating you've been about this."

"You only say that," I told him, "because you think this was Ray's story. 'The Tale of the Drifter,' or something like."

"Whose story was it, then, may I ask?"

"Mine."

He just shook his head again.

Will we ever know what is true in the world, especially about sexual crossover? I guess not. The data is secret, the informants are inarticulate, and they are probably too shaken by their experiences to report fairly on them. We have to take the word of writers; but writers are mad. We try to be gallant, however. When I ran into Ray in the Pines Pantry near the end of the summer, I waited for him to check out, and, outside, apologized for baiting him.

"Sure, huh," he said. "It's all the same."

"No," I insisted. "No. I was tough around you, as you said. It's unforgivable. So don't forgive me. Just register my apology."

"Hey, sure." He put his hand on my head and patted me. "Sure, pal." His hand slid down to my shoulders. "I know you were only doing that 'cause you liked me."

I looked at him smiling away. The touch of his hand was forgiving, which suggests that he knew what I was doing, which tells us that he *is* more aware than he acts—but that way more madness lies. Life in New York.

"How are you getting on with your new people?" I asked.

"They're okay. Kind of taking me twiceways. First she likes to screw me with a rubber thing, and then I go on and do him. It's fun but it really makes my hole ache."

I was still watching him, noting him down; I couldn't help myself.

"Carlo's really a great guy, isn't he?" Ray said.

"We all think so."

"I always liked that Carlo."

Carlo had said, "Why don't you ask him?" and so I did: "Ray, it couldn't possibly make any difference now. You're off to a new job with moneyed people, and Dennis Savage won't mind anyway at this point, and I don't know why, but *I* do, because I'm not sure I can live in a world in which Dick Hallbeck is interchangeable with Jim Packer. So look . . ."

Walking, we had reached the ferry plaza, where we would separate, he to the west and I to the east, and I glommed him one last time, and there were the utterly untroubled eyes of a man who doesn't need what you have. But I asked anyway.

"Are you Perry Hamill, a former teaching assistant in a Hawthorne-Melville course at Bucknell?"

He smiled and gave the tiny shrug, and nodded me goodbye. He started off. I didn't move. He sensed that, and, ten feet off, stopped and turned. Two men with their groceries standing at the harbor.

"Are you?" I said.

He smiled and looked me spang in the eye and whispered, as he turned to go, "Wouldn'st thou like to know?"

Uptown, Downtown

A tour through the gay metropolis.

My friend Lucky very recently made his first trip to New York. He saw it as a great theme park, an agglomeration not of neighborhoods where different cultures flower but of sectors where entertainments present themselves. The West Village was Gayland, Fourteenth Street Scuzz Avenue, the Lexington IRT Terror Train. Most impressive to Lucky was Midtown, which he termed Businessville.

"Wow," he opined, as dashing men in dress kit stalked past us, dotted here and there with important-looking women. "It's swank!" Lucky lives year round in a pair of jeans; for solemnities he may go as far as to don a T-shirt. "What do you call those things they're wearing?"

"Suits."

"No. The handkerchief in their high pockets."

"We call those 'quibbles,'" I replied, thinking fast.

"Do you ever wear a quibble?" he asked me, as we walked on. It's petty to kid an Angeleno; too easy. But Lucky is so receptive to colorful trivia that it's a form of sustenance, a way of making love to him. He dragged me out on long walks, from the two big museums bordering the Park down to Wall Street, from Sutton Place to Hell's Kitchen. Every now and then I'd stop in front of some dreary brownstone and invent a backstory involving Theodore Roosevelt,

Boss Tweed, Texas Guinan, and others such, as Lucky shivered at the closeness of history, the wonder of having a past compounded of closed systems fiercely abutting one another. Who was the hero, the villain, the dupe? Which was the risky, the wealthy, the happy district? Where were the theatres, the bordellos, the banks? Visitors always think New York is like their town, but bigger. New York is not like any other town. It is all dupes, all risky, and its own theatre. To be young, beautiful, and Angeleno is to know nothing of parish phenomena, of the advantages and penalties of helter-skelter sectorization, of the inevitability of epoch. When I first came to New York, the upper west side as a cultural place stopped dead at about Seventy-third Street; north of that, it was nothing but hardware stores straight to Poughkeepsie. Now it's one great pecan pie as far as the eye sees.

Somewhere, Lucky heard the word "gentrification"—meaning instead of being overrun with roaches you're overrun with Akitas—and he wants to see an example. I take him to Chelsea, but we find little evidence of Coming Up. "Where's all the gents?" asks Lucky. He laughs. He has made a joke. But the many men in tank tops and net shirts grow rigidly sober as they pass us, reading Lucky's stomach and thighs. There's no fun in New York; everyone's too busy cruising, the only activity common to all the sectors.

Lucky notices the general malaise. "I thought New York was like one big party." It is; but no one's invited. Some make an entire evening out of rejection, lining up outside discos to turn their facades into wailing walls; others scheme to learn the phone numbers of the great, and dial to thrill to a "Hello" they daren't answer.

"Take me to the fun part," Lucky urges.

"That's not what New York is for," I almost say. Then I think of the Madcap Heiress of Seventy-fourth Street, and decide it is time Lucky saw the east side.

The Madcap Heiress was born to clown looks as well as a fortune, and has played the one into a unique comix and the other into a credential of glamour. In the Village, guests are lavish presents to be unwrapped. On the west side, guests are the intelligentsia. At the Madcap Heiress', guests are an audience to be charmed and scandalized. All queens are funny: because the only other thing they can be is bitter. But this queen is insightfully ridiculous, like Dali's mustache. To be absurd in a sullen world is a surmise—as those Park Avenue tramps know, shouting lurid nonsense at the officers of the Corporation as they lope up the street in their ties each weekday evening.

The Madcap Heiress is thrilled to see us, but sighs profoundly as we step in. "Utterly worn out," he says. "Crazy Bunny came for lunch and brought that awful Dizzy Wizard. The two of them rendered me helpless and then played with the toilet flusher till the whole apartment was . . ." Now he takes in Lucky. "Little Lamb, who made thee?"

Lucky had offered to put on a shirt for the east side, but I figured the Madcap Heiress would prefer him *al fresco*.

"I like your quibble," Lucky told him.

"Completely baffled."

"He means your handkerchief," I put in.

"Oh, my . . . *quibble*, yes. My . . . Crazy Bunny gave it to me, had you heard? For when I came back from safari. He lifted it from Bergdorf's, there's no doubt. Did you know I was on safari? Hunting and tracking or so?" He purrs, admiring Lucky. "Actually, I went on Jewish safari. Just like the real thing, except all the animals are in cages. Darling, who *is* the boy?"

"He's my western friend Lucky."

"Could I have seen you in a movie?" the Madcap Heiress asks him.

"Yes."

I'm startled.

"*Cousins Who Rim During Shavuous*, or something?"

"*Brotherly Love*," Lucky corrects him amiably.

"A movie star in my apartment! Utterly floored!"

"You made porn?" I ask Lucky, before I can stop myself.

"Come see the famous view!" the Madcap Heiress cries. "You don't have anything like this in the West! The Contessa Pigoletto came all the way from Milan for my famous view! Well, and for a certain Greek-American electrician. But still."

It is a spectacular view, a right angle of glass scanning the center of town—to the extent that this episodic town has a center.

"The billion lights!" our host exclaims, taking Lucky's arm. "The heights of rage and ambition! Right before our eyes, four hundred nobodies are becoming overnight stars through acts of indescribable corruption, one hundred sixty-five statesmen are selling secrets, seventy-eight people are trying to cure their herpes with leftover Kwell, and twenty-three innocents are being murdered by strangers. And you're unnerved, you . . . explosively ripping object . . . because here you are in the city of passion and awe, and all you know is brotherly love. Is there much love in the west?"

"Depends on who you run into and what mood you're in," Lucky replies.

The Madcap Heiress turns to me. "So *distingué*! Will he move here?"

"I'm only here on business."

"Terrified to guess what kind."

Lucky is a hustler.

"Are you up for another movie perchance? *The Shoulder Caps That Devoured Biloxi*? *The Incredible Abdominals That Never Stopped Moving In and Out*? Or just *Young, Cute, and Lewd*?"

Later, Lucky asked me if the whole east side was like this. Of course *none* of the east side is like this, but after a while all of Manhattan is, because the rhythm of its humor takes the tempo of the queen and the gauge of its glamour observes the queen's imperatives. My friend Tim came to New York bearing the open cool of Seattle and the precision of Washington, D.C.; two months after he arrived, he was referring to himself as The Marquise.

If the Madcap Heiress is basic Manhattan, then so must be the east side, for there are no Madcap Heiresses anywhere else. The rich don't live where you live; they live where they live. A century ago, they had one of their meetings and decided that the rich sector was east of the Park. But New York's rich is strange, like everything else in New York. If Lady Bracknell moved here, where would she abide? Only the very East Fifties would look right to her, but they move too fast. Bank Street would be slow enough, but the wrong chic. Put her on West Eighty-second for a week and she'd be mugging Puerto Ricans. New York is too commingled. It's densely shared.

Lucky appreciated the Madcap Heiress. Effortfully polite, he asked about Crazy Bunny and the Dizzy Wizard, not realizing that these, like many of the people we know and count on, are fictional characters. If I had asked the Madcap Heiress about Crazy Bunny, he would have been peeved. You're to listen, not ask. But devastating aliens may derail the patter. "Why, dear heart, Crazy Bunny is very simply the natural enemy of Colonel Snapper von Turtel, and you must take care, when they call, not to ally yourself with one or the other. So gruesome." He moved closer to Lucky. "Keeps you busy." He drew his finger along the curve of Lucky's left pectoral. "I love it when they fight." He circled the nipple, bold and high on the muscle. "I'll give you five hundred dollars if you let me taste your quibble."

West siders routinely attack the east side, I imagine because the west side is a slum. It acts like one, too. Here, only the gays are men; the straights are shapeless wimps in joke-shop eyeglasses. In a Yankees cap they think they're preening, and when a weightlifter walks by they sneer. Lucky failed to notice them. He saw the Korean fruit stands, the boutiques, the old folks on the benches—and these are New York, but not New York enough for him. There's too much there here, too many sights that obscure the character of the place. "Where's the intellectuals?" he asked.

"They live in New Jersey."

I took him to a west side party, so he could sample Manhattan wit. But the guests were glued to the television—not even entertainment-center video, but network ooze. At least it was Public TV. I blushed for New York at the sparkless comebacks thrown at the screen, but

Lucky wouldn't know irony from babble; just hearing people talking fast intrigued him. Half the gang were straights, so they couldn't understand why he was shirtless, but they were too afraid of the answer to ask.

Guests came and went. The notable arrival was a tall but undergrown character who managed to be brutally bald and excessively hairy at once. He made numerous philosophical statements, each as valid as the advice you get on a cocktail napkin, and went on to put–down assessments of the hobbies, professions, and eating habits (remnants of Chinese takeout were strewn about) of the entire room. Then he settled down to some concentrated mugging of a program about a recent American assault on Everest. Lucky had tuned the rest of us out; mountains fascinate him. So, I expect, did the climbers, of that blond, bearded, lanky, affably laconic type that always turns up on documentaries of the outdoors. They were clearly as exhilarated as challenged, and I could see Lucky realizing that there is no one like this in New York. He was sad; he had hoped there would be mountains here. There is no one like this in L.A., either, but there are some in Oregon, whence Lucky derives.

"Why do you do it?" an interviewer asked a climber.

"Because you're a schmuck," said the hairy baldo.

"Say, excuse me," Lucky began, and I froze. The last time Lucky said, "Say, excuse me," he chopped three San Franciscan teenagers into messes on Sacramento Street for making homophobic allusions. Like all Oregonians, Lucky is easygoing except about one thing for which he will not only fight but die—everyone raised in the state gets to choose his thing at the age of fifteen, then must stick to it for life, even if he leaves home. Lucky's thing is mountains.

By hap, the fight was taken out of Lucky's hands, for the others had had enough of hairy baldo, too, and they more or less harried him out of the party. Or maybe they had suddenly realized why Lucky doesn't wear a shirt: he punches bad guys.

"You must take care not to ally yourself with either side," the Madcap Heiress had warned us, so we flee both west and east and proceed to Below Fourteenth Street, a city itself. Here, many of the principles of uptown are observed in reverse. Dressing for success is despicable; punk, prole, and various nonaligned grotesquerie are the norm. Moving fast and intently, as if one's day were full of Enviable Destinations, is suspect; downtown, you lurk, wander, or at most stroll, and going into a trance every block or so is good taste. Up north, everyone carries something—an attaché, a gym valise, a tiny shopping bag filled with leisure-class chotchkes; down here, everyone is openhanded. In the caverns of Businessville, street musicians, breakdancers, and monte sharps are intrusive; around Washington Square, they're the only things happening.

I hate it here; everyone looks as if he might glow in the dark. Lucky loves it. "Look at you!" a woman in a Mohawk enthuses at him, apropos of I'm not sure what, and a couple of uproarious kids covered with tattoos call out, "Hey, Jive!"

"I thought New York was unfriendly," Lucky says.

"That's not friendly. It's cultural harassment."

Stand anywhere in Manhattan, and no matter how busy you look or how involved in conversation, a crazy will come up to share the most idiotic secrets. Once in a movie theatre, the man in front of me turned around to say, "This is the night when I like to eat cabbage, but I'm afraid of how it smells."

"Hey, Jive!" Lucky echoes, pleased with it.

"Friendly?" I mutter. "It's a city of lonely maniacs."

"*Hey,* Jive!"

"Don't do that."

He tousles my hair. "You have to loosen up."

"If New Yorkers loosened up, this might as well be Cincinnati. And if my hair must be tousled, it ought to be by someone old enough to be my father, not by . . ."

"By what?"

Now I tousle his hair and he cries, "Hey, *Jive!*" and a black baglady across the street warns, "Children! You play nice, now!"

"This is New York," Lucky whispers, not for me to hear. "This is the jive."

We move on to Christopher Street, gay tourism's Bridge of Sighs, but Lucky is pensive and watches with but one eye. "What does 'lewd' mean?" he asks.

"Well . . . going around without a shirt and making porn movies could be thought lewd."

"Are you sore at me for that? The movie?"

We take in street ballet: a lot of skin, and anyone not in shorts is a goon. Two devastatos, approaching on the same side of the street as imperious as nabobs on howdahs, burn glances each into each, pass on, turn around to look again, both, and, at the same moment, turn and move on.

"What's the matter with this place?" Lucky asks. "Don't those hunks know how to cruise?"

"They weren't cruising. They were admiring themselves in the mirror."

"I take it back about New York being friendly. I'll bet I couldn't even give it away here."

It is a city of browsing eyes. The favorite question is "Should I have heard of you?"—but the words mean "What are you like in bed?" As a rule, trolls are the most impetuous (they will do anything to be liked), hunks the most inspiring (but hard to reach), romantics the most expert, and cynics the most intense. Which are you?

"Show me another sector," Lucky suggests. "I don't need this one so much."

"This is the gayest part, you know."

"Show me the most New York part. The most . . ."

"Typical?"

"Yes."

Is there one? Lucky's tour tells me that there scarcely are sectors at all, that all New York's parts are equal, because everyone goes everywhere. The architecture varies—glass and chrome stupas in Businessville, cast-iron frames in Soho, belts of brownstones. But the characters are often interchangeable. I note lawyers on St. Mark's Place, artists in the East Eighties, Poles in Yorkville, Italians in Chinatown. Mr. Peachum assigned his beggars their uniform and location in John Gay's London. Is someone assigning New Yorkers posts and routes? We need a sense of neighborhood, a disintegration of atmosphere. We need muzzles and handcuffs on all straight male teenagers, a ban on radios, and the death penalty for littering.

"There is no typical part," I tell Lucky. "It's consistent right the way through."

"Then show me the opposite of typical. The outstanding place."

"There is none."

"I know one. I'll take you there." It was my apartment.

"See," he showed me. "You have no famous view and no Crazy Bunny."

"I can see the whole of Fifty-fourth and Third."

"You won't when the new office building goes up. And you don't wear a quibble. Or have friends who come in and mock everything other people believe in."

"Like Chinese food."

"No one can come up and bother us," he goes on. "No one has strange hair or dervish clothes."

"Dervish?"

"Wacko."

"I thought you liked dervish behavior."

"Not in my friends."

"Lucky, don't you realize that New York is the city of the dervish? My apartment isn't atypical—it's asylum."

"That's why it's outstanding."

"Resistance is taboo! They don't like to let you take shelter here. That's why Bloomingdale's clerks are snotty and cab drivers play loud horrendous music on their radios. Privacy is offensive. The week I had my phone unlisted, people who hadn't bothered with me in years accosted me on the street, demanding the new number." I pace, I worry, I exult. "Death to spies! I am invisible!"

"I have to go to the airport," he says.

"Now?"

"Now."

With Lucky, everything happens without warning. He picks up his satchel, shakes my hand, smiles, drops the bag, hugs me, won't let go. "Do New Yorkers do this?" he asks.

"Only when you're here."

"Any city with friends," he observes, "is a nice city. The others aren't nice. That's the difference from one to another."

I consider offering to keep Lucky in New York—he'd be better off as a houseboy than hustling. But I doubt New York could stand Lucky on any terms. Thieves and crazies, yes. Queens and ruffians, surely. And vicious wimps especially—New York can't get enough of them. But brotherly love is an affront.

At that, could Lucky stand New York? After he goes, alone in my apartment, I practice saying "Hey, Jive!" in an affable manner. A dangerous silence ensues: and I hear the city screaming.

Kid Stuff

A tale of taboo and regional style, from which some readers may turn away in confusion or distaste.

There isn't all that much to do in The Pines on the best of days, but there is *nothing* to do when it rains. I keep Monopoly and Risk on hand just in case; but one must be prudent. Once, one of my best friends landed that summer's Hottest Man on the Island and brought him to my house thinking we were all at the beach. Instead, the two of them found six of us huddled avidly around the Monopoly board. Worse yet, quaint show albums were tooting away on the stereo—the kind with Helen Gallagher or George S. Irving. Worst of all, someone had just landed on Boardwalk, and Teddy Anders, who maintained a hotel on the property, announced that this was the most exciting thing that had happened to him all summer.

Well, the Hottest Man on the Island took a penetrating look at this pathetically maidenly tableau, dropped a withering glance upon my friend, and strode off. As the others gaped in bewilderment, my friend slowly told me, "I will never . . . never . . . never . . . forgive you for this." And he never did.

Mind you, I don't defend this point of view. One cannot be having sex or hunting for it every minute, even in a place as rampantly erotic as The Pines. Still, perhaps a day-long Monopoly game is too comradely an activity for the ruthless beach, too fraternal. Do you want to be known for a hot house or for clubby chastity?

At any rate, you can't be hot when it rains, and I recall one afternoon eight years ago when sheets of water were ripping down as if the next Flood were upon us: Dennis Savage, his lover Little Kiwi, Little Kiwi's fiasco of a dog Bauhaus, Carlo, Ron, and I. All possibilities in reading, eating, and laundry had been exhausted. There was nothing left to do but lie around grumping, one activity Dennis Savage really excels at. Conversation lagged, till he suggested we trade Shameful Anecdotes. "We could start," he said, "with The Worst Thing I Ever Did to My Lover."

"How could you choose," I wondered, "from your many thousands such?"

He sat up, ready to strike. "Or you could tell us once again how you and your brothers committed incest night after glorious night right through your childhood and how it's just a typical American sport and *no one* would think you a gang of debauched cretins for a little thing like that."

"He committed what?" asked Little Kiwi, waking up.

"We didn't commit incest," I said. "We slept together, in total innocence. Haven't you seen puppies lying in a pet-store window? That's all we did. Doesn't everyone?"

"I never did," said Dennis Savage.

"I don't have a brother," said Carlo.

"I always locked my door," said Little Kiwi, "to keep out the scary clown monster."

Ron just blinked.

"What's more," said Dennis Savage, "I have never heard of any brothers sleeping in the same bed except yours. How does such a thing occur? What, do you wink at a brother and say, 'Who wants a backrub?'"

"I don't remember how it got started," I say. "I suppose someone was afraid of the dark, or had a nightmare, or was cold. We had a whole floor to ourselves, and one of us would just . . ." I trailed off. They were looking at me as if I'd told them we used to waylay strangers on the turnpike and chop them into sausage. "All I can say is it felt very normal to us. My older brothers used to carry me into their beds, and I did it with my younger brothers, or they'd pile in by themselves. Sometimes all five of us . . . I guess we just wanted company."

The rain beat even more heavily.

"They would carry you where?" said Little Kiwi.

"Nothing happened, I tell you."

"*Winesburg, Ohio,*" said Dennis Savage.

"*Nothing* happened?" asked Ron. "Sexually? Are you sure?"

"We'd just snuggle up like bunnies."

"You know," said Dennis Savage, and I braced myself. "First it was dear little puppies; and now you say bunnies, suggesting visions of velveteen and cartoons and chocolate shapes with nougat eyes. But in real life bunnies are notorious fuckers. And I find it strenuously curious that you ladle out these tales of unapproachable *pornofamilia* and act as though you were merely playing hooky from Bible class. Are you telling us that five males—some of whom were heavily pubescent and others of whom were toothsome and easily overpowered—spent some ten years in bed and never touched each other?"

"He committed *what*?" said Little Kiwi, just grasping what we were discussing.

"A five-some!" said Carlo, impressed.

"All we did was sleep!"

"I know of . . . a couple of brothers," said Ron. "I mean, I know about two brothers who did have sex." He gulped, glancing at me. "I believe all five of you could have been together in bed and not . . . done anything. But it does happen."

We waited, listening to the rain.

"I wonder if Bauhaus is gay," said Little Kiwi. "Sometimes he walks funny."

"What brothers?" Carlo asked.

"In my town. Southern Indiana. You know, a little industry and a lot of farming. Three banks. One post office, two schools. See, the reason I know about this is it happened to my best friend. Tom Coley. I guess he had to tell someone, so he told me."

Ron is of that thin, pale-blond, long-necked type that doesn't get noticed at first. At second, you think, "Who *is* this boy?"

"I'm not saying this is common. I always think a lot that happens depends entirely on chance. Not on birth or education, you know. Money. Things. But just who's near who at the right time. Anyway, Tom had a brother named Elton, two years older. They could have been twins, except Elton was bigger and broader because . . . well, you know how much difference two years can make in your teens. I'm not telling you that Tom or Elton were big wheels, now. In school, I mean. Football captains or debating chairmen. But Elton was a slick guy and Tom was . . . a good fellow. Did I say that he was my best friend?"

Everyone was still, listening.

"Well, this happened when Tom was in ninth grade, Elton in eleventh. See, their father was dead and their mother had this snappy job as a legal secretary. In a lawyer's office? And she always worked late. So they had the house to themselves after school. She taught them how to heat up canned spaghetti and TV dinners because she didn't have the time to cook for them. She really worked hard. Everyone in town thought she was the mother of the decade.

"Anyway, as Tom told it, one afternoon after school he was toweling off from a shower and his brother came in from *his* shower and they got to speaking about this and that." He grinned. "In our casual midwestern way, you know. And somehow or other Tom ended up on Elton's lap, just talking about . . . I don't know. School. Their father. Maybe going to college. Except they're both completely bareass and Elton has his arm around Tom's shoulder. And you know how close brothers can be sometimes. And while they're talking, Elton is kissing Tom. Just little pecks, like . . . like conversational punctuation. You know, a sort of brother thing. To cheer him up. You kissed your brothers, didn't you, Bud?"

"Never," I replied. "I scarcely shake their hands. I run when I see them. They're worse than the scary clown monster."

"Oh. Well, maybe these two brothers were different because they had no father and their mother was away so much. They had to be kind of each other's parents sometimes, I guess."

"Pecks?" asked Dennis Savage. "On the cheek?"

"Well . . . actually . . . no, on the mouth. Kisses. Little demonstrative kisses between two brothers."

"Little between *what?*" said Little Kiwi.

"The thing is," said Ron, "that although neither of them would mention it, they both had hard-ons. And the kissing got . . . hotter. They were still talking, but in between they were virtually making out. They had their arms around each other and Elton was playing with Tom's genitals, and smoothing his skin, and stroking his hair. And I guess somewhere along the way they had stopped talking and were openly working on each other. And Elton got up and steered Tom over to the bed, and stretched him out on his stomach, and went into the bathroom for stuff, and when he came back he got right on top of Tom and screwed him. But you should understand that when Tom told me about this he underlined how careful his brother was with him, how gentle. Slow. And you know what was funny was they never seemed close in school or anywhere else like that. I mean, they *were* close, but they didn't make a big thing of it. It was like no one . . . knew about them. And then, after that first time, they started to take it up regular. Every day, same thing. They'd start talking and kissing in the chair, then move to the bed. And after each screwing, they'd talk again, waiting to get hot some more. And finally they'd roll over and collapse, and when their mother got home she'd find them lying in each other's arms."

"She knew about it, then?" said Carlo.

"Oh, no. She thought they were taking naps together. Two brothers who were so close they would talk themselves to sleep after school. She was worried about their not having a father figure, so it was nice that Elton was looking after Tom. Maybe it sounds more like the south than the midwest. They're very physical down south. Demonstrative. The midwest is almost as squeamish about personal contact as the northeast."

"Just a minute," said Dennis Savage, from upstate New York: snowman country.

"Oh, come on," I said. "Would you call New York a relaxed, friendly, demonstrative city?"

"Not while you're in it."

"Gentlemen," said Carlo, raised in South Dakota. "The northeast *is* tense. I think that's why Bud's talk of sleeping with his brothers sounds weird. If you were from like Georgia, it would seem natural. And that's why Ron's tale is so interesting. It brings sort of a decadence to a place where we all thought men are men."

"And little brothers are nervous," said Dennis Savage.

"No, that's just it," said Ron. "Tom became very dependent on his afternoons with Elton. As far as I can gather, they never referred to it even in strictest privacy. They just did it. Every weekday, without fail. Over and over, the same methods every time. Elton sitting in the chair, and tilting his head at Tom, who would walk across the room to him. And if he got home first he took off his clothes and lay down to wait for Elton. There was nothing else in his life. He went through ninth and tenth grade in a daze because nothing was real to him except their . . . their . . ."

"Dates," said Carlo.

"Trysts," said Dennis Savage.

"Tango practice," I offered.

"Their love," said Ron.

"Of course, they already loved each other as brothers. They had a natural closeness. You know. But when they made it physical, it didn't just deepen. It became . . . I don't know how to explain it. It was not as if Tom had made a lover out of a brother. It was as if he'd made a *lover* into a *brother*, made him . . . I don't know, permanent, absolute. Close in a way no best friend can hope to be. And Tom made up this dream that he and Elton would stay like this for the rest of their lives. Keep on spending afternoons talking together and going to bed and falling asleep, and nothing else would matter. It's a strange story, isn't it? A strange dream to have for your whole life. I mean, the point of growing up is that you cut yourself off from the closeness of your family. You've already got everything they can give you in forming your personality. Your feelings, your emotions. They're all done with giving your character its shape. So you move on. You get married and start your own family and the whole thing repeats itself. Okay, you stay in touch with them and solidify the bond at special times. Christmas. A fiftieth birthday. But you don't stay a brother for the rest of your life, do you?"

"Not a younger one," I said.

"Imagine," he went on. "Imagine two men living somewhere, on a farm or something. And all they're doing is loving each other, and they're brothers! Can you imagine that? It's like being in the Boy Scouts for fifty years. It's . . . what is it?"

"It's a very sweet fantasy," said Dennis Savage, "in the wrong historical age."

"Anyway. Tom knew it couldn't last much longer. Because once Elton got out of high school and got a job . . . and some adult self-assurance . . . and learned how to talk to women, well . . . it was Elton's moving-on time. It was a terrible period for Tom, because they weren't breaking up over some curable incompatibility, or going through that crazy period some lovers hit after two years. They were breaking up because . . . well, because once upon a time Elton was horny as heck and women weren't available and Tom was. See, the bizarre part of this romance was that only one of the two men was gay. Think about that—and both of them knew it, too, I'm sure of it. It's like the birds and the bees without the birds. And then one day Elton was out of high school, and the next day he got a job, and some time after he got a little apartment over the record store. Drove him crazy Saturday nights when it was open late. And so of course Tom . . ." Thinking of it all, Ron paused, distracted.

". . . came out of his daze," Dennis Savage suggested.

Ron nodded.

Silence.

"I don't know," said Carlo. "Is this a sad story or a happy one?"

"It's a true story," said Ron. "That's what matters."

"Yes, but did they ever finalize it?" I asked. "Did they . . . well, did they ever say something to each other? About how they felt? What they had—"

"The midwest," said Ron, "doesn't work in that style."

"It's not what you say," Carlo suggested.

"You mean," I went on, "that never once in that two years those boys spent in bed did they say 'I love you' somewhere in there? Not once?"

"It's not what you say," Carlo insisted. "It's how you are made to feel."

"You have to remember that we aren't direct about our emotions. Not like New Yorkers, anyway. We're a country of poker players. Bluffers, you know?"

"Did they ever get into bed again?"

"How could they?" Ron replied. "Once Elton had his own place and was hitting the singles bars and smartening up his smile at the waitresses and such, what would he need Tom for, I wonder? You have to be fair."

The rain pounded on. Bauhaus shifted position. Carlo coughed.

"Anyway, it was as plain as it gets. There was that day they went out walking on a Saturday. Just walking. You're aware that two men might take a stroll with a lot on their minds and not say anything about it? This was like that. They weren't seeing each other much by then, just when Elton came home for dinner. And Tom didn't want to visit Elton in his apartment because . . . well, I'm not sure if he ever did know why. If you ask me, he was afraid to be alone with Elton and not go back to bed with him—afraid of having to face a formal parting of the ways. Because so far, no one had said anything about it. Yes, it looked as if it was over. But technically it was still an open question."

"Some affairs truly never do end," said Carlo. "It may turn out that you'll never fuck again, but you don't know that till years later."

"Tom knew then and there," said Ron. "Because they took this walk. And you can imagine how Tom felt—I mean, this was one of the very few chances he had to be alone with . . . his lover. And they were just ambling around, seeing what was doing, and they ran into a girl from Elton's class in high school. So it was like, 'What are you doing now?' back and forth, which is what you tend to do in the midwest for the rest of your life—unless you come to New York. And Tom was just waiting till they could politely go off on their own again, but it was dragging on and finally Elton invited her to join them for coffee and she said yes. And there they all were, Tom just so miserable and saying practically nothing and Elton and the girl flirting above and below the table. And of course finally they went off together, and Tom went home alone, knowing that was how it was going to be from now on. Tom was one thing and Elton was another, and he had to face up to it. As we say in the midwest, 'That's how the river gonna flow.' And this is where the story ends."

"Didn't they ever . . . say *anything* about this?" Dennis Savage asked. "It seems a somewhat brusque way of dropping a lover."

Ron was quiet. So were we; we could hear his breathing.

"Well," he said finally. "It really isn't the way things work out there."

"You keep saying that," I put in. "And there is something to it, I understand. But is this a story about a place or about people? My guess is every story is about people, even if the way they think and talk and act and, I don't know, maybe even make love . . . even if all that typifies the place they're in."

Ron nodded, but he said nothing.

"I mean," I went on, feeling crummy for pursuing Ron's feelings—but hell, if I'm going to write this story I have to *know* it—"what next passed between Tom and Elton?"

After a bit, Ron said, "Well, you're right. They did . . . refer to it once. At Elton's. Tom had taken up visiting there every so often because it was so clear that it was over that he didn't feel any more left out there than he would in the center of town. So he went over, and Elton and he were talking about Tom's college plans. He was going to be the first person in his family to do more than high school, so that was big news. And Elton was asking him about his major and so on, and after a while it ran down, and Tom knew it was time to leave but he just kept sitting there. You know how that feels. And Elton sensed that somehow, and he looked at his brother for a real long time, looked right at him. And Tom looked back. He was thinking about their two years together, and knowing what they were, and not asking for more, not even once more . . . just telling Elton how much . . . how important it was. How happy he had been. And Elton sensed that somehow, all that, and he . . . he nodded. Real solemn. As if to say he understood. And then they both got up at the same moment, and went to the door, but when they got there and Elton had the door open he suddenly closed it again. They were going to shake hands just then, you know. But Elton took Tom in his arms and he held him real tight. And he said, 'You're such a pretty kid.' He said that. And they stood there and held each other, and I swear it was as if . . . as if . . . I don't know. I don't know what it was at all now." A tear rolled down his cheek. "But he was so . . . damn . . . wonderful to me. So wonderful." Another tear. "We never fought. We never quarreled in our entire lives. About anything, never. And he came to all my track meets. Do brothers do that? All the time, I mean? I felt so safe with him. Jesus, I . . . I *don't care* who knows anymore. I *don't!* And let me tell you something—after him, all those gorgeous New York attitude hunks who think they're God's present are just pieces of ham to me! Pieces of fucking ham!"

"Canned ham!" said Dennis Savage, thinking to keep it light.

"Rotted canned ham," I put in.

Carlo, one of New York's most incurable gorgeous attitude hunks, made no-no fingers at us.

"He did *what?*" said Little Kiwi, finally.

"Oh hell," said Ron, wiping his eyes. "Isn't anyone hungry?"

He was shuffling lettuce and eggs when I came into the kitchen. "I thought omelettes and salad and this Italian bread," he told me.

"Terrific."

"You beat the eggs, okay?"

As I did, he said, "I was never going to tell anyone that. Not ever."

"Where'd you get the name Tom?"

"Oh, he *was* my best friend. Tom Coley. He died in Vietnam."

He set me to washing greens and cutting radishes.

"Are the others shocked?" he asked, quietly.

"Just Little Kiwi, and he's extremely unsophisticated, remember.
He didn't even know about lesbians till last week."

"Know what about them?"

"That there were any. Where is Elton now?"

He stopped, thought, patted my arm, said, "Stay here," and went to
his room to get a photograph of Elton taken at the last Thanksgiving
party. "Dayton, Ohio," Ron explained. "He's the superintendent of a
mattress factory. It's a good job in those parts. That's his wife Carrie,
that's Elton Jr.—they call him Tony—and that's Mary."

This Elton did not align with the one I had imagined pulling Ron
into his lap and leading him to bed. He was half bald, working on a
paunch, and sported an entirely dismal beard. Nice family, though.

Then Ron produced another photo, a dog-eared black-and-white of
two boys in swimsuits at the edge of a lake, and I gasped. Ron, I could
have guessed, would have been a spectacular teenager. But Elton,
perhaps fifteen then, his arm around Ron's shoulder, was about the
nicest-looking thing you ever hoped to be related to, or slip into bed
with: and, as Ron points out, sometimes you get both.

"Now that you've heard my story," said Ron, "are you ready to
admit that you and your brothers . . . you know?"

"Now that I've heard your story, I wish I could. But the truth is, all
we did was sleep."

He shrugged. "You may be better off that way. At least you came
out with no expectations. I had a tender, handsome man take me
through the hard parts of late adolescence, so I missed a lot of pointless anxiety. But where was I supposed to go next? I've been looking
for another brother ever since." He buttered the omelette pan. Typical

Pines: we have every kitchen apparatus known to man, including an artichoke guillotine, yet we're always out of clean towels. I think Bauhaus eats them.

I had one last question. "I can believe that an essentially straight man might pillow with an available male for two years out of adolescent horniness. But why would he then turn around—just as he's about to reform, so to say—and call you a pretty kid? Rather new-wave lingo for a midwestern straight. It seems sadistic, somehow."

Collecting the cutlery, Ron said, "Or generous. Maybe he was telling me what I needed to hear. As long as you're throwing someone over, why not let him think he means a great deal to you?"

"Surely you did. You don't sleep in someone's arms for two years without meaning something to him."

"Well, that's true." He was folding napkins. "A few years ago, at Christmas, Elton and I were joking around—shouting and punching each other, you know? Kid stuff. And Carrie asked us if we had always been this rowdy. And he said, 'No, when we were teenagers we were very serious around each other.' He said, 'Sometimes it was as if we were the only two people in the world.'"

"And you rent your garment and screamed that yours was a love that would never die."

He smiled, heaping dinner onto trays. "I kind of laughed and nodded and we went on to the next thing. Let's face it, gays have to do a lot of acting around the rest of the population."

They had the Monopoly stuff all set up when we brought the food in, and Carlo said, "There should be a Monopoly where you play for men instead of properties."

"There is," I reminded him. "It's called the gay world."

And, as the rain battered on, we got down to the really serious business of life: putting hotels on Boardwalk and Park Place and waiting for Dennis Savage to come around and land on them and go bankrupt.

The Preppie and the Clone

An east side romance.

Carlo decided that he wanted a preppie lawyer and no one could talk him out of it.

"It's not for you," we told him.

"Their vested suits," he would reply.

"You'll be bored, Carlo."

"Their luncheon clubs and business talk," he would go on. "Their fox trots, tennis rackets."

"What would you speak about?"

"They went to Harvard University! Look, I'm tired of hunks and stars. I want something different this time. Maybe someone over forty. I like them . . ." He grew blissful.

"Ripened," Dennis Savage offered.

"Practiced," Carlo corrected. "And they're nicer when they're older."

"Grateful," Dennis Savage observed.

"No. They just have the time to be generous."

I grinned at Dennis Savage's lack of expertise. But then his taste favors bashful youth, and we habitually take our reading of romance from our own narrative, neglecting all other data.

It was the Friday after Christmas, a television afternoon at Dennis Savage's: one of those amusingly wastrel days New Yorkers sometimes

122

schedule before plunging back into the grid of themes and ambitions and opinions that stretches across every social intersection of the town. Dennis Savage was free of his teaching duties, I was taking the afternoon off, Carlo was as usual living on unemployment, and Little Kiwi, on temporary enforced leave from the mailroom of BBDO because he had bitten a coworker for calling him "a derogatory epithet meaning an aficionado of oral gay sex" (as Little Kiwi put it, after working it out on a piece of paper), had been packed off to the grocery with his fey Godzilla of a dog, Bauhaus. We other three had settled down to cruise the soaps for skin. Strangely, instead of suburban bedrooms and health clubs, all we could find were political intrigues in exotic places, with heroines in tattered gowns crying, "No, Mark! Don't leave me here in the jungle, alone with the Ishtar Ruby!"

"Whatever happened to love?" I asked. "I thought soaps were about romance."

Dennis Savage scoffed. "Soap opera is about the illusion of romance. The characters fall out of love as fast as they fall in."

"Falling out of love is easy to do," said Carlo. "It can happen overnight."

We stared at him.

"You should go into it," he explained gently, "without expectations."

"You say this, after wishing for a lawyer?"

"I need a new adventure. I'm so truly bored with having a hot time and trading Circuit buzz terms. I want . . . I want someone I can *electrify*. That's what I want! Hot men are neat, but they already know everything, don't they?" His eyes lit with a wild surmise. "I surely believe I want a virgin!"

"Back to the sixties," Dennis Savage breathed. "Remember when no one knew how to do *anything*?"

"A lawyer with a terrace," Carlo went on, dreamily, "and a bulging briefcase."

"He'll be dull, Carlo," I warned.

"He won't, because we'll fall in love. Don't you know that everyone is good in bed when he's in love?"

A key clicked in the front door and Little Kiwi marched in with the groceries, the mail, and dire Bauhaus. "You're watching *soap operas?*"

"The best people watch soaps nowadays," I told him.

"The best people," he answered, "are otherwise engaged."

Carlo winked at him, and, suddenly shy, Little Kiwi turned away and threw his raincoat onto Bauhaus to watch it go. In the kitchen, sorting out his haul, he called out, "They didn't have Froot Loops, Snug, so I got Count Chocula."

"Snug?" Carlo echoed.

"*Froot Loops?*" I cried.

Dennis Savage blushed. "Little Kiwi, I believe it's time for your nap."

"Dennis Savage eats Froot Loops!" I exulted.

"Well, *you* eat zwieback and milk!"

"So I do . . . *Snug.*"

In the ensuing silence, we heard Little Kiwi slotting things into cupboards and watched his raincoat crawl evilly around the living room.

"What's new, *Snug?*" I asked.

"I could really enjoy tearing your head off."

"Little Kiwi should go first," Carlo told him. "He blew the secret."

Little Kiwi joined us, happy as a hatter. "He wouldn't hurt me," he announced. "He likes me a lot." He ruffled Dennis Savage's hair. "I guess I shouldn't have called you Snug, though," he added in a whisper.

"How long has it been now?" asked Carlo, looking at them thoughtfully.

"Four years," I said. "And they still sleep face to face, hot breath steaming their cheeks."

"Has anyone ever told you," Dennis Savage asked me, "that you are a vicious rotten oik who is completely fagola?"

Little Kiwi was taking in the television; a woman in a nun's habit was shouting, "Lars! Please, Lars! Don't rush off in search of The Golden Cone of Calcutta!"

"Soap opera is dumb," said Little Kiwi, picking up his raincoat. Bauhaus continued to slither around the floor, his eyes closed, growling.

"The conversations are funny," Carlo admitted.

"No class consciousness," I put in.

"It's not realistic," Little Kiwi insisted. "Out of nowhere, two people meet and kiss and shack up, and a few episodes later they're slapping each other. People aren't like that."

"Sometimes they are," said Carlo. "Like if they get to know each other too well."

"How could you know someone too well?" Little Kiwi asked. "That's what love is for." He came over to Carlo. "Isn't it, Carlo?"

Carlo smiled at him. "Sure it is," he said.

Carlo was so serious about finding a lawyer that he harangued me about throwing a lawyer party so he could examine them and make a correct selection. Ridiculous. Everyone thinks I know suitgays because I live on the east side. On the contrary, you know whom you know and where you live has nothing to do with the case. Anyway, the only lawyer of my acquaintance is my cousin Ellis, who is straight, married, and the father of two splendid children. There didn't seem much point in setting him up with Carlo.

"Ellis?" Carlo said at a planning session in my apartment. "That sounds right. Where did he go to school?"

"Dartmouth."

"That's what I want! Fill a room with those and—"

"I know!" said Dennis Savage. "Hugh Whitkin!"

"Hugh!" Carlo sighed. "The names they have!"

"We were at Hamilton together, and he went on to Harvard Law. He knows a hundred preppie lawyers."

"Would he give Carlo a party?"

"Maybe I should skip the party and take Hugh Whitkin."

"Uh-oh!" Dennis Savage and I said in chorus.

"Is that a no?"

"Carlo, didn't you say you wanted a virgin?"

"Has Hugh been around?"

"Somewhat," Dennis Savage admitted. "When they discovered the Stone Age paintings in that cave in Spain, his phone number was on the wall."

"Is he cute?"

"Abnormally handsome," I said. "Nice shape. No muscles. Straight golden-blond hair . . ."

"I *love* Hugh Whitkin!"

"No Hugh Whitkin for you!" snapped Dennis Savage. "He's a jaded son-of-a-bitch who'll chew you, spit you out, and still have time for a lunchtime quickie with the mailroom boys."

"Look, I'm not exactly a novice—"

"No Hugh Whitkin or no party!" Dennis Savage walked to the phone, opened his address book, and laid his hand on the receiver. "I can set you up a party at Hugh Whitkin's or I can forget about the whole thing. It's your choice."

"Wait a minute," I said. "Carlo has been around the block, after all. I don't care how lurid Hugh Whitkin is, you can't throw a lion to the lions."

Dennis Savage slowly shook his head. "Choose, Carlo!"

Carlo chose. "No Hugh Whitkin."

"Attaboy."

But when Dennis Savage turned to dial, Carlo winked at me.

I should say something about Hugh Whitkin, though it grates me even to introduce much less develop him. He would make a dandy villain on the soaps: the smooth cad who will woo you till you grow to need him—at which time he tells you you're a dead issue. If Carlo is the gay brimming with romance, Hugh Whitkin holds as much romance as a colander. He is everything I despise in gay, closeted, selfish rich, politically resistant, and classy without culture. There was a time some years back when I moved with a nobby crowd. We were conservative in that old-fashioned, anglophile, James Burnham way, and dressed up when we socialized, and disdained a good many things. Eventually I realized that a conservative gay is about as valid as a Jewish Nazi, and Hugh Whitkin—the maximum leader of this crowd—was the main reason why.

I broke with my friends not so much for political reasons as for psychosexual ones. What did they think of themselves? What did they believe they knew of the world? What kind of men did they like? Little. Everything. Wimps, like themselves. You can't lead a successful life thinking you don't deserve one, or voicing preferences for the good old days of the men's rooms and the vice cops, or referring to the annual marching festival as Gay Shame Day. The first time I heard one of the crowd lament "the lost glamour of the tea-room rendezvous" my mouth fell open, and I disgraced myself passing heavy commentary at Harry Apgar when he brayed that line about "the love that dare not speak its name" becoming "the love that wouldn't shut up." Then, on a Gay Pride Day, when Hugh Whitkin smirked about "gay shame" I held very still—maybe I'd heard him wrong. But no: he smiled at me, daring me to challenge him; I think he knew I hated him before I knew it. I thought about it for a long while, as the others stirred about me and I refused to move out of the way of whatever was going on and everybody got the idea that I was going to do something horrible.

I didn't. I left and took a long walk home to think about it, and finally realized that I had been keeping company with men who embodied the straight's comprehension of gay: self-hating, devious, dreary pixies, as fearful of sensuality as hungry for it and terrified of women who aren't terrified of men. Solidarity of kind, to them, meant not comradely support but cold bodies to fit around the brunch table: a guest list for glum amusement between work and sleep.

The more I thought about the company I'd been keeping the angrier I got, till I was storming home promising myself never to see any of them again—and not to waste any words explaining myself, either.

I was resolute. But I feared I'd suffer a bad case of *pensées de l'esca-lier*—going over and over what I should have said when I had the chance—if I didn't confront one of them. And I knew which one.

I called Hugh and told him I wanted to see him. The sooner the better. Maybe now. He laughed. "Everyone's worried about you, the way you hurried off. But I'm not worried, my friend." He laughed again. "I never worry because I have nothing to worry about."

Carlo is right in assuming that lawyers have terraces, and Hugh's is spectacular, a wraparound overlooking the East River. Chivas in hand, we went outside, Hugh sardonically smiling, as if he knew ex-actly what I was going to say and was ready to trip me up.

I began, "I'm going to tell you straight out—"

"What's that line from Oscar Wilde," he interjected, "about being absolutely candid when you have something unpleasant to say?"

I tried smiling sardonically back at him, but my sardonic lacks something in crust.

"Please go on," he said.

"I'm here to tell you what I think of you."

"My dear fellow, why on earth would I care what you think of me?"

That's a great comeback, boys and girls: no matter what the other says in reply, he comes off a fool. While I regrouped to renew my assault, Hugh moved closer to me, touched my arm, and said, "Have you ever made love to someone you loathed?"

Startled silent, I tried to overwhelm him with a bold cool, and stared into his eyes. But you can't stare down a man as handsome as Hugh Whitkin; you can only stare at him.

"You're on the wrong side," he told me. "You're going to be, the way you're headed. Leather jackets and mustaches and those circus-freak rags in the back pocket. Is that how you fancy yourself? Walking around like a human commercial for debauchery?"

I should have realized that you can't win an argument with a law-yer. I wasn't even able to start one.

"You're a smart fellow," he went on, his voice low. "Reason it out. You're not some pouf roughneck from Scranton. You're one of us."

Smiling, because he never worries. "You're going to be miserable if you join up with the wrong crowd." He touched me again. "Don't you realize that no one in America cares whether or not you're quietly homosexual? It's the gay stuff they hate, that's all. This public flogging of their feelings. You think the men upstairs are going to allow this filth to hector them indefinitely?"

He was stroking my hair, mesmerizing me. I was letting him. It came out a whisper when I said, "I hate you."

"No, you don't. You don't even wish you could."

"I'm not one of you."

He touched my tie, the handkerchief peeping out of my blazer pocket, the stripes in my Brooks Brothers shirt, as if taking inventory of my worth. "Linka Oelrichs remembers you from Friends Academy. She says you were in *The Boy Friend* together."

"She was thrown out in her senior year for rimming Phoebe Wadsworth in the common room without a permission slip."

"Linka Oelrichs heads the *Times*' Vienna bureau. Her brother Colbert is going to be the junior senator from Connecticut when the time comes. The family has been running their share of the Northeast for four generations."

"Cole Oelrichs is a bloody fucking crap-headed dildo and so are you," I said, but I had my hands on him then, pulling his jacket off his shoulders, remembering what I went through as a seventh-grader, five hundred miles from home and trying to fit in with the likes of Cole and Linka Oelrichs and various apprentice Hugh Whitkins, a pouf roughneck from, as it happens, not Scranton but Wilkes-Barre, one town over, and I suppose if I had given Hugh a beating I would have gone home feeling better but then I would never have known what it's like to screw the most elegant man on the east side.

Of course his theme, so to say, was that I *was* one of them, that I took him kind for kind, affirming that his patrician breeding and antique fortune were decorations as essential to the correct life as were the strains of orange and brown in his golden hair. But more: as he had never shown the slightest interest in me physically, alluring me and allowing me to be allured *and* to act on it was a lovely slur, a derogation fit for the blue book. At least I gave it to him gutter-style, standing in his bedroom, with our shoes on and pants down. And when I was about to leave I said, "To answer your question: Yes, I have made love to someone I loathed. Just now."

He was sitting on the bed, pulling off his shoes, and he laughed as I walked out. He laughed because he has nothing to worry about.

Even eight years later, I wasn't sure how glad Hugh would be to throw a party for a man he'd never met, a particularly gay man at that, and a distinctly unpatrician gay man, but for all Hugh's Us and Them he's probably as curious about what the other side is like sexually as the rest of us are.

I asked Dennis Savage if Hugh had remarked about my participation in all this.

"He said he's looking forward to seeing you again."

"Did he say . . .?" I caught myself just in time; Dennis Savage was watching me as Aschenbach watched Tadzio. No—as the hotel manager watched Aschenbach watching Tadzio.

"Is there something you haven't told me?" said Dennis Savage. "About you and Hugh Whitkin?"

"Of course," I replied.

It was the night of the party; we were dressing Carlo out of my closet. As someone who has lived his entire life on a wardrobe of T-shirts and corduroys (Carlo's trademark; supposedly he has never worn a pair of jeans since he came to New York), Carlo was naturally as dazzled by the accoutrements of the dress-up life as Poles, Greeks, and Norwegians were said to be by the stupas of Manhattan as their emigrant boats pulled into port.

"Look at these!" he cried, seizing my little clock cuff links, heirlooms I never wear. "Earrings that tell time!"

"Don't you ever buy new clothes?" Dennis Savage fussed, pawing through my shirts. "You must have gone through high school in these."

"I want a striped tie, okay?" said Carlo. "And perhaps I may have been wondering if I should change my name."

Dennis Savage carefully looked at him.

"Well, they're all going to be Ellis and Terence and Perry, right?" Carlo continued. "Maybe I should seem like one of them."

"Maybe they're as tired of their scene as you are of yours," I ventured. "So, like, opposites attract."

"Yes, okay. It's just . . . I do believe I thought of a name I might use. A party name, as you truly might say."

Dennis Savage, straightening Carlo's tie, said, "I don't like it already."

"Say, Coco," I advised Dennis Savage. "Why don't you concentrate on designing the outfit and—"

"*What . . . name . . .* did you think up?"

Carlo chuckled at him and patted his shoulder. "Whitkin McHugh?"

Dennis Savage slammed the closet door.

"I just thought—"

"We had a deal! No Hugh Whitkin! No thinking about or impersonating Hugh Whitkin!"

"Oh, gee."

"I *knew* he'd pull this!"

I took Carlo over to the mirror so he could see himself. He looked terrific as always, and a little different—wiser, maybe—and he saw it and grinned.

"Look," he said.

Then we collected Little Kiwi, bundled into a cab, and rolled up to East End Avenue to Hugh Whitkin's party, a soap-opera casting director's dream: two dozen men only a woman could love, cute but not sexy. Still, after a career of men called Slim and Blue, this was what Carlo wanted. It was quite some do, with catered food, a bartender, and a waiter. Little Kiwi had his first Perrier and sat upside down on the sofa, Dennis Savage performed fraternity nostalgia with Hugh, and I helped Carlo circulate.

Smooth, boys and girls. But Hugh always is smooth. He greeted me at the door like a dear friend welcoming me back from having been lost for two years in The Cloisters. Somehow he seemed backlit, as if Greta Garbo had lent him William Daniels, and, of course, the debonair flurry beyond the entryway was impressive, with the most delicate chamber music on the processed tape and the most admirable hors d'oeuvres on the passing trays. "Guess I won't need this," Little Kiwi whispered to me, showing me the box of Raisinets he had slipped into his breast pocket.

Yes, smooth; still, I don't like these parties. I prefer the lit gatherings—tense, yes, but brilliant. This lawyer crowd could talk (1) mortgages, (2) Wall Street, and (3) shop. Someone with prep-school tact led me to an alleged fellow opera buff who turned out to have seen only three operas, all of them *La Bohème*. As my favorites are *Les Troyens*, *Les Huguenots*, and *Francesca da Rimini*, we had little to share.

Carlo was a wow. He was too intent on finding his fate to be shy and too thrilled with the *richesse* of archetype to worry about how he appealed to them. Yet as he charmed them they were unsure how to charm back. "Where do you play squash?" one lawyer asked Carlo.

Imagine.

After squiring Carlo through the ranks, I went over to Little Kiwi and dished the gang with him. He hasn't much to say but at least it's a familiar mouth. Dennis Savage joined us and we watched the circles form, close, and reform around Carlo. Whatever buildup Hugh had given him to assemble his crew, Carlo was living up to it. Hugh thought so, too. Slowly he turned, step by step, inch by inch. When Dennis Savage and I got to them, Carlo was merrily enlarging on his San Francisco past to an audience so enraptured they were dribbling scampi onto their vests.

"Cockdudes?" Hugh was saying. "Cuddleboys?"

"Yeah, see, the cockdudes would spread out these mattresses," Carlo was telling them, "and they'd go out on the street to round up some cuddleboys," as he shifted his focus to Hugh, "and then . . ."

because Hugh had taken Carlo's hand in his own, "you see . . ." and
they locked eyes and somewhere great bells went clang.

Hugh took Carlo's other hand. "Yes?"

"They lay the cuddleboys on the mattresses."

"Ah."

"And they . . ."

"Tell me."

". . . they . . ."

"Yes."

Carlo grasped Hugh's shoulders. "This is a nice party."

"What do cockdudes do to cuddleboys?"

"I'm not allowed to talk to you."

"No one is."

"They loosen the cuddleboys up. Cream them up."

"Do they, now?"

"You're so handsome."

The other lawyers had drifted away; one thing a lawyer knows is
timing. Carlo and Hugh kissed as Dennis Savage shook his head.
"Get your coat," he told me.

Dennis Savage refused to discuss it; not a word. Of course Carlo
had gone for Hugh. It was not blond hair after dark that he wanted,
nor innocence after experience. He wanted mean after pleasant—or
so I guess. Carlo had known hot without menace, fun without substance. Every other day he would tell me, "I've just fallen in love,"
but once, in one of those profound confessional sessions he abhors
but gives so much to, he told me he had very seldom been in love in
any real sense. "Very seldom," he had insisted. But was this love? In
his several months with Hugh, Carlo's chest sprouted hair, his head
whispered gray, and his stomach, so slightly, began to sag. He aged.

"It's astonishing," I said. "Dennis Savage and I tease each other
about being jaded and decadent, but it's really because we happened
to be there when Stonewall sexuality exploded. We were witnesses,
more than anything else. But you, Carlo. You have done all this,

everything. Yet every now and then you take some man to bed and suddenly the world cracks apart. You're like a kid wondering how far he'll get the night of the prom. Do the men with the most sex know the least about love?"

Carlo took out a bag of grass and butt papers and prepared to roll a joint. He can do it one-handed. "What was your first time like, Bud?" I didn't answer; it was not a question but an opening flourish. "Mine was in the back of a truck, when I was seventeen, on my way to New York. I hadn't even crossed the Mississippi then." He sorted the herb, flicked away a bit of twig. "This guy was driving a moving van filled with furniture. Someone probably got himself transferred from Denver to Toledo. Took his wife and kids and went on ahead. Anyway, the mover picked me up. Big fellow, bearded, rough hands, fancy green eyes. He flashed them every other second. Your typical gay kid's nighttime fantasy." He licked the paper, nodding at the recollection. "My first *real* time, I mean. All the way. I was scared, but I knew I wanted him, and I thought, There's probably a road in if I phrase it right. Because he kept looking at me, you know? Heavy looking. Two times, it's gringo rivalry. Three or four, you remind him of someone. Ten times with green eyes, he wants to fuck you." He folded the joint, lit it. "And that's what he said he wanted, right there in the cab of his truck." Took it in. He smokes too much, but other than breaking hearts it's his only vice. "He said he wanted to cornhole my cherry. Those words. Those words, Bud." He looked at me. "I'd never heard the term but I knew what it meant without thinking about it and I wasn't afraid. I was glad. We were passing a very empty stretch of road and he made it clear we could pull over and do it or he'd dump me right where we were. And I told him I'd be glad to let him cornhole me. He looked over again, the biggest look yet. What a fool I was. I was smiling, so relieved, after all that fumbling I had known in high school. And you know what he said? 'I don't want you voluntary.'"

He proffered the joint. I shook my head.

"Anyway, that's how I got to New York, hitching with truckers, and I swear every single one of them fucked me. One took me to a motel in the afternoon, one got me out in the trees behind a Howard Johnson's, and one gave me twenty dollars to do it with him in front of his best friend—to settle a bet, he said. A bet. Okay. But there was one you should know about, different from the others. This very man took me to his mother's house in some small town in Ohio. It seemed the same as the others at first—me face down and him on top, no talking, just the gentle pounding in the darkness. See, they were all men and I was a raw kid, so that was fair. But I wanted to find out what it was like on top, making someone happy like that. Because that's what it is, isn't it?

"Anyway, this guy with the mother. He wasn't much to look at, I guess. Kind of clumsy. Said the wrong thing a lot, you know. Laughed too much for nothing. But he was very nice, and I wasn't used to nice men then, especially not big ones. Big men truly aren't nice where I come from, you know. They're tough. Okay. That's how we grow them. Anyway, this guy . . . I can't remember his name now, but I can see him as clear as I see you. Brown hair, kind of scraggly, the hair that never looks combed, like. Brown eyes, bushy mustache. Gigantic shoulders, like he's been carrying stuff all his life. Arms, too, big. Chest. Not cut up. Fleshy. With a light dust of hair and nipples as big as a woman's. Stomach just starting to loosen up. Squared-off ass, big junk. Oh, I truly see him. I see him, Bud." He put the joint down. "He was the best of them all. He shouldn't have been, but he was. Very basic, slow and certain. That means something, anyway. And like we were lying around talking and I asked him if I could take a turn and fuck him and he said okay, and it was totally different from then on. The moment he turned over and I got behind him I felt . . . more involved, somehow. What could be more involved than being fucked, right? But this was. I sat on him and stroked his sides as if I was giving him a massage, great long strokes all the way down him, and each time he let out a deep breath, like he was struggling not to moan. The lights were out, but the bed was by the window and a ray of light from a street lamp was hitting him just at the neck where the hair ends, and I thought that must be the sexiest piece of flesh a man can have, just there. I ruffled the bottom ridge of his hair and he gave out this incredible sigh. We were using soap, you know, dipping it in a little bowl of warm water. It was like stepping back fifty years into the past. Like something *The Policeman's Gazette* might have known about but wouldn't care to mention." Stirred by the recollection, he paused. "Soap and a little bowl of warm water," he went on. He cocked his head, seeing it again. "We had dinner with his mother, and then we went upstairs, to a little room under the slope of the roof. Maybe he kept it especially for this. When we got up there, he said, 'What we need is some soap and a little bowl of warm water.' I guess I remember details like that more than I do what a guy looked like. But I remember this man. The way he looked all stretched out under me. The light on his neck. As I soaped him open, he began to spread his legs, bit by bit, wider and wider. And I thought . . . well . . . that I *knew* him somehow, like I was closer to him than . . . than anyone. He was my ally. My teammate. I was a real jerk about getting my cock into him. I guess I must have thought it would just slide in, but it took some practice. I had to pull him up on his hands to work it all in, and then we froze like that. I could scarcely breathe. I was filled with some wonderful feeling and I didn't know what it was. Never felt that before. Never." He paused again to relight the toke, nodding at some thought. "Well, so we hunkered down again and I began to fuck him and all I could think of was him, this man I was hitched up to, legs and arms and torso. All the way, right? All the way is how they put it. I kept saying his name over and over." He looked at me. "Jed. His name was Jed. Jesus, twenty years ago. Jed. And then I knew what the feeling was—I *loved* him. It was love! I did, I felt it. Him, that man, his skin and his muscles and his neck. Not just sex, not even just good sex, but love. I swear to God. I loved him. And I put my head down on his so our cheeks sort of touched, and I like nodded slightly, so my hair brushed his. It wasn't wild at all. It was serene. It was like . . . maybe like giving something to him and keeping it at the same time. That must be sharing. All the way. And when we broke apart, I grabbed him in this hug of death, and he laughed and said, 'You're a real live wire.' It may sound crazy, but I actually considered staying on with him, living in that house, in that room, maybe. With the street-lamp light and the little bowl of warm water. I didn't even care if we never fucked again, I just wanted to . . . I . . . what? *Touch* him. Say his name. And then he shifted over and put his arms around me and he nuzzled the back of my neck. And, do you know?, I was crying. My whole body was shaking. Lying with my head on those big chest muscles sobbing like an infant while he comforted me. I finally calmed down, and we lay there for a long time. Maybe an hour. We weren't dozing, either. Just lay there, nothing doing. All the way. Then he suddenly said, 'I'm forty-six years old.' That's all. I waited, and at last he said, 'How old are you?' And I told him. So then he put his hand on my head, stroking my hair. Playing with it. And then you know what he said? He said, 'You're going to be so happy.'"

"And are you?" I asked.

He stabbed out the joint, rose and aimlessly crossed the room, deep in thought. He came to a halt at the Victrola, lifted the lid, idly inspected the machine.

"Maybe I should have stayed with him forever. It was like that first night for a few days, and then I started to mind it when he'd roll me over for his turn to top me. I didn't want him to know me the way I could know him."

Here Carlo turned back to me. "And don't ask me why. Don't ask me anything. I just didn't. So I came here. And then San Francisco. Then back here, home. And I tried all the types and all the scenes. I had everybody. I did it and I did it, with the musclemen and the tender kids and the stars and the straights. But never again did I feel the way I felt that night in that little town with the ray of light on Jed's neck. I guess I wonder what would have happened if I'd stayed with him. What if that was love, that time? I want to go back to the way that . . . happened. That stranger. And maybe Hugh is the only stranger I have left."

"Even now?"

"Almost. Maybe. The way he lies on his stomach, waiting to be pleasured. There's something in him." He shrugged. "On the other hand, he's such a soft thin shell of a guy. God, does he need a gym." He turned to the window, watching the ironworkers bulling up the frame of the block's new office tower. "There's nothing as excellent as a big man. A really big, wonderful man. If I were a big man, I'd be happy."

"Carlo, you *are* a big man."

He turned back to me and grinned. "I only look big."

"You know, every other day I pass one of your ex-es. They always ask after you. Steve Bosco is moving back from Seattle. He wants to call you."

"Big Steve." He smiled. "He's a teddy bear. Every Sunday he made French toast in the waffle iron. He shouldn't call, though. I'm not free yet. But the bad things always end. Trust me. The good things hang on forever."

"So it is bad?"

"Not . . . not the way you think. See, I know Hugh is mean, so he can't hurt me any more than the nice men can help me. It's only your true friends who can hurt you, right? When they get mad at you."

I said nothing.

"It'll be over soon. I'm waiting for something."

"What?"

"You think I'm a sheltered sweetheart like Little Kiwi. Dennis Savage won't speak to me, did you know that? He gets off the phone so fast you'd think his building was afire."

"He wants to run you out of gay."

"You're all wrong about me. See, I'm truly not a cuddleboy. I'm a cockdude. I can risk anything."

"What are you waiting for?"

"I can't call it by name. But I'll know it when he does it."

He did it the night Carlo turned forty at a surprise party I threw in his apartment. The ruse was a peacemaking visit from Dennis Savage, piled on a dinner date Carlo had with who knew whom; and the guests were assembled an hour ahead, decorating, cooking, and drinking. What a comparison to Hugh Whitkin's lawyer party: half the group were in T-shirts, leather and lumberjack flannel lent an air, and Big Steve Bosco wore nothing but a netted pouch and running shoes.

Little Kiwi, in charge of the food, took offense. "His chest hair is infiltrating the lasagna!" he cried, carrying the platter back to the kitchen. "Make him wear something!"

"Be gentle," I warned him. "He's an affectionate elder who wants to stay in touch"—hanging on forever, I almost added, like a soap character.

"His hands are too big. He's always hugging people!"

"That's the mode of his circle. Don't be a monopolist, boy. Learn the modes. Welcome diversity."

He eyed me warily. "Will there be a quiz on this?"

"Lights!" someone cried, and out they went, but the footsteps traveled past the floor. "False alarm."

I took the lasagna back out, but had to drag it right back in again because in the darkness someone had slipped an ice cube into Big Steve's pouch and now he and several others were chasing around the living room in lighthearted melee.

"Is it true that Carlo is dating Hugh Whitkin?" Little Kiwi asked. "Snug won't tell me."

"Why do you call him Snug?"

He smirked. "I better not say."

"You can tell me."

"Like fish!"

"Lights!" This time was it, and we huddled grinning as the door opened. You know the festive moment, when the victim walks in and someone yanks the lights on and everyone screams "Surprise!" But this victim walked in with Hugh Whitkin and they were in the middle of a fight.

Hugh, of course, fights in undertone and Carlo never fights. Still, it had a nasty edge, the two of them framed in tight doorway light while the rest of us stood unseen at the far end of the living room waiting for no cue.

"You don't get to ask those questions," Hugh was saying. "I'll tell you what you can know. Everything else is none of your business."

"Enough for tonight, now."

"No. Oh, no." Hugh grabbed Carlo's elbow. "What do you mean by calling Randy Pinkerton a bohunk, you ghetto slime?"

"It's just a word, Hugh. I don't even know what it means."

"It means that you are a shabby slut and I doubt that we can continue this relationship on any level."

Carlo slowly pulled away from Hugh, spilling more light into the doorway. "You're truly a beautiful man, Hugh. No one else I've been with had anything like your style. They had the gym and The Look, that's all. You're perfect. Yet they were all terrific guys and you're a grungy prick. Why is that?"

"You little whore," Hugh rasped. He was actually angry. "You godless Christopher Street savage."

"I'm tired of fighting, Hugh. Let's be gentlemen and shake hands." He extended his. "Tomorrow, if you still—"

Hugh cracked the flat of his hand across Carlo's face, someone snapped on the lights, Little Kiwi yelled "Surprise!" and what a pair of faces the party then beheld. Carlo looked like a Munchkin the day the house fell on the Wicked Witch and Hugh like a truffle trapped in a gumball machine.

Big Steve hulked forward with dishonorable intentions toward Hugh's health, but Carlo intercepted him with a cry and an embrace. "You look great!" Carlo told him. "I must get the name of your tailor."

Hugh took a long look at Big Steve's jaw, a fleeting one at Big Steve's pouch, and fled.

"It's my birthday, right?" Carlo asked us all as we milled about, laughing nervously. "This is my party!"

Once we loosened up, it *was* a party. Carlo spent much of it in Big Steve's lap opening presents, Rick Conradi did a drag act in the discarded wrappings, and Kenny Reeves taught Little Kiwi the samba.

"You were waiting for something," I reminded Carlo. "Did it . . . occur?"

He grinned and patted his cheek. "You saw it occur, my friend."

"So was Hugh the stranger you wanted, after all? Did you electrify him?"

"Hugh is a stranger, I guess. But not my stranger." He looked around the room, at something like twenty men he had known for about four hundred years in the aggregate, nearly half a millennium of buddies. "Maybe there are no more strangers in gay life," he said. "Maybe you can only electrify yourself. Listen, that's what Stonewall gave us, right?"

"Do me a favor? Go home with Big Steve."

He laughed. Dennis Savage signaled me over to the salad bowl to pick out the last few cherry tomatoes.

"Thank God that wretched soap opera is over," he said.

"If it's over, it wasn't soap opera. Soaps never end, you know."

"I don't recall how this got started, but I'd swear it was your fault."

"I know why Little Kiwi calls you Snug."

"If you *dare* say so much as—"

"It's because you electrify him when you cuddle, you cockdude, you."

He said, "You would have made a good early Christian, you know that?" But I could tell he was pleased.

Rope

Notes on S&M, set forth by outsiders as well as by experts.

Strenuous, black-hearted Dick Tangent asks me where Bobby is.

I say I'm not aware.

He knows I'm lying, and takes the double-crostic away from me. I still won't look at him; fine, he'll wait.

I give in and turn to him. "Look—"

"Hey," he cuts in, mock-amiable, patting my knee. "Hey, now. Because the longer he stays away, the worse it'll be for him when he gets back. Tell him."

"He knows."

"I want that little chicken here, and I mean today. By the time I get back from tea. That gives him three hours." He leans against the deck railing, facing the ocean and me. "What does he think he's doing, anyway? He knows he'll come home. He's got a case on me, whether you like it or not."

"It has nothing to do with me."

He nods once, slowly. "Now you're talking." He looks at the puzzle, cut from the *Times* and set on a clipboard. "You do these in pen?"

"Pencil makes too light an impression."

"Belts make a good impression. You ought to try them sometime. Tell Bobby what I said." He hands me the clipboard and saunters off.

I have always had back luck in my Pines houses. My first year, I roomed with a temper-monster and an alcoholic realtor who, before my eyes, jacked off his poodle, Amahl the Night Visitor, with his foot. The dog cried out like a plucked mandrake when it climaxed. The second year I jumped from a house as structured as summer camp to one so open no one got around to making dinner. I lived on Lorna Doones; and by September I looked like one. I tried going freelance the next year, but I hated being a guest, so I bought out the share of a friend who was suddenly transferred to Los Angeles, and ended in a small rectangle surrounded by deckwork and perched high over the eastern end of the oceanside Pines: with one S, Dick Tangent; the S's two wonderful Labradors, Mortimer and Gridley; the S's M, Bobby Hackney; and a coil of rope with which Dick terrorized Bobby.

No gizmos for Dick—none of that *Drummer* kit of clamps, enemas, whoopie cushions, Cuisinarts, seltzer bottles, and other jazz. Dick was subtle, tactile, confidential. Tying up his partners was not the start of his scene, but its ultimate threat. What he would do to you then was, I suppose, your worst fantasy, Room 101; anyway, he had Bobby paralyzed. I had seen them in bed lying so skillfully intertwined they might have been a pretzel; and chasing each other along the beach splashing and shouting like little kids; and staring at each other on the deck as the sun was coming up, not daring to touch except at the eyes, and then Bobby would turn at my footsteps and I'd see tears running down his cheeks.

It was a good house logistically. Dick ran it, and ran it well. He and I got along because his dogs and I did. He let them walk me, which was not unlike driving a chariot without the chariot. He did all the cooking, saw to the landlord details, and even enjoyed cleaning up. All I had to do was play secret agent with Bobby, who was forever running off in fear of and returning in lamentation to Dick and the rope waiting in the bedroom.

Now, Bobby, I should tell you, was a very disadvantaged kid. Poor family, chance education, no ambition training. God gave him something: cuteness to die—but this too turned out to be a disadvantage, because as long as he could remember, men had been seducing and raping him. His cousins, his uncles, the minister, delivery boys. He called them "pirates." Too slight to defend himself from their advances, he took up karate training; but the instructor kidnapped him. Then Bobby joined a gym, but in the shower room everyone could view his gigantic cock—another disadvantage, the poor kid—and pirates would drag him home and commit disorderly conduct upon him. I suppose he concluded that as long as he was born to be possessed, he might as well select a permanent dreamboat.

That Dick Tangent was. He knew the Three Secrets, more valuable than the Three Cards of Pushkin's Queen of Spades, to wit: (1) have a lot of jaw, (2) smile seldom but dazzlingly, and (3) walk from the ass down. For my money, his dogs were more fun. Mornings, I'd come out on the deck and they'd frolic about, then I'd lie down and they'd take turns leaping over me. Yet everyone I knew was suing for dinner invitations, and not to meet the dogs. Dick ruled these out. "Take your guests to the Monster," he'd say. "Read your lease. I cook for the house."

Besides, he was busy with Bobby. There were other folk on the premises, but we were all in our late twenties and early thirties, and things were beginning to break for us professionally. They were often away: filming on location, setting up a Denver office, whatever. So basically it was a three-character play, a *No Exit*; or no, a duet with an audience, so Dick and Bobby could shock me, worry me, delight me when they lived happily ever after for a day or two, then challenge me when their contentious bond snagged taut and threatened to snap.

"How's World War III going?" Dennis Savage asked, when I repaired to his house for relief.

"You know this is the skid row of The Pines?" I replied. He was far west, deep in the woods on the bay side, where the mosquitoes are so big they wear cock rings. "If Elmer Fudd came out, this is where he'd stay."

"We had shrimp scampi for lunch," said Carlo, tidying up in the kitchen.

"Watch out, Carlo," said Dennis Savage. "Dick Tangent's been giving him macho lessons. He got an A in Tying Castanets to Your Balls So People Can Hear Them Clacking, and now they're working on—"

"Congratulations," I told Dennis Savage, "on getting over your accident."

"What accident?" asked Carlo, a dependable straight man.

"The night of the Green Party. He was putting toilet water behind his ears and the seat fell on his head."

"Does Dick still have that rope?" Carlo asked.

Sensing dish, Dennis Savage grew rigid. "Carlo! Did you—"

"No. I was out of S&M by the time I came back east. Does he?"

"Yes," I said.

Carlo smiled, nodded, shrugged; what a life.

"He never uses it," I added.

"Till it's time to," said Carlo. "He's quite a character. You remember what happened to Bert Wisner after Dick put the rope on him."

"He vanished," said Dennis Savage.

"He moved to Brooklyn," I corrected.

"Same thing."

"No," said Carlo, putting the dishes away. "No," closing the cabinet. "He left the scene, and he got into porn and hustling, and then you'd see him panhandling around St. Marks Place, and he looked so pathetic men took him home just to cash in on that sense of . . . of little lost boy. He wasn't attractive anymore. He was helpless. Some men go for that, you know? Like they collect pictures of amputees? And Bert had been a very, very cute man. He could've gone anywhere. He blew it all."

"Because of Dick Tangent?"

Carlo shook his head. "Because heavy sex is fire, and some people are made of stone and some of paper. The stone people are good for S&M, but the paper people go up like tinder. They fuck their brains away. They trade life in for fantasies. They become obsessed by stone idols." He packed away the flatware. "No, not because of Dick Tangent. But because some people shouldn't do anything more than cruise and screw and do an affair now and then. Haven't I always told you that certain kinds of love are dangerous before the age of thirty?"

Dennis Savage and I carefully attend. Carlo is not a great reader of Proudhon or Dickens or Nietzsche. But when it comes to romance, thus spake Zarathustra.

"Dick is a very deep guy, very loving," Carlo went on. "A strong man can survive him, learn from him, even. But a kid . . ." He shook his head. "It's like locking an altar boy in with twenty Popes."

"That's Bobby, all right," I said.

"Have you ever been tied up?" Dennis Savage asked me.

"Not for sex."

"Maybe," Carlo began, "someone should—"

"Whoa!" says Dennis Savage. "Not for *sex*? Then for what, an international incident?"

"My brother used to—"

"I knew it!" he exulted. "Another chapter of *Pennsylvania Gothic*." He turned to Carlo. "You know how parents send clan photographs at Christmas? The Morddens send their portrait by Charles Addams."

"Your brother?" asked Carlo, amused.

"Well, you know. Brothers will fight. And ours were pretty severe. So, finally, rather than chance killing me, he took to tying me up. Formalizing the punishment, so to say. I'm not defending it, but it was rather sensible, wasn't it? After a while, I didn't even bother to struggle."

"Listen to him," Dennis Savage whispered. "Listen to corruption."

"No, wait," said Carlo. "I happen to know about this. He tied you to your bed, didn't he?"

"Yes."

"Wrists and ankles?"

"No. Hands to the bedposts."

He smiled. "You had an old-fashioned house. And then what? He'd talk to you, right? Sit on a chair next to the bed?"

"On the bed."

He shook his head. "It's a tiny little thing of a world, gentlemen. So many men—so few stories."

"Did someone do that to you, Carlo?"

"My father."

"My God," said Dennis Savage, "I'm surrounded by perverts."

"No," said Carlo. "It's just punishment. An act of the middle class, like cruising shopping malls and turning on a television. It's discipline. But it's also a kind of flattery, I think."

"What do you say to a man you've just tied up?" asked Dennis Savage.

"You don't tie up a man," said Carlo. "You tie up a boy. Your kid brother. Your son. Men do the tying."

Dennis Savage said, "The two of you. Sometimes."

"It can be a very honest moment," Carlo told him. "I never felt so close to my father. Other days, you know, he was like steel. So sharp, so full of himself. But when he tied me up, he was gentle. So open. Intimate. Even soft. I was never so conscious of him—of the hair behind the top buttons of his shirt. Or the veins in his hands. We had this game we called, 'I'm Going to Touch Your Eyes.' When I was a kid. It was just another name for tag, really. But later, it turned into this like . . . this touching game. Where he'd sneak up on me and pin my arms and touch my eyes while I struggled. And I did it to him. It probably sounds strange, but, you know, it's like kissing him. It is. And so that's what my father said when he was satisfied that I had learned to be good and he was going to untie me: 'I'm going to touch your eyes.'"

"And would he?" asked Dennis Savage.

"Oh, yes. My God, how I miss that!"

"I can do without the rave review."

"Men have grievances one to another," Carlo told him, "and they are bound to express these."

"What is this," Dennis Savage cried, "Bible study group?" He raised an index finger. "And they made to divide the people, that those who knew reason would not know love, and that those who knew love, yea, would not know reason."

We laughed, and Carlo said, "That's what S&M needs, a sense of humor. The trouble is so many men got into it too early—tied up like that . . . consoled by it, too . . ."

"Patterned," I suggested.

"Yes, that's right. That kind of upbringing can make you very solemn about it. It's funny you never got into the scene, Bud."

"I loathe it."

"Oh, it was so wonderful a few years ago. What we called 'San Francisco Style.' It was like getting tied up by your father. Nothing to fear. No weapons or anything. Some quiet talk, then the buddy stuff. It was lovely. *Fun.* It wasn't touchy, the way it is now. Philosophic and so on." He grew informally nostalgic. "Oh, one night . . . you know . . . Big Steve decided he wanted to fist me, and I said no, and he got nosy about it, so I ran out of the house and he chased me up and down the boardwalk. It was one of those sweater nights, everyone all bundled up inside, and here were these two naked men chasing through the place. Finally I just ducked into a house and there were four queens sitting on a couch doing cocktails, and I flattened myself against a wall and winked at them. Wouldn't you think they'd be glad to have me around, a surprise happening to them? But they looked at me as if I had thrown up on their . . . antimacassar or something. So when Big Steve poked his head in and said, 'Hey, you guys see my victim around here?' one of them stood up and pointed to me and said, '*And there he is!*' So Big Steve looked at them and looked at me, and he broke into this . . . this great laughing roar, and he took me out of there with his arm around my shoulder, laughing all the way home. And I just liked him so much for that. I mean, he was no S. He was just doing what everyone else was doing then. You know? But

of course he had never been tied up or anything . . . patterned . . . so
he didn't realize . . ." His reverie dwindling, he blinked at us.

"Realize what?" Dennis Savage asked.

"Oh." He smiled. "Jesus. Remember when we were the new boys
in town? Trying everything for the first time? Wasn't there one encounter in there somewhere when you felt you weren't just sharing
something with someone but . . . well, opening yourself dangerously
to him? Totally, sort of? I mean, like feeling him pressing against you
through your emotions? And imagine now . . . imagine if you saw
that coming and tried to close yourself away from it, because you
don't want someone knowing you so well. But the other guy won't let
go. He presses. He presses, gentlemen. Closer and closer. He invades
you. A stranger. And, like if you pleaded with him to let you be he'd
hold you and he'd soothe you. You know. But he'd keep coming and
you'd never be safe. Never. Never. Never." He took up a sponge to
polish off the counter, but just stood there. "You guys tell me, what
kid could stand up to that?"

"What's going to happen to Bobby?" I asked. "Is he going to get
hurt?"

"Dick Tangent doesn't hurt them. The way he does it, there are no
visible scars."

"What exactly does he do?" asked Dennis Savage. "Is it like with
your father?"

Carlo shrugged and sponged off the counter.

"What did your brother say to you?" Dennis Savage asked me.

"Not another word," I announced, "shall pass my lips."

"Those talks aren't meant to be shared," murmured Carlo.

"Just tell me one thing. Are you comparing this family discipline
routine to S&M?"

"Not sexually," Carlo replied. "Family discipline isn't sexual. But
S&M is more than sex."

The dogs pranced about me when I returned. The house was still,
and Bobby sat despairing on the deck as the sun went down.

"What am I going to do?" he asked me.

I didn't know.

"I can't stay here anymore."

I nodded, looked sage.

"Wherever I go, he'll find me. They always do."

If this boy lives to be thirty, I thought, he's going to have an *amazing* backstory.

"Tell me something," I said, sitting next to him. "Do you love Dick—I mean, *really* do you? Or is he just an available sweetheart?"

"Oh, what difference does that make?"

"To a lot of Pines beauties like yourself, no difference. My point is: are you in this house because this is the summer of love or die, or are you truly hooked on him? If the former, you can get away from him. He's not the KGB, you know. If the latter, maybe you should work something out with him, with less S and more M. Or maybe he actually has a deep and abiding crush on you and together you can—"

"You fucking asshole," he said sorrowfully.

I rose. "Go to hell."

"I'm sorry." He grabbed my arm. "Please don't leave me alone. It's just . . . you don't know what you're talking about. You don't work anything out with pirates. They come in where you are and they say they're going to be nice to you but they aren't, whatever you do. It just eggs them on. I've tried joking with them, and getting tough, and running like hell, and screaming for help, and crying. You name it. They just keep coming in."

"Coming in where?"

"They're pirates, don't you see what they are? They're *pirates*! All they care about is . . . is . . . "

"Plunder."

"What's that?"

"You."

"So what do I do now?"

The dogs came up, leashes clamped in their jaws: time for my walk. "Come on. We'll spin along the beach and talk about it." The dogs romped frantically ahead down the walk while Bobby paced what looked like a last mile somewhat behind us. Every so often the dogs would look back and bark at him. Cute doesn't score any points with them; they think he's boring. Mortimer growled.

"Even his dogs are pirates," Bobby muttered.

"Well," I said, as we reached the water. "The way I see it, you have only to decide whether to go on with Dick and take what he dishes out or drop him for someone who isn't a pirate."

He splashed around in the water to his ankles, head down, shivering in the gathering wind. He sighed.

"What does he do to you?" I asked, trying to connect Carlo's lesson with Bobby's theory of the pirate.

"You know what he does. He cockfucks me to death."

"Besides that."

"He tells me things."

"What things?"

"Adventures we could have, like."

"Such as?"

He looked at me a long while. "No," he said finally. "You'll get mad."

"Not at you."

He made a face, designed to look wacko but very winning, a face to energize a pirate. "Fantastic adventures, that's all."

I waited.

"Like . . . there's a war somewhere. And the soldiers wreck this town and take hostages. And they're in this barn and all the soldiers get drunk and they decide to snuff the hostages. So each soldier picks out a prisoner he likes . . . you know. It goes on from there."

"I'll just bet it does."

He shrugged. "I don't mind those stories. Dick's not the first man who told me them, anyway. It's just that sometimes he makes me tell them, too."

"What?"

"It's funny what you'll say once you get going. Horrible things. Horrible, terrible sexy things. All made up. Things that could never happen. It's like I'm drugged, like he's pulling something out of me that shouldn't be there. The more we do it, the more comes out." He shivered again. "It doesn't sound so bad, I guess, talking about it like this. But after it happens, I feel so rotten and crazy. I feel like he's going to turn me into someone else, almost. Into . . ."

A pirate, I thought.

"Did this ever happen to you?"

"No." Yes. "Not really."

"And then he gets so tense with me sometimes. They always do, pirates. They get sore so easily. Oh, please don't be sore at me!"

He sent this over my shoulder: Dick had come down to the water, taking all four of us by surprise.

"Please," said Bobby, approaching him. "Please, Dick," stroking his arm. "I'll be a good boy and I'll do what you say," putting his arms around him and resting his head against Dick's shoulder as Dick moodily rubbed his back.

"We're going all the way tonight, Bobby boy," said Dick.

Bobby shifted position and held Dick more tightly, his feet almost on Dick's as if he were trying to climb into him. "Dick," he whispered.

"All the way to rope," said Dick.

Bobby was quiet.

Dick looked at me without changing expression. "I'll cook steak and mickies on the grill. You can make the salad. There's peppers and scallions and carrots. Use olive oil this time, and drop the chives *over* the bowl at the last minute. Don't mix them in with the dressing."

"Dick," said Bobby, looking up at him. "Listen. Not the rope yet. Okay? Dick?"

Dick took Bobby by the hand and led him up the sand to the dunes. The dogs and I watched.

"Dick is about to start losing his hair, I think," I told Mortimer, who was pulling on a leg of my jeans, trying to get me to follow his master. "And Bobby is about to be patterned," I told Gridley, pulling the other leg toward the ocean. "Dick will touch his eyes, I bet."

At the base of the stairs, Dick and Bobby paused and spoke a bit, and Dick ruffled Bobby's hair. They kissed, a good long one. As they mounted the steps, Bobby turned to us and waved happily. Gridley barked.

"I think someone just got a reprieve," I said.

Mortimer grumped.

"Of course, we should consider the possibility that Bobby is made of stone in the first place."

Mortimer sat.

"In the middle of this riot, you notice, I get gourmet reproaches about the chives in the dressing."

Gridley sat. Mortimer dug a little hole.

"All of which teaches us that, sooner or later, every gay gets roped. Sooner or later."

Gridley snapped at a beetle.

"Boys, I ask you; which is better: to take your roping early and grow up sophisticated, or come out innocent and work up to it?"

They hadn't a clue. I would have raced them to the stairs, but it occurred to me that at that distance Dick and Bobby looked like father and son, or perhaps two brothers, and I didn't want to shake up the picture.

Raw Recruits

*Ranging wildly through the years of Stonewall,
and perhaps more a discussion than a story,
although the most drastic narrative event in all this
book darkens the final pages.*

I was graduated from the University of Pennsylvania in the class of
1969 with a degree in Medieval Studies, for all the good that did me:
none. Mother greeted my return with, "Help, the monster-child is
back!" My dad, more whimsically, told me how much my education
had cost him—"door to door," as he put it, meaning *tout compris*,
from the tuition bills to my train fares to and fro and even the dinners
at Bookbinder's when they jaunted down for a visit.

All told, he quoted a whopping sum. I felt guilty. I decided to
devote the summer to Good Works, such as tending bar at weekend
cocktail hours. (With recreational amenities and a convenient suburban location, my parents did a lot of entertaining.) My specialty was
Tequila Sunrises poured into huge goblets over cracked ice and
topped with lemon juice, the fruit so overpowering the taste of the
liquor that the uninitiated took them for a kind of art deco orangeade.
In fact, it's potent stuff. One Sunday morning we came outside to find
Aunt Agnes, Uncle Mike, cousins Jeffrey and Rita, their children,
three locals, and an unfamiliar dog all passed out on the patio, and I
was in trouble again. Worse yet, I intercepted the invitations to my
graduation exercises and hid them so I wouldn't have to go back to
Philadelphia. By day I tooled around the north shore of Long Island
with my high-school chums; at night I worked on a novel of dubious
virtue. By the summer's end, Mother had had it. Coming into my

room one night, she said, "Monster-child, we all love you very much
. . . but why are you still here?"

She had a point. First I negotiated a settlement—years later, when
I told my agent Dorothy the terms of the deal, she was impressed by
their generosity. "It's like a contract with Knopf!" she said, deep
praise. Thus endowed, I phoned an older friend who had once offered
the hospitality of East End Avenue, packed a valise, sat in with two
grad students of old acquaintance on their drive into town for the start
of the semester, and, in September of 1969, at the dawn of Stonewall,
I moved into New York.

Like everyone else of my ilk, I was unlearned in metropolitan style.
But one meets people. There's a name or two to call. One event leads
to another—the opera, say, to cocktails on a terrace. You'd be surprised what doors the right tie will open. Hugh Whitkin's, of course,
was one of them, but at the time I had no inkling of what I would
become, and value, and despise. I had skipped two grades of grammar
school and ended up somehow always younger than my attainments
warranted. I was unformed, the raw recruit. But I did notice that my
old society of mixed couples going steady and gearing up for careers
was ceding to a more complex fellowship, all-male, of brunching,
cruising, and tricking. When my old friends got themselves placed,
aligned, married, they would ask of a stranger, "What do you do?"
When my new friends asked that question, it came out, "What do you
like to do?" and it meant: in bed.

There was, in fact, a veritable old-boy network still in operation
then—possibly because counseling the new boy in town on the nature
of life was not unlike learning from youth about the nature of love.
So, anyway, I took the transaction to be. At length someone brought
me to a spacious co-op in the east eighties for advising by a wise old
queen.

"First of all," that worthy warned me, "you must have a best friend.
First of all. So?"

What was I supposed to say? I tried to look concise and untouch-
able, yet warm. Enigmatic. Big-city.

"Second of all, so? You must have a dream of success, a work ambition. Do not be a waiter, a bar pianist, a masseur. Be avant-garde, but be respected."

"So," I murmured.

"Quite," he rejoined. "Friendship, ambition . . . yes: then comes love, thirdly. Do not expect it. Do not look for it. Do not believe in it. Are you willing?"

"I beg your pardon."

"Will you renounce love?"

"Of course not."

"So." He smiled. "I just wanted to see. Of course you believe in love. Of course. I believe in love, in my many years. Yet I've never known love. Do you think that strange?"

"Not in the least."

"Sweet chicken."

"I'm not a chicken," I flared up.

He considered me.

"Nor am I. Do you suppose that's interesting?"

Would I ever be doing this myself? I wondered. Do all gays become queens in due course? So I looked around and marked what I saw, noted whither the culture tended. The wise old queen put forth his three rules and I had mine. First of all, queens and clones stay the same, but kids become men, or nothing. Second, all gays have, somewhere, a touch of queen in them—or let's say an instinct for rebellion. Last, once a gringo crosses over into gay he can never get back. To attempt to retreat would be like giving up all your friends, your sense of brotherhood, of affirmed self. Or so I guessed.

It was, in any case, the age of the clone. The wise old queens were passing on, or keeping to themselves in their gala co-ops, and I thought how different a wise old clone's advice to some newcomer might be, how very potent the urge to friendship, how disinterested the line on ambition . . . and what does a clone think of love?

To Big Steve Bosco, a king clone, I said, "Some are born clones and some attain it. Does anyone have it thrust upon him?"

"You're a funny guy," he said. That means that Big Steve missed a few words in the sentence. But then, I had noticed, large, humorous, loving men were attractive even without great savvy. Ah, what would you talk about, you ask? But the odd thing is that clones never run out of things to say to each other. Nor do queens—though they prefer to speak to clones, as a rule. It's kids who lack tongue, who really don't know what is being said from one sentence to the next, or who, lacking attention, develop irritating allergies: to cats, soap, porcelain, whatever will disrupt a lover's life.

Big Steve thought anything a kid did was forgivable, as kids were on the scene for one purpose: to be bunked.

It was great to hang around Big Steve, soaking up lore, for I was gleaning copy and every third word out of him was a term.

"Bunked?" our boy asks.

"Sure." Big Steve was cutting up vegetables for some huge elaborate salad to be delivered to some party along with cold-cut platters and a cake. Like many gay men in New York—fantasy masseurs, or "actor-models," or makers of tape collages for parties—Steve chose a calling that had scarcely existed before Stonewall. True, he did not invent the profession of caterer. But surely he was the first caterer to guarantee caped and cockstrapped waiters among his help—and the only caterer I ever heard of who made a point of closing the evening by passing among the guests entirely nude (a truly awesome sight) to treat the host to a fabulous smooch. "It tends," he explained, "to make them sporty with the tip." But I think he did it for the hell of it.

"What's bunking?" I asked.

"You know what screwing is, right?"

"Yo."

"You know about sleeping over after, where you kind of nest the kid you screwed in your arms so you wake up all nice and warm together?"

"*Sì.*"

He handed me a slice of green pepper, fresh, wet, gleaming. "And there's having a special breakfast, right? Like with honey toast or a farmer's omelette."

"*Do.*"

"What's that?"

"Yes in Welsh."

"So," he went on, "you put all that together in one night for a nice kid who deserves it, and that's bunking."

Who deserves it? I wondered, examining the cake, a humungous rectangle sitting demurely under wax paper and bearing a motif of music notes and G clefs on its frosting, with the legend, "To my sleeping beauty: best wishes on the birthday from Cleve."

"What's this for?" I asked. "Some uptown faggot?"

"Don't use that word," he replied, evenly but with a fierce command. Something else worth learning: some gays don't think we can use straights' expletives, even for our purposes. Faggot is not our concept, therefore not our word.

"Besides," Big Steve went on. "Besides. What for do you want to put down someone you never met? That doesn't hardly make sense." He handed me a radish. "Everyone's got something to offer, if you look in the right place."

His ability to get along with practically everyone was legendary; but everyone, in Big Steve's world, was gay. He not only lived entirely in the ghetto, leaving the West Village only to deliver and serve his collation, but literally did not know a single straight, did not watch television because it was all "straight stuff," and would not open a bank account because banks were ungay.

"Have you ever bunked a man instead of a kid?" I asked him.

He paused. "You mean did I bunk a big old clone, like me?"

"I wouldn't put it like that."

"That's what I am, anyway."

"It's just that bunking sounds like sort of a fatherly act," I said. "Where you make the rules, you take the initiative, you have the power. Right?"

"It works best with kids because they like to be taken over."

"As a rule?"

"Never met a kid who didn't. See the idea is, when they're young they don't have the experience, see? They don't know what to do. You have to teach them. You might almost call it a clone's duty, teaching kids. They've been raised by straights, so they're a little afraid of what's going to happen even though they want it. So you have to . . . what's the word?"

"Seduce them?"

He thought it over. "Seduce them. Yeah."

"Egad."

"See, you can't just take a kid home and say, 'I'm going to fuck you.' They'd run. Instead, you say you know this photographer who likes to shoot buddy pictures. Always looking for new talent. Kids like that—you can't give them enough attention, for some reason, even the really cute ones who've been getting attention since they were old enough to love. So you get them to take their shirt off, like you're just looking them over for the photographer."

He stops chopping up the salad to enlarge at ease. Big Steve is like a gay Gene Caputo, the ironworker: sex is the topic that covers everything.

"So you move them around a little. Let's see this angle, or like, fold your arms and turn this way. You get your hands on them, but it's very professional. You keep it clean. It's best to take your time. Then you say, 'This is very promising,' or something like that, and put in about what the photographer pays his models, because kids never have enough money. And you say, 'Let's try a certain pose like this.' You get them out of their shoes, sit them on your lap. You say, 'Look at the camera. Let's see you smile. That's a pretty smile.' Then you get them to drop their pants, and that's when you can start working on them. A little stroking here and there, and you're keeping it smooth. No kissing or like that, just slowly bringing them along till their body starts to tingle all the way to their toes. When you think they're ready to go, you can start kissing them, and when they put their hands up to hold on to you like little lost boys is the time to touch their behind. Not before. Because by then they know what's going to happen and they want it."

"After that treatment," I said, "Bob Haldeman would want it. What if a kid believes you about the photographer and just wants to pose for some money? What if he goes along with you because he's afraid you'll beat him up if he doesn't?"

He considered that for a bit, then smiled. "So what? I give them a real neat time."

I complained about this to Carlo, who was then, as Michael likes to put it, Big Steve's "current ex-lover." It seemed to me that Big Steve's technique was immoral, might well be taking in a number of innocents against their judgment. But Carlo, who has lived on the concept that good sex is its own morality, was not much bothered.

"That's his way of making friends," Carlo said.

"Oh, good grief."

"Come on. You and Dennis Savage and the other collegiates don't realize how difficult it can be for those of us who truly aren't born talkers. When we are trying to set up a social thing, I mean. Anyone knows how to talk sex. But getting to know someone, trying to make a friend . . . well, *you* always have something to say, sure. Big Steve doesn't. All he can do is cook and smile at you and . . . and touch you. That's all that man can do. And you have to make friends, don't you?"

"Hmm."

"Friends is how you survive. Besides, do you really think he's seducing anyone who doesn't want to be? Really?"

"You must admit, he's kind of overwhelming."

"Which would probably discourage anyone from coming home with him unless they were ready to go for it. For some of them, maybe the only way to come out is to have it done to them."

I thought of his tale of hitching across the country when he first came to New York.

"Admit it, Bud. Isn't that how you came out? Someone shows you what to do."

"Did he show you? Big Steve?"

"He truly showed me how to behave the next morning. I wasn't always so sure of myself, then."

"You're not exactly the kid type," I said. "A cuddleboy. It's odd seeing you in that position."

"There's a kid hidden away inside every clone, I sometimes think. Even Big Steve."

I wondered who might be more helpful to the raw recruit: a precise queen, dryly citing stylistic code, or an embracing clone, limited in what he knows but strong in certain manly virtues. Queens, clones, kids. As the years went by, I noted the new arrivals and heard dish on their metropolitan debuts, heard that this one had a smash gallery show in Soho, that that one burned out on drugs and whoring, that another was going uptown, trying yoga, or never seen by day, and that two others met one day, fell hopelessly in love, moved deep into New Jersey, and now would not come out even for brunch. Friends is survival, Carlo says, yet the recruits do not come to this city of utter trash and absolute power to make anything as mere as a friend.

I sometimes think.

But then comes an arresting exception and you have to reorganize your theories: as when Dennis Savage got bored one evening and hied himself to the theatre and there found himself next to a kid fresh from the midwest who agreed to go out for coffee and exchanged phone numbers and said, "I think you're a nice handsome man" when they parted—but that's just it, they parted: the kid would not go home with him.

They met for dinner and it went, I was told, really well. Yet still the kid would not budge in the indicated direction. A number of dates followed, after each of which Dennis Savage came running into my apartment like a fish whose scales have been stripped.

"He says he likes me!" Dennis Savage feverishly reported. "Now, why won't he let me—"

"Maybe you should send him to Big Steve for breaking in."

Dennis Savage paused, crushed by a thought. "Maybe he isn't gay?"

"Bring him over here for socializing," I said, "and we'll figure it out," realizing as I mouthed the words that I was showing signs of turning into a wise old queen. "On second thought," I added, "what do I know?"

"No, yes," Dennis Savage insisted. "Tonight at seven."

"Not good. I'll be doing my cartwheels then."

"Seven-thirty."

"That's seance hour," I said, panicking. I don't want to give advice. I want to take it. I want to be broken in, thrown around, snubbed, flattered, not paid for first-rate work . . . anything but regarded as a wise old queen. "Fuckin' A," I growled, to throw him off the track. "Fuckin' A. Let's pick up some bimbos and—"

"Eight o'clock."

"Gotta watch the Jets game."

"That's football. This is summer. They don't play football in—"

"Take him to Carlo!" I think I was beginning to scream. "Or—"

"Are you going to help me or not?"

Shattered, I collected the pieces of myself and shrugged. "Anytime."

"Eight."

At eight, Dennis Savage introduced me to a slender kid with floppy black hair, a blond's skin, and the most helpless cute appeal I've clocked yet. "Pay dirt," I—almost—said, as we shook hands.

"This is Little Kiwi," said Dennis Savage.

"No, Virgil Brown," said the kid.

I thought it over, surveying him. "No," I said. "Little Kiwi."

I served coffee—Little Kiwi wanted ice cream in his—and we talked of this and that. It was my job to get a bead on him, but he said little. He looked around a lot. He admired the antique model car that sits on my desk. He appeared to be perhaps fifteen, and was dressed in clothes designed to look like posters and menus. There was writing of some kind on every corner of him—we suppressed *that* damn fast— and, in all, the little he gave out revealed a young man unknowing, shy, and fearful. Later on, it turned out he was twenty and had done two years of junior college before coming east. But the oddest damn things spurred his fancy. A friend had given me an out-of-season pumpkinhead carving, and Little Kiwi asked me why it was smiling.

"I have no idea," I said.

"But I think I know."

He looked at me the way some waif might have looked at Horatio Alger the evening he launched his series of waif-makes-good novels. "Why?" I asked.

"He's smiling because he likes me."

I fought down the urge to pat Little Kiwi's head and went on playing the cocktail dandy with the two of them, but my mind was traveling. Are youths supposed to remind us of our own dear emergence? Or: was *I* that raw? This is the city of the debonair, is it not? Apparently unaware that one of our cardinal givens is that one does not eat four consecutive frozen Milky Ways out of the fridge of a man you just met that night (me), Little Kiwi ran on like a movement of one of those toy symphonies of Reinecke's day, with a plunk here and tinkle there. And finally everyone stopped talking. And Dennis Savage looked at Little Kiwi. And Little Kiwi looked at Dennis Savage, and how he looked was apprehensive. I felt *de trop* in my own apartment.

So I threw them out, and, at the door, as he shook my hand, Little Kiwi suddenly said, rather quietly, "I just wanted to be sure we were friends first," and he was looking at me but somehow he sent the message to Dennis Savage. Then they went upstairs to Dennis Savage's place and I didn't see him for three days. So it appeared that they had indeed become . . . friends.

And friends they stayed, which made it all admirably domestic, though it was some doing getting Little Kiwi out of his midwestern clownsuits and into something fit for life in the cultural capital. He took our advice in good faith, but there was a very great deal he didn't know, and sometimes, when things were explained to him, he became upset. You never knew how anything would hit him. A host of subjects, most of them sex but also talk of nuclear war and almost any social theory, would send him running to Dennis Savage like a lost babe found. And of course I would then get hell for the dread crime of Being Sophisticated With Little Kiwi.

Our circle in general found him amusing. All right, he was of age, but he *looked* so young; and he could find a turbulent whimsy in almost anything, as a child does. The rest of us brunched and dished, interpreted, analyzed. Little Kiwi romped and frolicked. In his life, the most risible acts were made conversant with the most sensible—as when he took pity on a stray dog and took him back to Dennis Savage's. Little Kiwi had had enough presence of mind to stop off on the way to secure food and plateware and even rubber toys, and he gave the dog a rather chic name, all considered: Bauhaus. (A bunch of us had been talking over Weimar at dinner the week before.) But the dog turned out to be eerie and pointless and klutzy, sort of a Carmen Miranda in Polish. Not long after Bauhaus moved in, I dropped in to find him parading around in one of those cardboard neck ruffs that vets put on animals to control their scratching a sore.

"What's going on here?" I asked.

Dennis Savage made a defeated gesture.

"Bauhaus saw an Airedale wearing that," Little Kiwi explained, "and he wanted one, too."

"Yes, o queen," I said, bowing to Bauhaus, "it shall be done as you command!"

"Oh, for heaven's sake," Dennis Savage roared. "Little Kiwi, take that foolish thing off that animal!"

"But he loves it so!" Little Kiwi protested.

My laughter made Dennis Savage yet more irate. "It comes off him, and I mean now—or he goes and you follow."

"We *will* go!" cried Little Kiwi. "*Come*, Bauhaus!"

But Bauhaus was very intent just then on doing a corn dance on his behind with his toy *Doggie News* in his mouth. Little Kiwi, perforce fending for himself, marched to the front door. When he got there he stopped, thought it over, lurched into the bathroom, slammed the door closed, and clicked the lock.

"And I'm never coming out!" he cried.

"As J. Edgar Hoover once said," I offered. "Okay, Mr. Smarty, you wanted a live-in boyfriend. Now what?"

"You might well look down on him," Dennis Savage whispered. "Yes." He nodded. His hands went out, palms up, like a rabbi's when a Methodist asks why Jews go to church on the wrong day. "Yes.

Because he's not educated. He's not particularly bright. His idea of gourmet food is you get fried chicken from a deli instead of in a TV dinner. But would you like to hear something personal from me? Would you?"

"Shoot."

"He's the sweetest damn thing I ever got close to. And the sooner you understand that, and share some of my joy, the more you'll know about the world."

"Love," I replied, "sure makes folks talk funny."

"You should hear me at night." He was knocking softly on the door as I departed—wondering why I had never noticed that the bathroom doors in our building have locks on them.

Alone of our squad, Carlo seemed to accept Little Kiwi without surprise—but then the rest of us kept viewing Little Kiwi's overgrown innocence in the context of our own watchful urbanity, whereas Carlo simply took him for a sexy child. He referred to him as "the kid himself." It shows how broad some men's views on sex can grow—beyond puberty, no age is inapposite, no place incorrect, no technique too radical. Everything is permissible because everyone consents.

Into this heady environment came one kid of my acquaintance not so much against his judgment as against mine: my houseboy Barry. Actually, he was more of an errand boy, as I wanted someone to run the street chores for me rather than disarrange the fastidiously coordinated office in which I not only work but live. A neighborhood kid not yet out of high school, and in a permanent state of quarrel with his parents, Barry had somehow or other taken up odd-jobbing along the Circuit at five bucks an hour. He was good at it, too, reliable and even imaginative at figuring out a substitute for a grocery item that wasn't in stock anywhere. His personal life, however, lay in disorder. One never knew for certain where he was staying, whether he was still legally a student, or even what his last name was. (He seemed to have several.) It occurred to me, too, to wonder how he had first launched his career as kid servant to gay men, and I imagined a wise old queen

version of Big Steve suavely alluring him with money and praise—
who knows?—even love.

I heard of Barry from a friend who was using him as a maid two
afternoons a week. His apartment had always looked like Calcutta.
Suddenly it was orderly; it gleamed, a showplace. Pieces of furniture
hitherto hidden under dirty clothes were revealed, to charm, and his
windows, once as dark as stained glass, lapped up light.

"Did you move?" I asked.

Barry came out of the bedroom just then, brisk and ready.

"All clear," he said.

We met—he had a soft handshake but a nice, slightly distracted
smile—and my friend his employer recommended him to me. He
was right, I realized: a cocktail dandy really ought to have someone
running tackle for him at the grocery, bank, laundry, and so on
(though, I must say, there's nothing like a walk home from The Food
Emporium at four o'clock in the morning with a cache of gourmet-
counter apricot-strudel cookies in your bag to remind you that you are
a New Yorker). I wondered if hiring Barry would spare me a New
Yorker's most onerous perquisite, shopping at Bloomingdale's; but this
was idle exercise. Barry and I struck a bargain right there on the site,
and, after he left, my friend said, "Believe me, you won't be sorry,"
his voice grinding like a burlesque attraction.

In fact, Barry tended to bring out the campy-seducer tones in older
men, which annoyed me. He seemed clearly to be a naturally unat-
tainable straight kid who had berthed his way into a field that calls for
tact and resourcefulness but no great intelligence or initiative. Yet,
every so often, when he would trundle in as I labored at my desk, I
caught allusions to passes made and, it sounded as if, not waved away.
I began to ask myself if I was being encouraged to make a move on
him. I thought back twelve years to Big Steve and his seductions; he
would have loved Barry, who had the scrubbed prettiness and pregym
slimness to coordinate with Big Steve's protective tenderness.

Like anyone else, I enjoy taking advantage of those encounters that
present themselves like ripe fruit, waiting to fall into hand should you
but reach up to pluck. But this was 1985, and like almost anyone else

I had become apprehensive of people who, like Barry, may for all I knew have been tanking up on bodily fluids. In fact, much as I liked Barry, I resented being tempted, and took to being elsewhere when he was expected. Finally one day he left a note for me: "Can I please talk to you about something?"

I stayed in for his next visit, and we talked. Rather, he rambled and I edited. He circled around a number of subjects at once, as if unwilling to confront his truths; I stopped listening to his words and tried catching the overtones. Suddenly he was saying, ". . . and Joe's mother said I couldn't stay over with him anymore, and she, like, told Alan's mother and *she* said okay, the same goes for her. Now, it's go back to my so-called parents or . . . or what? That's what I was asking, maybe."

"Maybe. Barry, exactly how old are you?"

"I forget."

"You know the term, 'jailbait'?"

"Look, that's not the problem. Mr. Lavery says I can live with him and be his houseboy, like. I just wanted to ask you what that means. You know, all together."

"It means you put out."

"To him?"

"No, to Princess Di. Who else, but to him? And his friends. Not to mention the hustlers he'll call in from time to time to enliven the action. Arnold Lavery is one of the shadiest characters in the east fifties—and that's saying something."

"His whole apartment is black."

"Do you like him?"

"Sure."

"You do?"

"He's my best customer. He says he's going to take me out to Fire Island when it's summer. He's even going to buy me . . ." He stopped. "Sure," he said.

"Buy you what"

"Just some clothes, he said."

I realized why Carlo could not share my disapproval of Big Steve's aggressive tactics. There *are* kids who are going to find their way onto the scene one way or another; and Carlo, wiser than I, knew that those who don't go Big Steve's way fall into the hands of an Arnold Lavery. For all our collegiate professionals and dashing brunches, this is still the city where those two opposites, beauty and money, dangerously attract. I wondered if I ought to send Barry to Big Steve for salvation, but Big Steve couldn't afford Barry. A kid without love or ambition doesn't want either. He wants luxury, and to be wanted, and not to care about anything.

"Barry," I said, "what is this talk about? Do you want me to speak against your moving in with Lavery, or to approve of it?"

"I don't know. I like thought . . ." He rose and looked down at the floor. "What exactly does it mean to put out?"

"You know what it means—the works."

He looked at me for a bit, then crossed the room and, without a word, left.

I tried to bring Carlo into the case, but he was too moody to help, and the little he had to say unnerved me. Like Barry, he was incoherent, but, unlike Barry, Carlo had a theme. "It's over," he kept saying. Then there'd be silence.

"What's over?" I asked.

He patted my arm; he wanted to be nice. But he couldn't phrase it properly and I wouldn't understand if he did.

"Tell me what it is," I urged.

He looked tired, as if he had lived through six or seven Hugh Whitkins inside of a month. In shorts and a T-shirt he seemed not sexy but sloppy, his hair going every which way, his face dark with stubble, his feet too big. We were in Big Steve's tiny apartment, where Carlo was, as he has been on and off over the years, something between a lover and a guest.

"*What's* over?" I demanded.

He said he was thinking of going back to South Dakota, and this was so absurd I could not address it. Carlo is the most metropolitan of gays, not in sophistication or wit but in strutting independence. I bet if an extraterrestrial, from a planet where the beings grow rather than carnally conceive their offspring, happened down to earth, and saw Carlo ambling along a summer street in his cords and striped polo shirt, grinning as he gave the world a once-over, the visitor would say, "Now I know what sex is, and sex is gay."

I made some joke about Carlo blowing the state of South Dakota wide open.

"It's the dishonor, I guess," he said. "More than anything else." He was looking out the window, and when he turned back to me he missed his footing and had to steady himself. He shivered as he tried to smile, and I realized he had been drinking, though he seldom does, and never in the daytime. "I haven't been able to figure it out exactly," he went on, "but that's how it seems to feel. The dishonor."

At least now he was talking.

"Because," he said, "the ones who go on having sex will die. And the ones who don't aren't men anymore. They might as well be . . ." He sat back on the couch. "Oh, what might they be, after all this?"

"Queens."

"Or dead," he whispered. "They might as well be dead."

All over town, men were having these talks. Some had actually quit the metropolis for small towns in Maine, Florida, Wisconsin. Some had gone to stay with their parents, who were startled but glad of the company. Others simply lit out and fled the stricken city, like Boccaccio's *Decameron* crowd. But those Florentines at least took something of great value along: their company. I couldn't imagine a gay man who had known Stonewall City living alone in the straight world.

"What's South Dakota like for a gay?" I asked.

"It isn't. There is no gay in South Dakota."

"Then why go there?"

"It's the only place I know, besides . . . these places. I want to think of getting along somehow. Your parents' is where you go when you can't go anywhere else. Isn't it?"

"When you're tired of gay life," I offered, revising Dr. Johnson, "you're tired of life."

"That's the nail on the ace, Bud. I *am* tired of life. This life, here.

I'm a man. I can't get along on bull sessions and . . . remembering. It's like your hands are tied. I have to do what men do."

"You told me once, 'Friends is how you survive.' Now you're telling me you're planning to live without them?"

He crossed to the refrigerator and took out a bottle of vodka, three-quarters empty. "I don't even know where you're supposed to keep these." He took a short swig and came back to me. "Do you want a glass?"

"I don't drink before dark," I said.

"When your hands are tied it's always dark." He went on drinking. "Don't tell the others. Especially the kid himself. He looks up to me, doesn't he?"

"He looks up to all of us, one way or another. He's like the local kid brother."

A long swig this time. I thought back to the days when my brother Jim lived in New York and his friends would sit around assessing the mysteries of life and love, each with his own bottle.

"I know I'm hurting your feelings, Bud. But this brotherhood is going to be a dead dream soon, and I don't want to see it die. I think he looks up to me most of all, anyway."

His voice caught and he turned to me, crying. I started toward him. "No, get back," he shouted, waving me off. "Not to soothe me. I've done this show already, I know how it works." He went on, not wiping his eyes. "I can know what it's like in South Dakota and I can't know what it's like here anymore. That's the ticket, I truly believe. Big Steve was so mad at me last night, he made me sleep on the couch. He said I was a traitor and he wouldn't let me in his bed. In South Dakota there are these truck stops. Then he came in here and he turned on that lamp over there and he stood over me for a while. I was awake. I could hear him there. I didn't pretend I was asleep but it was dark so maybe he didn't know I was awake. You nod at the truckers real gruff, and if they nod back you go outside to their rig there. See, and he knew and he said, 'Get up, Carlo.' He sounded angry and I thought he might lick me for a minute. Because, you know . . . but he didn't touch me. They have everything in the back of their wheels. Towels, jelly, toke, cold beer. That's the whole life for them. They can be real men to you or they can be nice. There is no way to tell aforehand."

I'd never seen anyone cry like that, the tears roaring out of his eyes like those plastic-enclosed twenty-five cent globes of children's chotchkes spilling out of a broken machine.

"Carlo," I said.

"Shut up and please listen. This isn't joking. So Big Steve . . . he told me he didn't think it right that us two should be in separate rooms when we could be fucking. Because buddies like us were put on earth to take turns making each other happy. There are some things we tell each other, I recall. Some of the truckers have real long hair in the back because they're hoping someone will shoot a remark and they can slam the shit out of them, and they don't care where they are when they do it. They shouldn't have it that long. He said, 'Get up,' like that. And I said we should use a rubber and after all these years he is not going to do that with me, he said. That isn't buddies."

He was gesturing about the apartment, showing me where all this happened, and still crying.

"Well, I said it's taking precautions or nothing and that's how it is going to be, and he said it'll be how he wants it, and that's all the way and a rubber is like washing your hands with mittens on and he doesn't even have any and since he's trying to be nice to someone who doesn't deserve it and don't let him lose his temper, and Jim Fetters, who you wouldn't know because that was in tenth grade back there, he had gone out to a truck stop and he had this black eye all the next week and everyone said What happened? and he was just *white*. And don't tie my hands, that's all, because . . . because Big Steve and I had our troubles sometimes but he never hit me before. He just hauled off and hit me. But I don't have a black eye. And he kept going back there, shut up, and he kept getting these black eyes. Because Big Steve hit my jaw. He's my best friend, Bud. Even more than you. My best buddy. There are things we tell each other, and they started calling him Black Eye. He was proud of that. He even tied me up, he was so mad, and you can pray all you want to but that won't change anything, long or short. And I couldn't fight him back. I can, but I couldn't. They get the preachers out to talk to you. I don't see how they can tell, but they can. Preacher tells you, if you're that hard up, he'll do you right there, why not? They call you son. All of them. He tied me up. And I told him, Jesus, don't tie my hands. Don't tie me up. Maybe someone at the truck stop or a preacher but not you. Get back, this is not joking. Don't tie me up, I said. And he could see I wasn't joking. But he always had a weakness for that stuff . . ."

He was weeping now, but he had leaned back and thrown his arms out along the top of the couch as if discussing a quirk in the plot of the latest movie.

"Jim says it's been going on since the whole state was just forts and I expect it'll keep going on till all the gays are dead and it's just gringos and truck stops. I told Big Steve because he ought to know. And he was listening then. He untied me and put a blanket on me, and he went out. He hurt me very bad, Bud. Not just hitting me, though. Because I saw his eyes. And he was still mad when he came back, but he was lying next to me and holding me and that's all. I heard his eyes. The preachers tell your parents if you don't let them do you. He's still mad now. They say you were a wanton with Jim and you'd best be separated. We hardly did anything at all. They say the devil's in him. The devil's in his cock. His cock is talking to him, leading him astray, man shouldn't have a cock that size, that's a nigger cock or something, you got nigger blood? And your folks start praying, and the preachers are telling this to the town, the shame all over the town. They even hear it at the truck stop, nigger cock. They're waiting there now. I never hurt anyone, that's what I told them. Let me do you, they go, I won't say nothing. Never hurt anyone as long as I lived. Don't tie my hands. It isn't healthy. Some of those guys at the truck stop would do anything, but I wouldn't. Jim did more than I did. I tried to tell Big Steve, it wasn't hitting me, it was tying me up. He didn't have to do that. He knew he didn't. I thought Jim was giving himself black eyes for the attention. He didn't have to. He said it was a blunder. See, he can't say I'm sorry so he says he blundered. I told him I wasn't going to be fucked anymore, I was going to be top from now on. And he said he wanted me to be happy but I'm a rat. There aren't happy rats, are there? Because they know they're rats. That's why you always see them running around and hiding. Because they know people hate them. But people only hate them because they act like rats. Preachers are happy. Parents are happy. Jim was happy. He had his own devil. So we talked for a while, and then it was morning. This morning. I didn't sleep last night. I said, 'How could you tie me up like that?' He said he'll do worse to me if I don't stop being a rat. He says everyone's going to hate me because I'm a rat. And he looked at me the way those other guys did because I . . . they saw how easy I was going to be because I . . . wasn't ever really tough like them, I only . . ." Suddenly he began to sob again. "I'm not a rat after all this," he said, lurching to his feet, swaying, dropping the bottle; and I leapt up and grabbed him and told him to stop and took him into the back room and put him to bed while he whispered, "Get back, it's over" every twenty seconds. And "Don't tell Big Steve." And "Did I stop crying?"

It took me quite some while to find the aspirin, because it turns out that Big Steve keeps it in the refrigerator. I brought two tablets and some water to Carlo, who was asleep; but I woke him up, explaining that he had to take aspirin to stave off a hangover.

"Later," he said, turning over.

I almost threw the water in his face. *"Now."*

He swallowed them dry, and said, "You won't be mad at me, will you? I can only do one mad at a time."

"I won't be mad."

He nodded. "The devil's in everyone. Even Diana Vreeland. But why did he tie me up, anyway?"

"He tied you up because he likes you."

He looked so sad then. "Everyone always liked me. My whole life. Because they wanted to pull my pants down. That's why I got so big, Bud. At the gym. Why should Big Steve be any different?"

"He is different," I said. "He tied you up because he loves you. You

remember that guy you told me about on your way to New York way
back there? The one with the little bowl of warm water and the soap?
The one you said you loved? That's what you are to Big Steve—only
you've stayed that all his life. That's why he tied you up. He wants to
keep you in New York."

"He went to Seattle for two years."

"To try to forget you."

Carlo looked at me. "Oh, Jesus hell. Did he tell you that?"

I shook my head.

"Then how . . ." He wiped away new tears. "How do you know?"

"Because I was in that movie. We all were."

"I'm not a rat."

"Go to sleep, now."

"Don't go somewhere."

"Huh?"

"I mean, don't go away yet."

There was a bit of silence then.

"Did I say terrible things?" Carlo asked.

"You said . . . interesting things."

"About Jim Fetters?"

"Somewhat."

"Don't go. Okay?"

"I'm just getting something to read. As long as I have to play watch
and ward."

In the front room, I nosed into Big Steve's five-inch shelf, settling
on *The Silmarillion*—Tolkien is one thing Big Steve and I come to
terms on.

"Read me from some of that," Carlo said.

"Carlo—"

"Just till I sleep. Please, Bud."

"'There was Eru, the One, who in Arda is called Ilúvatar,'" I began, thinking that, if I hadn't left Pennsylvania, I would never have
found myself sitting on a bed in which Beau Geste lay listening to me
read fairy tales as he slept off the direst drunk of his life. A uniquely

metropolitan pastime. When I was sure he was asleep, I put the book down, and listened to him breathe for a bit, then left.

I never did get to talk to Carlo about Barry, to put it mildly; but Barry left my employ to live in as Arnold Lavery's houseboy. Just as well, that, for Carlo was in no tone to consider protecting reckless kids in an age that dishonors respectable clones. Our set tried to rally Carlo, but he resisted, out of fear, I imagine, that we would talk him down. Get back: he did not want to be soothed. He may well have moved in with Big Steve precisely to hop himself up, to force his own issue upon himself.

I was saddened. Yet he was right in a way. For it is the newcomers who recall to us the explosive truth that veterans live very near to the idea of fate: the Barrys and Little Kiwis who put the Carlos in perspective. What unites us, all of us, surely, is brotherhood, a sense that our friendships are historic, designed to hold Stonewall together. It is not rebellious sex habits that define us as much as the rebel coterie itself, the act of not bothering to adjust to gringo procedures. It is friendship that sustained us, supported our survival, and friendship that kids need more than seductions by Big Steve Bosco. For—not to put too fine a point on it—the difference between Barry and Little Kiwi is the latter's friendship with Dennis Savage, and Little Kiwi instinctively knew that, and so he held back on the touching till he was sure he had a friend. Barry, however, doesn't share that concept, that feeling of particular need—and where Barry is going, he'll not have many friends.

Carlo, who had more friends than anyone I know, left for South Dakota quite suddenly, just as the summer was getting under way. He did not call, and heaven knows Carlo doesn't write: my doorbell rang, without a summons from the doorman, because Carlo had just been to Dennis Savage's, and now it was my turn, and then South Dakota's.

As if making up for his demonstrative plaint at Big Steve's, he was taciturn, yet almost like his old, easily carried self. He smiled a few times, if adamantly, and when I offered him coffee he said he had to keep moving.

"Could I have your address?" he asked.

"Carlo, you've been coming here for over a decade."

"I don't know the number. I just know where it is. I thought . . ." He was looking out the window at the site next door; one crew was attaching the curtain wall, another setting down the wooden forms for the concrete on the second-floor roof. "Another shirts-off day in New York." He turned to me. "I thought I might send you a letter."

I went to my desk to write down the data; when I was at *Opera News* ten years ago, we all got business cards, which I never used. Over the years, they've made ideal note stubs. I pulled one out, and, as I marked it up, Carlo said, "Look."

"Oh, her," I replied.

He was gazing at one of the workers, who, for several months, had been coming around at various times of the day to stare into my apartment. Perhaps he was fascinated by the thousands of books and records in view, or trying to figure out what the hell I was doing in by day when I should be out working like him. Who knows? Maybe he was entranced by my Bemelmans.

"He's kind of cute," said Carlo.

"Under the hardhat he's bald."

"That's not his fault. Sweet bod."

"Lugging things around all day will do that to you. Here." I gave him the card. I had included my phone number in case of emergency.

"Have you ever spoken to him? On the street."

"Never saw him on the street. Maybe he never *goes* on the street. Every time I look up, almost, he's standing there looking."

"He's sort of like a smaller version of Big Steve, isn't he?"

"My God, Carlo, you look . . . the way you used to look. Just now, like this. Carefree."

"Wave at him, Bud." Carlo pulled me to him, turned me to face the site, and the two of us looked out at the man. "He's lonely. How old is he? Thirty? Thirty-five? Italian. Lives with his folks. Never married. Dates when he has to. There are always those poor neglected girls who are glad to get any date at all. In between, he wonders what he wants. What he has a right to. Catholic, so everything he dreams of is forbidden anyway. But he looks in here and he senses somehow that you know what he wants. You can tell him. He doesn't know why, but he *knows* that you're clued in. That's why he stares at you. Help him."

Carlo waved.

"Now you," he said. "Give him a chance."

I waved, too, but the man stood there frozen, just watching, as he always did.

"He's shy," said Carlo.

"He doesn't know what we're doing," I said. "We might be making fun of him."

"He's a nice guy."

"How would you know a thing like that?"

"I can always tell." His grip tightened on my shoulders. "Bud. Don't see me out. I want you to go upstairs after I leave. The kid himself was crying before. Wave once more to him, Bud, with me, together."

We waved.

"Okay," he said. "I'll report to you on what it's like. We'll think about some things. You won't tell anybody what I said to you downtown, will you? Big Steve is really so truly sorry."

"Carlo—"

"No, Bud." He was holding me so I couldn't turn around. "Look, he's watching us as if we held his secret of life. There's always something somewhere else. I'm going to let you go, and I'm going to leave, and you're going to stay here, just like this. Okay?"

I nodded; the worker in the hardhat, fascinated by our melodrama, was still watching us.

Carlo let go of me, moved, crossed the room; I heard the door click open, but just then the worker waved at me, and by the time I turned Carlo was gone.

*   *   *

No one's irreplaceable, I told myself, as we went on with our dreams and dreads and brunches, which, on a really vital Sunday, may be formidably combined. But in summer the urban brunches dissolve in deference to the Island dinners—which can last even longer than a brunch.

I decided not to take a share this year, but Dennis Savage had finally gotten into a neat house on the ocean, in a reputable section of The Pines, so I guested. Each summer, old friends cross paths at the ferry, or the Pantry, or walking on the beach, and comparing the tones of the various years is an available topic. This year was generally thought unsuccessful, the weather boring, the ocean pugnacious, "and," as everybody pointed out, "no one's getting anything except older."

True enough. Pacing through the no-man's land between Pines and Grove, one would still run into the odd devotee here and there, never saying die in their come-hither poses, or even a nude or two. But where once one might have thought, "I should pause and collect that," now one wondered, moving right along, if the stranger had come out of a time machine from the 1970s. Anyway, there was less roaming now, especially in those old haunts; folks stayed buttoned up in their houses, and at night sometimes one had to strain to hear that former symbol of Pines in plenary session, a blaring stereo. Many people even avoided the beach on the sunniest days. They would lie around on their decks looking relaxed and content, but as you walked by you heard them tensely badgering each other.

When a grouchy wind assaults The Pines, Dennis Savage, of course, flies in the vanguard, and he was at me from the moment I set down my valise. Little Kiwi, however, was in a merry mood, though he would grow silent for a few minutes whenever Carlo's name came up; and though, more generally, The Pines as a culture tended to daunt him. Sending him to the Pantry for an item or two was like urging the Wicked Witch of the West to take a bath. He feared he'd be kidnapped if he dared the harbor alone. What he really wanted to do was stage little extravaganzas on the walkway that joined the two sections of the house's upper story. For anyone else, the walkway was a means to get from a bedroom to the bathroom. For Little Kiwi, the walkway was a stage.

I had scarcely arrived before he called down to me to sing "I Love To Walk in the Rain," an old Shirley Temple number that I had put on a cassette for him and which he played repeatedly till the neighbors threatened to mace Dennis Savage's apartment.

"I'm not in the mood," I told him.

"Sing it for him, you beast," said Dennis Savage. "He's been waiting all morning for this."

I started singing, in several of my favorite keys, and Little Kiwi dashed into the bathroom and promptly came back in a hooded yellow slicker and a Japanese parasol that belonged to one of the other men in the house. As I sang, he capered.

"Very nice," I said, heading for the fridge. Dennis Savage barred my way.

"He's not done yet," Dennis Savage said, through his teeth.

I sang some more, as Little Kiwi passed along the walkway, twirling the parasol. "Keep going!" he cried, darting into the bedroom to tow his dog out by the leash.

"It's Astaire and Bauhaus, the lovable Hollywood team!" he explained as he danced. Bauhaus had apparently been snoozing and was not happy to enter a musical revue. He whined and grumbled.

"Now this amazing effect," said Little Kiwi, taking a bag out of his pocket. The bag disgorged a few mushrooms, which Little Kiwi set up on the walkway. Bauhaus ate one as Little Kiwi hid behind the rotating umbrella and I reached the end of the song. Dennis Savage and I clapped.

"I've got plenty more of those."

"What a treat for later," I replied. "Much later."

Once things quieted down, it was again—for me, at least—The Pines as it has always been: our boy, his notebook, and a few intimate subjects. Your first years in The Pines you can't get enough of the beach parade, tea, the meat racks. After a while, the parade loses its glitter, tea is a chore, and—by 1982—the meat racks were pretty poison. The main purpose of The Pines, by then, is to provide a sanctuary from the outer world, a gay place. You no longer worry whether you're going out enough, dancing enough, getting enough. Just being there is being gay.

I prefer to lie around talking and writing. Dennis Savage, who as a schoolteacher has nothing to do in the summer, sat on the deck with me to watch Little Kiwi walking Bauhaus along the water's edge. Every now and then Bauhaus would break away and chase someone, and Little Kiwi would run off in the other direction. He says if he stays there, people yell at him.

"You know," I said, "this looks like a Paul Terry cartoon directed by Robert Wilson."

"I hate my work," Dennis Savage said.

I looked at him.

"Well, I do!" he said.

"I didn't make the world."

"You sleep as long as you want to, and I have to get up at five forty-five! And what's the point of pushing on those dumbbells to get them motivated? You speak to the cultured, and I speak to idiots."

"But you have free health insurance. And holidays. Seems to me every time somebody turns around in one of the boroughs, the schools declare a national holiday. I work day and night seven days a week, fifty-two—"

"Come on, you're always out playing!"

Someone was waving at us on the beach: someone in a crowd.

"Who's the kid?" asked Dennis Savage.

"My current ex-errand boy. Barry."

He was wearing a bathing suit so slight he would have been arrested at Cannes; but his friends were dressed—two of them, incredibly, in tropical suits.

"Look at the bizarre," said Dennis Savage. "Well, I'm going to see about dinner. Some of us run our own errands." He went inside.

"Who was that waving?" asked Little Kiwi, coming up from the sand with the dog.

"That's you without Dennis Savage," I said.

He looked after Barry's gang, remotely trudging, I would guess, to some furiously dreary cocktail shop. I was watching Little Kiwi, trying to see him in a bathing suit like Barry's—made of the material super-markets bag onions in—and attending those parties at which mon-eyed jitterbugs cop a feel while making small talk. I couldn't see it.

"What do you mean," Little Kiwi asked, "that he's me?"

"He's not you. That why he's in trouble."

Little Kiwi stared after Barry's group. He turned back to me. "He looked happy."

"He is, today. But he'll get messed up and that'll be that."

"Why would he get messed up?"

"Because no one cares about him. He's alone."

"No, all those people with him . . . won't they—"

"They're his leeches. They'll milk him for fun and toss him away."

Little Kiwi looked at me. In the dying light, I could see him watch-ing me carefully, knowing that I'm the one who says the hard things to him. Our other friends treat him like a kid. I treat him like a clone.

"Why are they going to milk him?" he asked me. "He was nice."

"Yes, he's nice. He's helpless. Trusting. Likable. That's the type they love to milk. If this were Paraguay, leftover Nazis would have him brought to a party to be whipped for the fun of it."

Dennis Savage came out. "It'll be barbecued chicken, some pasta, shiitake mushrooms for everyone's good health, and maybe something green how about?"

"I don't want to get messed up!" Little Kiwi cried, running to him. "The whippers are coming!"

"What have you been doing to him again?" Dennis Savage roared, holding him.

And Bauhaus barked at me.

"We just saw a chicken on the way to his barbecue," I noted.

"Is Carlo coming back?" Little Kiwi asked, his voice muffled in Dennis Savage's chest.

Dennis Savage looked at me. "Is he? He's your friend, mostly."

"Yes," I said. "Yes, he was."

Three Letters from South Dakota

I have corrected the mispellings, puncuation, and most severe infelicities, but here they are as he wrote them.

July 24

Dear Bud:

I told you I would be writing. You didn't believe me, I know. But this could be like those times when you and me would sit around and bullshit about the world. Only I'm not right next to you now. I always used to think you would get too heavy and I admit that once or twice when you were not around I thought about the things you said and I wanted to knock your block off. I even like argued with you, because I knew what you'd say, and I finally thought of the right answers. I'm glad you weren't there then, when I thought of the answers. I would really have pounded you.

My mom just came in and said, "Oh, are you writing to the Lord?" They do that here. They write letters to God. They don't mail them, of course. It's just to concentrate the prayer. (How they say it.) When I came back, they gave me a party, and it was like this. First, they all got here, aunts and cousins and things that I haven't seen in twenty years. So they all mass up, staring like I'm the figure of Jack the Ripper in the wax museum. Then comes the time when some of them go into one room to pray and the others stand around joking. It reminded me of some New York parties, where some guys went into the bedroom to fuck while some others stayed in the living room discussing opera. Because after that everyone had supper as if nothing had happened. And you know how there's always, always somebody who can't take their eyes off you but is afraid to say anything, but you can feel how hungry they are right across the room? Well, here it is my third kin Irene (which is pronounced Areenee around here). You can bet her folks and mine will be trying to set us up soon enough.

It sure was a crossword-puzzle thing, scooting around the old places. Everything's still there, I guess, but what about the people? And everybody calling me Rip, or old Ripper, or even Ripley (like my folks), mostly, because they don't go for New York nicknames around here. And my mom calling to me in the morning, and there's the Cream of Wheat just like before, which I liked to eat year round, even in the summer. And my dad grinning at me like I just broke the record at the Olympics for the four-minute mile or something. I guess they really are glad I'm back. They cry a lot, because they love me so much. This is the thing about parents that I will never get used to. They are a little different to each other, too, than I remember. Like they will pass each other on the way to different rooms and just stop and hug each other. It sure is a sight. I had to ask them not to treat me like that, and they said okay. I know what they were thinking— prayer is more certain, anyway. They are just trying to make me break down and cry. They call out crying for the Lord. You just have no idea what it's like.

I guess I cried plenty that morning you were at Big Steve's, and I wonder what you're going to do about that. Forgive me? (I hope.) You should have seen Big Steve later on, how sorry he was. But he started right in again. He made me tell him the names of all the people I love on earth, so he could count them. You know how I hate that stuff. I know I looked terrible that day, too, because I was drunk and it was not even afternoon. Did you think I was going crazy? But I never took drugs all those years, just toke. No poppers or anything. At least I have that. You might as well tell me what you thought of all what I said at Big Steve's. I hope you would tell me. Some of it was about

Jim Fetters, who still lives around here. But I am putting it off, meeting him again.

You know what's funny? The truck stop that some of us would go to for like a glory hole is now a Jesus Center. There are people with signs there—"Why Don't You Love Him? Because He Loves *You!*" and "If You Died Tomorrow, Could You Meet Him Fair?" It's like they were holding up cue cards for a big hymn sing. The one I like is "What Will You Do When He Comes?" I was staring at the sign and maybe smiling, and the woman who held it looked me right in the face and said, "You best think about it, because He'll be coming soon, all over the universe." And so many replies came to me. You know, like joking in the bars. Our kind of thing. But I just told her okay. They give you a booklet which tells you how to behave from now on.

The main reason I am writing is, I want to tell you what Big Steve said to me. But first I have to tell you something about him that you didn't know. I know how you get about a guy's profession, and how people are supposed to live in certain areas of town (like not Brooklyn, right?), and clothes and all. Like a tie. I did everything wrong, probably, except I don't think I ever lived in Brooklyn, even for the weekend. Anyway, way back there when you were still friendly with your brother, he mentioned something of great use, I think. To know about. It was about parents, that you can hate them, or call them every tough name there is, or hide from them, or not visit the house, or even like get married or something without telling them. And they'll always forgive you, he said. But where they draw the line is if you just lose interest in them. If you get neutral. That's where they draw that line. They can do love and they can do war but they can't do test patterns. And what I want to tell you about Big Steve is that he is like a parent. Like he's as good when an affair is falling apart and everyone's getting mad as he is when it's new and you're both so hot for each other all the time you don't get any chances to fight. But he can't deal with it when an old lover walks past him on the street as if he wasn't there. There's always got to be something. Anyway, what he told me was, he would give his life for me. Just like that. And I said, "Who wants you to?"

So he just went on about giving his life. And how many people were there that he would do that for. And how many would I?

Hell, have you ever thought about that? How many of those *you* have?

Well, I don't know what got into me, because I know he wanted me to say I would give my life for him. Because that was how he always was, that you shared what you were all the way. So like even on one of those nights when I topped him for a considerable full time, just as deep and slow as it goes, and we would doze off together just holding on, and what more could you ask? Except no, sometime later he'd be waking me up to say now it's his turn, because we have to pleasure each other. And I'd say I already am pleasured. He'd just be rolling me over. You know how he gets when he's after you.

Anyway, I said I wouldn't give my life for anyone, including him. And what I'm asking you is, Was that the fair thing to say to him?

So okay. Tell me what's doing with everyone, and say hello to the kid himself especially. Don't tell him this, but I truly believe I will have to remember the way he started to cry when I came over to say goodbye. I will have to. Because I kind of went for him to push him around for a joke, but he backed away from me, shaking his head. So now I started to make a list of all the nice things I did for you and the others all along, but then I thought that's too dumb. And you would know them anyway.

Remember to answer my question about what I should have said to Big Steve.

This is your old pal Carlo.

                                                                August 6
Dear Bud:

Well, you can see there's plenty of time for writing out here. Jim Fetters came over during dinner, which you will find shocking, but that's how we do things, at like six or seven o'clock. Because otherwise you can't find anyone home. Before, they're at work. After, they're in bed. That's our hours. I always love your rules about when to call, when to visit, and those things, like. You know what a New York attitude that is. But we have this midwestern language, where if we like a visitor we slap another plate down and if we don't we hold the whole thing at the door.

But Jim is an old friend. So my folks fussed over him, and said how's Marge and tell about the kids, and he did.

Now, you know, it has been about twenty years all the way, and Jim has hardly aged at all. It was my mom who opened the door, and when she said, "Why, Jim!" I felt guilty for not having gone around to him myself, us being best friends for so long all before. But the next thing I felt was just curious, and I got up and when I was at the door old Jim jumped me like a long-lost puppy dog, crying, "Hey, you big old Rip!" and stuff. Boy, he looked good. He truly did. He couldn't get over how I had grown. Of course they don't have gyms and all that here, not much. In Dakota we have a saying, "You don't make yourself into a clone, boy, you just better be born one." (That's a joke. We don't have such a saying here.)

So there was my old Jim. And my dad has already made a place at the table and we all sit around to hear Jim tell about his family, my folks just beaming away at us as if we were sixteen and talking out how the track season was shaping up. Then Jim asked what I had been up to all those years in the big New York City and my folks kept on smiling but their eyes sort of turned, you know. I almost imagined my dad saying then, "He was doing gay things in New York, which is a gay city, and now I'm going to switch him for it!"

You know what you do out here when someone comes back? You go visit all your old friends. It's sort of like if a New Yorker went around the Village looking up his old lovers. Imagine what you'd see. Some of them would be shacked up with new lovers and would they want you around? Some of them would be all alone and the sight of you would not cheer them up, would it? And some would be straight angry at you.

That's kind of how it was here that night when Jim and me went visiting, riding up the driveways to all these depressing houses. I guess the old gang didn't get to prove themselves. Everyone was married or living with someone, and even the guys I used to like didn't seem glad to see me. Jim was in rare form, like showing me off. He called me "Our New York boy from Dakota." Or maybe Our Dakota boy from New York is more like it.

You should have come along with us to get notes for your stories on dramatic pauses, because there sure were plenty. Jim was about the only one talking, most of the time. Meanwhile, all these little kids were wandering in and out, and one house was a real tornado, like there had been a married fight. After we left one place, Jim got real quiet, and after he started the car he said, "Hey, Rip, you think they still remember the trouble we got into?" About the truck stop and all. And his folks finding us together. The news around town, as I told you.

I said I guessed they did remember. And Jim didn't mean just *remember*—he means they don't forgive us. We drove back to my folks' and parked and took a walk around the yard. We have a lot of ground and things. Sheds and high grass and my old tree house, where Jim and I had a club when we were kids. No one else could join. And finally Jim said, "Oh hell." Like that. Just "Oh hell."

I said, "It's real neat to see you, good buddy." We weren't looking at each other. "I don't care about all them," I told him.

He said, "Me neither."

We walked around for a while, and then he stopped, and it was like an idea hit him out of the blue. He said, "I know! Let's get smashed. Got a bottle in my car."

I said great, but how about his family? He said it was all right, this was his night out, because it was like a holiday that I was back.

That's another thing we do around here that doesn't happen in

New York. Guys sitting around all night drinking. Maybe you could call this a Dakota brunch. My folks went up to bed not long after we started in, and my room is downstairs in the back, so we could make ourselves at home. And what do you know but Jim starts in asking me about New York and who are my friends and what we do. And hell, I told him. I told him, Bud. And he didn't play tourist on me, either. He took it. Sometimes he nodded, as if he thought that's how it was, all along. Nothing shocked him. And you know I have wild tales to tell if I loosen up.

I was stretched out on my bed and he was in the rocking chair, with the bottle between us. We drank it straight out, the way you do it here. One thing he said, was all the names were funny. Big Steve. Dennis Savage. He said they sounded like wrestlers on television. The only name he could relate to was yours, because we've got loads of Buds around. Then I said your name was really Ethan and he damn near choked his booze up.

Then I told him *my* name was Carlo. I explained about getting approached in the Eagle that time, and just in case you don't know about this, how this guy was looking for an escort for a friend of his. Or do you remember? That guy who owned his whole house by the river, and had his friend take pictures of me pretending I was going to hang him? He had a real noose there too, but it was tied all wrong. I fixed it for him, and he had this funny look on his face. Anyway, he took me to Key West, and after the whole thing was over he gave me five thousand bucks. *Do* you remember? (I guess that's a joke because Dennis Savage once said everything you hear goes right into the type-writer.) Well, Jim couldn't get over that. He kept calling me Carlo and shaking his head. And after I told him all I could about all of us, he said, "Rip, what does it *feel* like?"

He kind of stumped me there, so I said, "What does it feel like here for you?"

So then he got going about his life, and he said it plain away that he surely missed our adventures in high school because things slowed up after that. I could have said that seemed generally true from our drive around town. Jim said the only thing keeping him whole was his family, because his wife Marge is really great and they have a little boy just like Jim and a little girl just like Marge and they all play together and he reads to the kids and they all fall asleep in his lap. It sounded real cute, especially since I mostly remember Jim cutting these really Old Testament sort of farts in the library and riding his bicycle into a tree when the brakes busted, and other crazy stunts which do not exactly connect with him being a father.

He asked me how I could live without a family and I said my family is all the guys I was telling him about. Isn't it? But he didn't get that. He said no—a family like playing with them and learning from each other and living with them inseparable, and I said that's what we do. And finally he sort of got it, that my family is my buddies.

And I know what you're thinking, smart aleck, which is how come I'm *away* from my family, and that's just the kind of thing you always say that I have no reply to until I get home and think about it and wish you were handy so I could paste you a good one. Because you think you know everything.

Anyway, we were just into the second bottle when Jim started in again about, "God, you got so big, Rip," and "Why'd you get like that?" and "I'd be afraid to wrestle you now."

Which is how we got into trouble in the first place, because we used to wrestle naked, and the guy who won could make the loser do anything he asked. Like drink a bottle of ketchup. But one time we got into it in a different way. I know it was different because the other times we were just fooling around with it, but this time we went straight down the track, and all you could hear was us breathing.

You don't think I would remember something like that, at that age, no matter what the others do?

But the thing is, Jim asks me, What exactly did we do that time? I couldn't believe he forgot, after all the trouble we got into. I made him swear he didn't know. So he swore. Okay. And I told him, which was that I pinned him and I made him suck me off. And I like had to pin him again with his arm bent back, because he still wouldn't. But I knew he wanted to, anyway. And after he did it I started swinging on him, and I had him on his back holding his legs in the air gobbling him up when they found us, the preacher and his folks staring there right behind him. They must have known all along and called the preacher, because they were afraid to find us themselves. The preacher was so calm about it, he probably disappointed them. But then he had sucked us off himself often enough.

Old Jim was fit to be iced and put away for the summer when he heard about all this. I guess he really had forgotten. We were so pissed by then we started laughing, which is weird when you think of the terrible things they did to us. I guess the way we survived high school is I said anyone who said a word to us, I would put him in the hospital. And we already had a tough reputation because of hanging out at the truck stop. After all the laughing, we started getting teary, thinking about everything. So we took aspirin, a trick I learned from you, not to get a hangover, and I got up a jug of water so we wouldn't have to crash through the house when we got thirsty later. And I found a blanket. We sacked out in our clothes to sleep it off, just bundled up there. And Jim asked me if he should have come along to New York way back. Because I had asked him. He said, "Would I have had a family with New York names, like you? Would they have taken pictures of me too, and given me five thousand bucks?"

I told him, "You would have been a humdinger there, Jim."

We started to drift off, and I heard him say, "I missed you the whole time, Rip, because you're my best pal." So we went to sleep like that, and the next morning he was gone.

This is your friend, Carlo the Smith.

                                                            August 30
Dear Bud:

About time you wrote back, I don't care how busy you are. Or are you still mad at me? Because I know you are even if you won't say so.

You didn't answer my question right about Big Steve. I asked you if I said the fair thing. If I gave the right answer. I didn't want you to interpret Big Steve's question and turn it into something else. If he was really asking me if I loved him more than anyone else, why didn't he ask that? You and he really ought to get together now, and talk about love all the time, because that's all you guys want to do. You can't just accept something for the way it feels. You always want to know what to call it.

Anyway, I finally got off my butt and found a job, because that's another thing they do around here. None of that New York unemployment stuff in Dakota. My dad had a talk with me to see what kind of experience I had that we could put to use, and I burst out laughing, because what I have been is a hustler and a waiter for Big Steve's Kingdom Kum Katerers and a porn actor and a boutique clerk. But I was also a mover, and that's what I am again. I have to commute into Aberdeen in Dad's truck. It's mostly short-haul stuff in town, I can do it single-handed. You wonder why people want to move so much. They just go right into someplace as terrible as where they were before.

What did I tell you, that my kin would try to set me up with Cousin Irene? I guess they think I came back to change. Maybe instead I came back to be the same. I put them off, but they kept at me, and Irene's father called and said they're expecting me for dinner, so I just said okay and tooled off to town in the truck. If they won't take no for an answer, let them take yes. But I'm still not coming.

You're probably wondering after all this what I'm doing for fun. Well, it took me a while to find the right place, and unfortunately it's one of those real mean gringo taverns where every time the door opens every guy looks up to see if someone's brought a woman in so they can start a vicious incident. But I can't find a truck stop sort of place and of course we don't have any Ty's. The place is called Kicker's Bar and Grill, but I have this joke that it is really called Mars, because the men are all like Martians, you know. They can't talk, they can't smile, they can't do anything I'm used to from New York. You probably think they talk about sports or politics or women, but not even that. They don't talk, period.

The night I skipped dinner with Irene's family I was there. I spotted a guy who looked right, because he kept watching me. He was a big, bearded guy. I came over to his table and bought him a beer, and he turned out to be the most Martian of all, but I had guessed right, anyway, because he made me feel he was running his hand up and down my back just by the way he looked at me. That's a trick only gringos know how to do, because gays will do it by touching your arm, or smiling, or even by saying something pretty direct. Well, look, I know how the game is played, though after New York it's boring to pretend. Also, I have to tell you that even though this guy was no chicken, he was still younger than me, which just shows how things turn over, because I always used to be the kid. Probably for longer than I should have been.

We went through three or four beers each, and when you're drinking with a Martian it seems more like thirty beers. But finally we were near it, because he was staring real hard at me with a mean smile. He's missing one of his teeth. And when he was looking he leaned forward so our knees touched, and I could hear him sucking on his breath. His eyes were like fists. He said, "You want to try a little something new tonight?"

I said, "Like what?" real tough.

"Give me your right hand," he says, and he's reading my palm. "Look at what I see," he goes. "A tall dark stranger's coming into your life. With a beard on him. Tonight, looks like." Then he looks at me. "Right?"

"If you got a place," I said.

He laughs and says, "I got lots of places."

What he had was another dump over a store, like all the people I've been moving around town. He kept the lights out, and when we stripped he didn't take his shorts off, so I said, kind of joking, because it obviously wasn't, "Is this your first time?"

So he said, "What's your name again?" and I told him. And even though he already heard it, he starts using it a lot, like it's a new game he thought of. Then he says, "It's like this, Rip. You move around enough and keep your eyes open, you begin to realize that it ain't never *anybody's* first time."

I can tell you, it sure wasn't his. He said anytime I'm stuck for a place I can stay over some more, and I did a few times, and finally, without anyone saying this is what's happening, I just plain moved in with him. I guess that sounds familiar, huh? But you'd best not write to me anymore, since I'm not at my folks very often. This guy I'm with, whose name is Warren, is a typical supergringo. Anything he doesn't understand he puts down. Anyone he doesn't know he doesn't like. And he's a mean drunk. I tried telling him about me and like Fire Island and the things we do, and he got so nasty making fun of it that I just gave up. But at least he doesn't want anything from me except sex.

He did one strange thing, though. Just two nights ago, which I guess is why I had to write this letter, I got up real late to take a piss, and I was still at the pot when Warren suddenly loomed up behind me and tried to pull me around, and he said, "Where the fuck do you think you're going?" I said, "Let me finish this, will you?" and he was going on about he doesn't want me ducking out on him. It didn't take much to calm him down, because he was half asleep, and he even apologized, which is probably a first for him. But listen. When we got into bed he got all locked up around me, his feet and arms, like I'm his prisoner. I said, "Come on, quit it," and got him off me, but a few minutes later he came right back again. And then he started saying my name, and he said it over and over again.

Is there life on Mars? This is Ripley Smith, over and out. Please don't be mad at me anymore. Give Dennis Savage and the kid himself a hug for me after all this. And listen, whatever happens now, don't you forget me, boy! Because once you're buddies, it doesn't matter if you're there, just how you feel, and who you remember.

And what you can forgive. Okay, my friend?

The Hottest Man Alive

A symbolic tale, projecting the first years of Stonewall against the fall of a great man.

Of course Carlo wrote no more letters. He was settled in—as he prob-ably would be if you dropped him in Tibet, the Gobi desert, or Middle-Earth—with a hot man who could busy, then puzzle, then trouble him. With our resident hunk departed, my circle closed ranks and went on with love and work. But we all felt the lack—not just of Carlo the person but of Carlo the type, for the ideal confraternity blends all kinds. Ironically, I was thinking of this when I ran into a hunk even more essential than Carlo, or perhaps just more public.

It was late one night in the winter after Carlo left us, one of those bad, bitterly cold nights New York can throw on without warning. I was trudging along Third Avenue watching for a cab when I saw a tall, broad, and familiar-looking man heading my way. He seemed to recognize me, and came toward me—where had we met? My mind jumped to pluck a name, a place, from cabinets marked College Chums, Pines Housemates, People I Enraged at Parties (a dense file), and People I Charmed at Parties (surprisingly thin). As he neared, I started to smile, but he came too close, backed me against a car, and said, "I'm hungry. Give me money or I'll hurt you."

Shoot, this *would* happen just when I'm starting to get famous. Because, damn it!, I am not giving these creeps my wallet on de-mand. Anyway, it's too tempting to bluff them down. I disconnected one footpad in the Village by grinning and nodding and speaking Russian; and when a kid fell into step with me on Fifty-seventh Street and said this was a holdup and he was armed, I told him nothing doing unless I saw the gun, and he ran away.

"Hand it over," my present assailant growled, bending my arm behind me, "or I swear to God I'll break it off."

He glared, to persuade me with bitter fire; but then recognition struck me, and I looked down at his left forearm to find the tattoo of a shield inscribed, "No. 1."

"Clark Ellis," I said, and he relaxed his hold on my arm in surprise. I had remembered where we had met before.

We had met, actually, twice, the first time in one of those "backdate" magazine stores where *Popular Mechanics* and *Boy's Life* had their sections, *Demi-Gods*, *Tomorrow's Man*, and *Rustic* theirs. *Rustic* bemused me as the name for a physique magazine. Here was not just the suggestion of the fact of beauty, but the sighting of it in a rural setting—putting real men into imaginary gardens. I was alarmed, alerted. Demi-gods did not exist; but hot farmers might.

One *Rustic* model in particular caught my eye. He was utterly unlike the dowdy hunks that prevailed in those days. They seemed to aim at an impersonalized ideal of flexing, a mere prowess. This one model, on the contrary, threw himself into his photo, aimed to reveal his personability, an expertise. At a time when a 1950s cover still hung over the emerging gay opulence, his parts suggested a sexy cartoon, each feature bigger than you could remember seeing on real flesh. The smile, above all, held me. It was more than dazzling: penetrating. It said, Forget the come-on—we're already there. The culture is here and I am among you. I had seen bedroom eyes before; this guy had room-at-the-baths eyes.

"Clem represents the new breed of poser," his caption ran, "with his conqueror's physique and sensual mentality that knows there is more to life than pitching hay and spreading the seed. We were glad to schedule his second photo session, but for some reason he never called." The oafs, I thought. Teasing me with availability and un-availability at once. Wise oafs: for it worked. That day, my teenage eyes wavering before the cashier's in fact dully tolerant gaze, I bought my first porn rag. I thought of these magazines as my textbooks in gay, though they taught me as much of fantasy as of truth: about what to hope for as well as what to expect. Over the years, some extraordinarily popular mechanics thus changed my suburban boy's life, but Clem's image stayed with me. Sometimes I wondered what his real name might be, as if a key turned into truth might make the fantasy all the more real.

I learned his name at Kern Loften's end-of-summer bash at The Pines the weekend before Labor Day in 1974. Kern's good qualities included a genuine palazzo, the hope of making his parties the greatest ever, and the ability to fill his rooms with his friends, their friends, and no one else. Private parties, without the bar-tension that the big public dos observe. The imposing bodies tended to belong to the bourgeoisie of the gyms, capable of love—not to the pornothespians who drifted in and out of the scene and were capable of anything. But Kern was rich, and some of his friends were rich; and the rich tend to hire help. Maids. Waiters. Lovers. You could always tell the hired lovers by the way they grinned: they already had what they wanted.

Entrance Kern's parties and he treasured you for life; to that end, an amazing soprano and I had put together a cabaret of show tunes, wacko Victor Herbert side by each with Harold Arlen art torch, the truth of sound musicianship fetching art back from mere diversion. We went on well after two A.M., made a hit, and spent the rest of the night basking in prominence. Sometime before dawn I started awake from a doze in one of the bedrooms facing the ocean. The house was dimly buzzing; someone had covered me with a blanket. A large figure stood gazing out at the sea. He turned as I stirred and said, from the shadows, "Nothing works, right?"

I wasted a smile in the darkness and said, "That depends on what you believe in."

He came toward me. "What do you believe in?"

"Will," I said. "Intelligence. Charm."

"What if you can have only one?" He sat on the edge of the bed. "Which would you take?"

It was Clem. I was so startled I blurted out something I had stuck into a story a few days before, one of those gnomic utterances that keep your mouth moving when you daren't speak your mind. "The wise," I said, "are troubled, for they trust only themselves and wisdom. The talented are twice troubled, for they trust only themselves. But the beautiful are most troubled, for they trust no one."

He thought it over, looking at the ocean. "You got that right."

His left arm rested close enough for me to spot the marking, "No. 1." He caught me, and said, "Got that in Denver. This incredible guy. The *most*. I think I thought he was straight. We ended up in this fleabag joint drinking, and he just went after me and did things like . . . like he'd invented sex that night. Hours and hours of it. We finished off the bottle as the sun was coming up, and I suddenly felt drowsy, and he said, 'I slid some stuff in your glass.' Strokes my arm and says, 'Right here, okay?' I didn't know what the hell . . . and when I woke up, he was gone and I—"

"Clark." Another stupendous man stood in the doorway.

"Coming." He rose and joined his partner, two carved idols breathing life into each other. Then he turned back to me. "Will," he said. "If you get your choice. *Will*."

"That's swift, because I've got plenty of will."

"What was that again about the wise are troubled?"

I repeated it, and he listened as if memorizing. His friend, chuckling, said, "The beautiful trust *no one*?"

"Neat piano playing, by the way," Clark Ellis told me, clapping his friend around the shoulders as they left.

"Thanks," I said to the empty room. The sun had nosed up; it was day, and the gang poured in.

"Clark Ellis!"

"What did he *say*?"

"I kiss this room!"

I told them, "He said the most important thing in life is will."

"Will who?"

"No, the most important thing is—"

"Politeness!"

"Sensible hats!"

"It's Sunday, it's The Pines, it's Kern Loften's," I announced. "I'm delirious. Everybody shut up and get out."

"What did he say?" Dennis Savage insisted.

"He told me how he got his tattoo."

"Number One!" they all echoed.

"The hottest man in The Pines!"

"The hottest man *alive!*"

"He'll never grow old."

"His ass will never fall!"

"Such hair—"

"That jaw—"

"He'll always—"

"I don't remember you," he said.

"How about not mugging me and I'll take you to dinner?"

Sarge's, the all-night deli, was a block away. He wouldn't look at the menu, kept searching me with his eyes, and said nothing to the waitress. From absolute aggression to complete passivitiy; strange. I ordered him a hot turkey sandwich, mashed potatoes, salad, apple pie, and coffee. I ordered myself a cheeseburger deluxe and coffee. So it worked out well, for if I'd gone home unmolested I'd have been stuck with cottage cheese and a hard pear.

"Cheer up," I told him. He had not aged badly, and, being naturally big, he had not lost his heft. But his expression was that of a man who never smiled, not even tentatively and certainly not dazzlingly. That did not jibe with the Clark Ellis I knew of.

"I don't remember you," he said again.

"How does a man as gala as you are end up mugging people? You were the King of Gay. You could have had anyone you wanted, and I know there's money in that. Why aren't you a millionaire model? Why didn't you let rich slobbos ply you with watches and yachts?"

He just looked at me.

"Spectacular men don't end up poor," I went on. "They *don't*."

The food came quickly, everything at once, and he fiercely dug in. He must really have been hungry. He had cleaned up when I was halfway through.

"I want more," he said.

I called the waitress over. "The same again," he told her.

"How about a different pie this time? We got cherry."

"The same, the exact same," he said, grabbing a fistful of my french fries. "Turkey, apple, gravy, coffee, everything the same."

"One exact same coming up," she echoed, walking off.

He polished off my hamburger.

"Clark Ellis," I said. "Clark Ellis."

"Hot shit," he replied. "Tell all your friends another beauty wasted out. They're bored and lonely but their rent's paid, right? They're ahead of me."

"I think they'd be sad."

"Everybody's sad. Nothing works."

"How did you end up mugging people?"

"I broke a rich guy's crystal ball."

"That'll do it every time."

"I fell in love with Bill Post so I didn't buy the briquettes and I smashed the crystal ball into a thousand million pieces. And I wrecked the house and robbed them. So they threw me out of the whole world."

"Where do you live?"

"I don't."

Silence.

"Who's Bill Post?" I finally asked.

"What are you, a reporter?"

"Not unlike."

"You remember the pink boy with reddish-brown hair and hazel eyes who played Frisbee all over the beach in navy blue speedos? Your summer of 1980."

Who didn't remember him? I had seen this kid and his Frisbee, as had all others that odd summer, when, for once, the night weather lost its clever bite and took on the seamy intrusiveness of summer nights anywhere. Men I had known as professional smirkers would pace the boardwalk morose and sullen.

Like this man, now.

"I always thought of you riding high," I said.

"I didn't . . . I couldn't control it."

"The way you smiled . . ."

"I had those jobs, those messenger gigs. You know? The East Side co-op run. They're always sending these packages to each other, you can guess of what."

". . . as if you owned the world."

"They all expected me to fuck them. Like no job's legit. Everyone's a hustler or a buyer. So who needs a whore who won't screw?"

"This is one exact same," said the waitress, bringing the food.

He paused, holding his fork, stared at me, and nodded. "Appreciate it," he said, and ate.

"Clark Ellis fell in love with Bill Post," I murmured, trying out a first line. "It was late one night in the winter after Carlo left us . . ."

"Sure thing and so what?"

"Nice pairing. Man and boy. Dark and fair. Knowledgeable and pure."

"He *was* pure. The sweetest chicken there ever was. I am telling you this. But he didn't know shit. He was like me: wake up, listen to the time pass, take a spin in the gym, answer the phone, and go party. Letting it happen."

"Didn't you ever try to . . . well, do something?"

"Make the contacts? Talk them up? Every day. Planning. Everyone was so helpful, too. You know why?"

Silence.

"You *know* why. So finally one day you really are a whore. Not even an errand boy. Just a piece of ass."

"So," I recommended, some years late, "you pull yourself away."

He nodded.

"And?"

He shook his head. "Not so easy. I had Bill to watch over. He was taking what they gave, always said yes. Turn my back for an hour, he'd be doing some new drug, or picking up street cock. Always yes. But I was the man he loved. Know how I know? Because he wept when I flipped him. Only love makes them cry. The others smile. Hustlers. So many are hustlers, and that's why nothing works. Good sex is easy. Man, it's easy. You know what's hard? Love is hard."

"Smile for me."

"What?"

"Nothing."

"Smile for me," he repeated. He had heard. Be a symbol, Clark Ellis. Dazzle us, remember? The culture is here and you are among us. Or no, that was years ago, and the culture has since expanded, broken into factions—political, professional, sexual, intellectual, racial. It is no longer a question, sheerly, of identity, as it was when I was young: of learning that you were among us, that we had an *us* to be among. As he ate, I ran through my file of Hottest Men Alive. Did they all end up alone on the streets? Odd: many didn't appear to end up at all. Yes, there was the black-haired sex model with the unbelievable jaw who was made heir to a millionaire's estate and became a hit-and-run realtor, leaving slivers from the Brooklyn Bridge to Yorkville; or the Australian dancer who collected gasping crowds on the beach at the skater's house and who went on to a not unprominent TV series. Yes but. It seemed as if almost everyone else came to a dubious end, could come but not *dwell* among us. One rather expects it of fast boys, born to burn out; but a sizable man somehow suggests aggressive survival. *Will.* What is will but a sense of self-importance;

and is this not what size demands, looks like, is about? Is this not why Bill Post wept when Clark Ellis flipped him?

"What does 'flipping' mean?" I asked.

He held his coffee, recalling something, and, I hope, very nearly smiled.

"That's when they're done on one side, so you turn them over." He put down the cup, dark again, murky, as if fog masked our table. "He had the smoothest skin. If you knew where to touch him, he'd do anything. Anything. He howled when I laid him. Howled like a dog. God, he was beautiful."

"Now that you've had the appetizer," said the waitress, ambling up with a coffeepot, "how about some real food?"

I took the check.

"Bill let them use him up," he went on. "He fell in with a fashion crowd. Those parties where straight couples are selling drugs in the bathroom? He was going to be this one's houseboy, and then that one's. You know that street? They kept passing him from hand to hand, just another hot kid. And he'd let them, that was the stupid part. Some nights he was so drugged he didn't know where he'd been, come staggering home to me. Got so I had to beat him up. It was the only way to straighten him out, scare him. It would work, too. After, he'd crawl into my lap and say he'd be good and I'd tenderize him. I bet he loved that most of all, even more than laying. We'd just sit there, listening to each other breathe. And I thought, If only there was some *job* I could find, something to do that didn't connect with all those parties and the money, the phone ringing . . . and someone asks for you by your code name, and you're broke . . . so what else are you supposed to do?"

"What happened to Bill?" A Barry, I thought. A kid and a clone.

"Those fashion guys ripped him up. Filled him with junk. Said to him, 'You're a star.' See, they were trying to break us up because I was telling him what to do. I was with Lorenzo Fell then. You know him?"

"Of him."

"The ugliest mcgoon between Ocean Beach and Albania, I used to call him. Treated me like a servant, him and his pals. 'Clark'll do the honors, of course,' he'd say to some horror, and I'd have to take it to bed. Why do ugly men always have ugly friends?"

"They don't."

"You don't know shit. Who do you know?"

"I have to give you references?"

"Rich, I mean."

"Kern Loften."

"Yeah, I remember him."

"Nice fellow."

"Listen, anyone starts nice," he tells me. "Then comes life, and watch. Money changes them. Careers. Power."

"Looks?"

"How can looks change you? Looks are what you are. Looks are what change."

"You can't change your looks, surely."

"What's a gym for, then? Mustaches and beards? Clothes?" Don't you know *anything?* his tone said. Aren't you gay?

"Anyway, they were pulling Bill away from me. Lorenzo was in on it, the whole gang of them . . ."

The waitress and her coffeepot. "It's a little late to start a new elephant," she tells Clark as she pours, "but the chef might save you some of the moose if you feel like dessert."

Clark looks at her.

"That's a joke, honey," she says, taking off.

"Don't you ever laugh anymore?" I asked him. Smile for me.

"They made it so we could never be together. They were telling him the Coast, movies. Not porn, real ones."

Movies with *will.*

"We had to meet in secret. And all I could say was, 'Who were you with?' I didn't mind it for myself, because I know how to lay a mcgoon without getting dirty. But he was just a kid. Didn't know how to protect himself."

"How does one protect oneself with a mcgoon?"

"You pretend they're going to fall into an acid bath the day after. Maybe you're going to push them."

I forked off a bit of his pie and he pushed it to me.

"Finish it. I had some money saved, and I told Bill, 'Let's ditch these guys and set up shop. You know, porn, catering, hustling. I don't know, maybe all at once. Cook the food, serve it, then lay the host. It happens, doesn't it?"

Yes.

"But they got to him. Made him afraid. He had it going and he thought he'd lose it if they dropped him. They were going to take him to Europe after September. So like when I heard that, I just freaked. It was so heavy in my mind, I couldn't . . . I didn't hack it out right. He told me he'd never go away. When I was tenderizing him, sure. And I saw him cry so I thought it was all right. But then they'd get ahold of him, and he'd change his mind. Every minute at Lorenzo's, I'd worry what Bill was up to, what they were doing to him. And this one evening, we were hanging around the deck, and one of Lorenzo's toads sort of squirmed into position and said, 'Won't someone rub my back?' and Lorenzo pointed at me, like I had to. This fucking *toad*! And then one of those junky kids that always hung around Lorenzo came out and said, 'We're out of briquettes,' looking at me as if it was my fault. It's my job to get them, okay, but not to count them or something! They were all looking at me like I was . . . I don't know . . ."

"Someone they couldn't forgive for being beautiful."

A deep breath. "I left, and went to find Bill. I thought, You know, that's it. Fuck their briquettes. Listen. *Listen*, Jesus, he was gone! They'd just picked him up and took him away!"

"Where?"

"Where? Someplace Europe, where. Who *cares* where? They got him, slid him out from under me, just about. Figure it, how I felt. But, listen, Lorenzo had this crystal ball in his house. Something special, like there's no others but that one? Handmade, or something.

Had it in the center of the living room, and you had to be all this careful when you got near it. They held seances, telling the future. Lorenzo would dress up and do this cackly voice and say what would happen to you. You could always tell who was in favor with him from the fortune he told. He thought that glass ball was the hottest thing on the walk."

"Hotter than you?"

"Man, Lorenzo didn't know what hot was. He was even afraid to be laid. Wasn't even a *man*! All he did was suck and tips."

"Tips?"

"Nipple stuff. Ugly guys are so—"

"And you broke the crystal?"

He looked back on it. "Yes." Nodded. A story. Something happens, changes your life. "Into a thousand million pieces. Right in front of them. Shithead dufos. I picked it up, and I aimed it at Lorenzo's head, and I . . . *threw* . . . *that* . . . *mother*. And, man, they screeched like butchered cats. So I took them and smashed their fucking skulls together and I wrecked the whole place—furniture, clothes, even the walls, man, the whole *place*! The place, The *Pines*! And, the whole time—figure it—they were lying around sobbing in these . . . *positions*, like it was a *movie*! And I took the cash and split. They couldn't call the police, because I controlled some very heavy input on Lorenzo's Colombian connections, you taste? But they did something I couldn't fight back on—I didn't even know about it at first. This Dr. Conover, who runs the VD mill on Lexington? He's one of the gang. They got him to spread the rumor that I had AIDS. You should have seen how suddenly it all went away. It *all*! Friends were like strangers, and strangers . . . weren't there. Guys that used to stand around talking to me on the street, hoping I would say, 'So let's score'? Nothing. Didn't see me. Didn't hear me when I shouted their names. Your word is out, see? Suddenly everyone was a phone tape with no tape in it. And that's like suddenly you are unemployed. No prospects. No contacts. And that is the end of your career."

"Why didn't you try another town? San Francisco?"

"They give it away there, man. I'm an employee, so what do you want? A whore. Do you know what a whore is? A man without will, I swear."

He was about forty-two now, and still amazing. No doubt everything would catch up with him; already his eyes were as troubled as a prophet's. There was but one Clark Ellis, but many stories like his, of men dwindled from dish mythology into unemployment checks and evictions and fizzled jobs and injudicious hustling and death by drugs of pleasure. Smile for me, No. 1.

"Everyone can't have heard a rumor started by a single clique," I said. "It's such a big city. Couldn't you—"

"No. Stop." He held up his hand. "Just listen to me, okay?" His hand was shaking. "Because it's . . . it's more than that." He set his hand flat on the table, laid the other atop it. "The AIDS thing was just . . . it was to scare off the fancy-pants crowd. The mcgoons and the money. That's the part you see—on the ferry or in the Saint or at a big theme party. That's the part you know. That's your gay life. But there's more than that part. Stuff that doesn't come out all the time. It's there just the same, and it's connected to the fancy part. You don't know about it, maybe, and your friends don't. But it's powerful. It knows about you."

Whatever it was, it sounded like Santa Claus; and he saw me fighting a smile and glumly nodded.

"Listen to something else. The same thing, but it's different. Listen. The world. You got your high-school football team and your college, and then some job and GQ clothes and your plastic, and you think that's the whole world. Everybody's world, okay, right? So someone didn't make the football team. Some got better jobs or more plastic or a dishwasher in the kitchen. So it's still the same world, isn't it? Don't look serious, just answer!"

"You haven't asked a question."

"Is that what you think the whole world is?" he almost shouted.

We both looked up guiltily at some movement in the room: the waitress again, with the coffee. "Now, now," she lightly warned, pouring. "He's probably upset," she murmured to me, "because he didn't get enough to eat."

She had cut into our momentum, and there was silence for a bit. "I played football in high school," he finally said. "Quarterback. Really the hero. There wasn't a girl in the whole school I couldn't have, including the teachers. And there was this guy on the team. Your strong silent guy sort. Never said a word to anyone. Good athlete, though. Good man. Good grades, even. He was . . . you'd say anything to him, he'd just nod. Last game of the season, there was a rumor that the cheerleaders were going to lie down for us, win or lose. Maybe it wasn't that big a deal, because they weren't exactly the singing nuns before that, but it had a quality. Like a pact, I guess. Something special for the team. It was like a party within a party, like it starts in one house and then a few of us get the signal and go somewhere else, with no parents or horny sophomores around. So we make our exit, and drive over to the duck pond. Real spread out there, dark, and it's got all these little hills and trees. Good place for the kind of thing. You can't tell who's doing what. And the guy I told you about, I saw him go off by himself and I followed him. We talked for a while. I mean, I talked and he nodded. He was really nervous. So I said, 'Come on, let's take a drive,' and we did that, and we parked somewhere, and nobody's saying nothing. Sitting there, fine. He's looking straight ahead, as if there was something to find in front of us, which there wasn't, and I'm kind of aimed at him. And suddenly he puts his hand on my thigh. He's straight back against the car seat like he's trying to smooth his way right through it. And then he looks at me, and I told him to go ahead. I should have known all along. He was so tense, I whispered to him to take it easy. So then I started to open up his pants, but he bolted out of the car and ran into the trees and yakked his guts out. Never saw anyone barf like that. Now he's probably a doctor with a big house and four kids somewhere in the Sunbelt and he never thinks about anything." He shook his head. "Now, why did I tell you about that?"

He looked sad and confused. I wondered if Bill Post had ever seen
him so.

"Was it like that for you?" he asked. "Back then? First time?"

"Well . . . nobody threw up."

"Why the hell not? It's always like that. It's supposed to be."

I thought of Carlo and the man with the little bowl of warm water,
and the excitement Carlo knew then that he could never retrieve.

"Why did you tell me that?" I asked.

"It was . . . about something. About the whole world. Things you
don't see that are in the world."

Stuff that doesn't come out all the time.

"I wanted to tell you what happened to me," he pleaded. "To show
you that there's more going on than you know about. That's why it
happens. It wasn't just Bill or Lorenzo or telling everybody I had
AIDS. Sure, you start on the squad and you go to the parties, and I
guess in a way Fire Island and all that is more of the same. Making a
different squad and going to other parties, but the same deal about
who's allowed and who isn't. Who gets in. But look. When you start
to slip, you fall into some really gruesome deals. I mean, some guys I
know started dealing and they got so into the honey they took it and
took it till they exploded. Or some guys got into shady porn. Or those
waiter gigs where like all the guests are so friendly and they're all
giving you stuff and you don't know what the hell it all is till you wake
up three weeks from last Tuesday with half your head watted out,
wondering how many people touched you and where." He took a
deep breath. "Or you can report for a video date and take your
chances." He gazed at me, the broken impresario of hot. The whole
opera's gone bust and Rigoletto ran off with the scenery. "You know
about those?"

"They tape you . . . in sport."

"You can even join a service for it. Unlisted numbers and so on. I
mean, you could pick someone off the street if you wanted, but some
of these people are into such kinky scenes that they need guys who,
you know, perform the specialities. And that's how you go down,

brother, let me whisper it to you. Because once you turn pro at this kind of thing, it isn't just Lorenzo Fell and his pansy sidekicks. It's the bottom rung of all the money you don't see. All the people who've done everything before they get to you, so, like, what's left to jolly them? But they'll figure something out, won't they? And that's what you'll do. Because you need the bread. Because it's there, you, in the dark rooms and all those eyes watching you. Maybe you can't even see them, but they see you all right. You hear them. Jesus, you can hear them *looking* at you, that's how heavy. Or a guy alone with a hundred whips and then this monster comes out of a door smiling at you like you're a piece of Danish and he's hungry. Or wives holding the camera, want to catch you porking their husbands. Video dates. Dark rooms and faces in a circle, that's what it is. And maybe anyone might do a spell in that world—but what if you're stuck there forever? Why didn't you get something better for yourself, huh? Why are you here? Why is this you?"

He stopped. "Say something," he told me.

"No, go on. Whatever it is."

"Why? What's the point now?"

"So I can understand about the other world."

"It's the same world," he said, slowly. "The same world." He leaned forward. "Okay," he said. "Now listen. This one time, I go up there. Huge place. Servant at the door, this way please, and I go in."

And I'm thinking that if Carlo didn't have Dennis Savage and Lionel and Big Steve and me and a few other friends to keep him busy and talk him out of things, he might have come to one of those dark rooms.

"They've got this kid tied to a chair. Sixteen, seventeen. Really sweet boy, scared as hell."

Or that it's not U and non-U but luck. The luck of finding the right apartment before the crunch hit, of not going down the street when the bad guys are waiting, of running into someone you half-know on a day when you feel the way George Will looks and the half-friend says, "Let's get ice-cream cones," and the next thing is the two of you are singing the entire score to *Follies* and you've made a friend for life. Or the luck, simply, of being one of the ones who doesn't take ill.

"All these people in suits. Sometimes they're in costumes and sometimes they're wearing like a plastic garbage bag, but these people were all dressed up. And the head man says, 'This boy is no fun at all,' meaning the kid, 'so you're going to liven him up for us.'"

I was thinking that this boy would look like Bill Post, for thematic symmetry, but Clark Ellis—as if reading my map—shook his head and said, "This chicken was pale white, like ivory, and very thin, with brown hair. He was no winner, just a stray kid. You know how many of those there are in this city? People were petting him, and they'd watch me, and pet him some more, and the man says, 'Let's see you, ace.' While I'm stripping they're getting the camera set up on this tripod. And the people were coaxing the kid toward this bed, and he's fighting them and he keeps looking at me. Just think of that, because the two of us are naked and everybody else looks like a party at the UN or something. I mean handkerchiefs and flowers and like feathers and lace. Fans and capes. And this kid was scared."

Like the football player in the car.

"The man gave me a gizmo like a combination carburetor and carrot grater and says, 'Slide this on your cock and fuck him.' Over on the bed the suit people were holding the kid down, and what do you think they look like? Grinning, like oh boy, some fun? There was nothing on their faces at all. See, they're holding this little boy down to watch his ass get all tore up, and nobody's home. Anyways, I told the man I didn't like the look of that piece of his, and he says he's got three big ones to lay on me if, but otherwise nothing, and what's my service going to say when he tells them I don't put out."

"This isn't the world," I told him. "This is land's end."

"That's why I'm telling you this story. Because you think that. Because you think everyone's got a place to live and enough friends and something funny to do on Sunday afternoon, don't you? You think Lorenzo Fell's as bad as it gets. Christ, all that fucking money! If only you knew about it, man. You would sure feel different in one of the dark rooms they got." He shook his head. "That rich friend of yours. King . . ."

"Kern Loften."

"He doesn't give dark-room parties, does he?"

"No, he gives very nice parties. Very official gay parties." The kind, I almost added, that you attended in your time of glory.

"He doesn't tie kids up and have them fucked with something you could cut your way through a jungle with, does he? He doesn't tape it? He doesn't have this woman in a mantilla or something who's looking at the kid and saying, 'Maybe get a towel for the blood, somebody.' Does he?"

Not exactly. Once Kern cut me off for weeks because I told him William Burroughs, despite a deplorable world view, was one of the greatest writers of the day. "How can you praise that kind of thing?" Kern asked while forgiving me. "Are you a New Yorker or aren't you?" And I replied, "What's a New Yorker?"

"He doesn't lay three bills on you because to him that's pennies and he wants to see what happens when you torture a boy who doesn't know how to make the exit? That's a neat sight to see, isn't it? Brings a lump to your throat."

There was silence then. Finally he said, "And so." He nodded. Gestured mildly. "And so. Good story, huh?"

I'll see what I can do.

"So they got this rope from somewhere and I said I don't need it. Look, I outweighed the kid by a hundred-ten pounds. He's just lying there, not even struggling anymore. I pulled a guy out of the crowd and gave him the camera and told him to be creative. And I scattered the people at the bed and pulled the kid up and stood behind him, like I was demonstrating him, you know. Showing him off. I felt him up but he was so scared he wasn't getting on. The camera was right on him and he kept trying to turn away from it. So I took him around through the guests so each one could touch him and kiss him, and they all got into that, stroking him with the camera on him. And soon he was hot. And they were getting pretty wild so I had to control

them. That woman who asked for the towel? She was dancing in and
out like the native princess in a jungle film. I looked over at the head
man, and he was pleased. It was good for them, so I could make the
bread without hurting the kid. I turned the scene around on them,
see? I sat the kid on the bed, and I waved the camera guy in close,
and I made the kid look right in there, at whatever it is. Then I asked
the kid, 'Who are you afraid of?' He swiveled around to look at the
head man, but I caught him back and I asked him again, with my
hands on his neck, thumbs right on his throat. He was so damn
sweet, he didn't understand what I was trying to do for him. But he
saw my eyes, and I pressed his throat a little, and he got it. So then I
said, 'Who are you afraid of?' a second time, and he said, 'You.' And
then he was begging me not to hurt him, and crying, and that was it.
That was all they wanted. Some of the others ran up and held him
down again and now they were laughing and cheering us on and I
could fuck him so gently and it didn't matter because I'd given them
what they wanted. The man gave me five hundred dollars and I got
dressed and I left the dark room and now, you tell me, Is that the
world or is this the world?"

"What?"

"That dark room there—or sitting at this table now?"

"What happened to that boy at the party?"

"Drinking coffee like this, talking about it. Maybe they're showing
that film somewhere this minute. Some guy's showing his wife so they
can hot up enough to fuck. Maybe that's the world. That's what
works. Money making adjustments for mcgoons. Ask a mcgoon how
he's doing. He's doing great."

"It's not too late, you know," I said. "You're still a beautiful man—"

"Sure," he said. "Sure," holding his head, lowering it to shake and
be sad and bewildered. And he said, "The beautiful are most troubled, for they trust no one."

"Where," I asked him, as quiet as a nail in a coffin, "did you learn
that?"

He was still, didn't look up. "You told me. Didn't you?"

"Yes."

"Where?"

"At a party. In The Pines. It was—"

"Help me." He raised his head, stiffened, and looked sharp, as if apologizing for the outburst, for needing anything. "Please. Something."

"Kern Loften," I began, "always thought you were the hottest man alive. He'd probably send you to a doctor first and so on, but—"

"He gave that party."

I smiled. "It all comes back. Who was that man you were with? He was almost as—"

"He's dead. A lot of hot men are dead because they were hot. You should know that."

"Well, Kern might take you on. I could call him." A thought hit me. "What about Bill Post?"

He shook his head slowly. Dead also? Gone? Sometimes they simply vanish.

"I could call Kern tomorrow."

He nodded, and so we left it, but he seemed in no way relieved, and when he got outside he told me not to call anyone for him. Not Kern and not anyone. The wind had puffed up, the kind that burns your ears. We clearly could not chat it out. I said, "Do you want to come home with me?"

"Yes. And I'll smash you up and wreck your apartment and take everything you have."

There was a moment, just a flash of a bit of time, when I could see him trying to believe he meant it. I kept it light: "Better not, the doorman'll fuss at you. I think it's Ramon tonight, and he's—"

"You played the piano. With the opera lady."

"Yes."

"What do you do now?"

Well, for starters, I'm going to write this story. "Do you want me to call Kern for you?"

"No."

"You said, 'Help me.'"

"*No.*"

"Why?"

"Because nothing works and everybody dies. Because it hurts."

He was about to turn, and I grabbed his arm and said, "Smile for me."

"No," he said. "*Why?*"

"To show me you're all right."

He looked at me for quite some time, then, and finally shook his head. I watched him walk off. After fifty yards he turned and stopped. We got into a kind of standing contest, then he came back and said, "What does it take?"

"Will," I said.

"No. To make you get lost?" But he grabbed for my hand and squeezed it, against the words, and patted my shoulder. "Go home," he said. "Okay?"

I grasped his left arm to see that caption of his again, No. 1, and I looked up at him, thinking maybe I would see the rest of him as he was, there among us once, really the hero, but his smile had busted into a thousand million pieces because nothing works. Because what you hope for isn't necessarily what to expect. And I am not a demonstrative fellow with people I don't know and Clark Ellis is very reserved, as many great beauties are expected to be, and the weather said move!, and I was so crowded with recollections of how matters have proceeded in those Stonewall days—which exactly coincide with my years in New York—that I scarcely knew how we ended up holding each other; but I would not make much of it, boys and girls, because I expect we were simply celebrating a pungent nostalgia, or marking our shared belief in certain things many others do not believe—or perhaps because it seemed correct punctuation, and easier than smiling. It was cold, and Clark Ellis went away.

When I reached my building and Ramon unlocked the door, I told him, "The beautiful are most troubled, for they trust no one."

And Ramon, who never smiles, said, "Good evening, sir."

Sliding into Home

In which unities of time, place, and action are observed—but not that of character, for even The Pines, Stonewall's most compact ghetto, may contain an intruder here and there. And herewith the author takes his leave.

I heard a strange voice ask, "What flavor of ice cream would you like, Virgil?" as I came up the walk. I opened the door to the patio, and stood facing a handsome, fortyish man in an outfit one rarely sees at The Pines, slacks and the kind of striped shirt you wear with a tie.

"Who's Virgil?" I asked him, though I knew very well.

"Don't listen to him!" Little Kiwi shouted, rushing up.

The man, completely at a loss, looked from him to me.

"If you're the garbageman, we don't want any today," cried Little Kiwi, trying to push me out.

"Don't call him Virgil," I told the man, using my valise to drive Little Kiwi back onto the porch.

"It's my name!"

"Yes, but it throws everything off."

"Then you're so mean," he said, "that I won't introduce you."

We introduced ourselves. The man in the outfit was Dave Bast, who had just moved to New York from Cleveland.

"How on earth," I asked, "does one move to New York in 1985? There's no place to move into."

"Unless you buy," he said.

"Ah. A professional."

Like me, he had come out for a stay at Dennis Savage's house in midweek, when the other renters were job-bound in town. Dave Bast had been about to secure the lunch matter at the Pantry when I walked in.

"Little Kiwi's flavor, by the way, is Frusen Glädjé vanilla almond."

"Whose . . . what?"

Little Kiwi sulked.

"You'll have to go slower on this for me," said Dave. "I've only just got here and everyone is . . . well, kind of a stranger."

"Whose friend are you, anyway?"

"No one's really. See, I was Seth Brown's paddle brother in college, and—"

"*Paddle brother?*"

"Our fraternity. St. A's. It's just a . . . term. Read 'big brother.' Or 'sponsor.' Or something such."

I was impressed. For those of who you don't follow collegiate Greek culture, St. Anthony's is invariably the top house on campus, sporting not only the wealthiest and nicest guys but also the best looking. (Another interior contradiction in straight: if they're so stuck on women, why would they fill a frat house with gorgeous men?) When I left for Penn, my dad advised me to avoid St. A's—"it's kind of la-di-da," he warned me. I'll say. His idea of a sound frat was ATO, his old house, which turned out, not surprisingly, to be the third-toughest jock house on a campus noted for tough jock houses. In my first year at Penn, the first- and second-toughest jock houses were dissolved by university decree for hazing enormities. ATO was thrilled: number one at last! An ATO friend of mine, Bob Morgan, urged me to pledge the house, but I figured I'd already had everything ATO could offer just growing up with Jim. I went to St. Elmo's, a sort of vapidly sweet frat that had lost its building in a fire a bit before and had rebuilt in red brick and glass. It stood on Locust Walk, the main drag of the frat system, right in the heart of the campus, but it looked too neat and mod next to the Gothic mansions that characterized Penn's Greek community. (Funny how that word keeps slipping in.) Once, I left a group of friends in front of the house; it was the pledges' weekly night for dinner with the brothers. As I left, one of them said, "That's his fraternity? I thought that was the science building."

"St. Anthony Hall, huh?" I said, taking in Dave Bast. "No wonder you're so well dressed."

"It's supposed to be my junking-around duds."

"By Pines standards, that's black tie."

He smiled. "I guess I'm doing everything wrong. It's bound to happen when you fall in among strangers. I came to say goodbye to Seth before I left, and he . . . see, we've stayed in touch all these years, and I've known Virgil since he was a sprout. Seth asked me to look in on him when I got to New York."

I turned to Little Kiwi, sitting quietly with his back to us as if he were a figure in one of Samuel Beckett's plays. "You mean you're related to something human?" I asked him. "You actually have a father?"

"Now I will never talk to you again *forever!*" said Little Kiwi, leaping up. "*Come*, Bauhaus!"

Bauhaus didn't; Bauhaus seldom does.

"I better walk you down to the Pantry," I told Dave, as I ruffled Little Kiwi's hair. "First time out here can be tricky." Little Kiwi turned and put his arms around me; he's vulnerable to affectionate demonstration.

Dave regarded us quizzically. "I thought," he said. "I mean, it isn't the customary thing to . . . is it?"

"How do I know till you ask?"

"I understood there was someone else . . . in the picture." He looked like someone who catches children with their hands in the cookie jar, then gets flustered when they fail to act guilty.

"There is someone else," I said, stroking Little Kiwi's neck. "Dennis Savage. He'll be along presently. In fact, he's not someone else, he's some*one*, the whole thing. Right?"

Little Kiwi nodded. He's the only gay I know who reached his mid-twenties having had carnal intersection with one man and no others.

It's an accomplishment of some kind, certainly, but Dave looked as if he were seeing something he shouldn't.

"Why doesn't Bauhaus come when I say?" Little Kiwi asked.

"Why don't you train him to?" I replied.

"I don't think he'd respond. He has such an artistic kind of temperament." Little Kiwi turned to Dave. "We may be putting on some shows later, so you should get set."

"Why do I have the impression," I asked, "that if this were the 1970s and we could still have sex with all the trimmings and not spend the following week waking up screaming, I would nevertheless be spending my trip watching you put on shows?"

Little Kiwi thought about it. "Because," he offered, "my shows are a legend of the Island."

I was about to respond, but I caught sight of Dave, and he was a sight. If he had known the kid himself since he'd been a, yes, sprout, then he couldn't have been surprised at what passes, in our set, for quaint charm. Yet he was staring at Little Kiwi as if . . . I don't know, as if the kid were exposing essential secrets.

It occurred to me then that I really had no handle on Dave—had no idea why someone so oddly out of tune was there at all. Who was he, besides a friend of Little Kiwi's family? As we walked along Ocean Boulevard—about a mile of wooden slats four feet wide—he said, "If my wife and I had had kids . . . a little boy like Virgil, say . . . I guess I wouldn't be here right now."

His wife?

"I guess raising children can wed a couple in a way that ordinary mating can't. Sharing that flesh-and-blood thing, really, that creativity. Putting those little people to bed, and holding them when they're sick. Then they ask those funny questions, like—"

"Why are you here right now, on a gay beach?"

"I discovered I was gay after being married for twenty years."

I think he expected me to congratulate him or mount some club demonstration, but I looked at him in disbelief. *Nobody* discovers his sexuality after being anything for twenty years; you discover it in youth, when it forms. And anyone who says otherwise is a bloody fucking liar.

"Anyway, if Amy and I *had* a whole family, I guess I would have let that carry me along."

We walked in silence.

"She was very nice about it when I told her," he finally said. "She didn't believe me, of course. Maybe I didn't even think she would. But I guess after twenty years of sex, they can't be expected to believe you're a faggot. She told me she figured there was another woman and that I was trying to spare her feelings."

More silence.

"Maybe we got too used to each other, after all."

He was carrying on a one-man conversation, answering questions I hadn't asked.

"I sort of knew about Virgil all along, so his dad was the first person I told. With his son and all, he'd have to understand."

You're really good-looking, I thought, but I don't like you. I'm not sure why.

"I caught Virgil here just before he left town, and he said if I was coming out I ought to do it here, because Fire Island is like . . . well now, I'm not sure I remember all that he said. I gather this is something of a homosexual amusement park, and as far as—"

"Just follow the walkway there past the ice-cream stand," I said, pointing. We had reached the harbor. "You'll see it."

I felt him gazing puzzled at my back as I marched away, leaving the impression that he had committed heavy faux pas. But so he had.

"What's the idea of inviting that gringo clown out here during my stay?" I called up to Little Kiwi when I got back.

He was on the balcony again, playing with the fancy umbrella Dennis Savage had given him for his birthday, the folding kind with a wooden handle colorfully painted and shaped to resemble a puffin.

"What clown?" he said. "Uncle Dave?" Suddenly he switched to a raspy voice as he animated the umbrella, handle side up. "Dave is no clown, *gskwark*! This is Randolph the Puffin speaking."

"Oh, not this again," I moaned.

"He's the nicest man in Ohio," the puffin said.

"Randolph," said Little Kiwi, "let's—"

"Just a minute, kiddo, he is *not* nice. He swindles a woman for twenty years—no doubt with lots of shadow-fucking along the way, whereupon he comes home and says, 'Not tonight, honey, I'm beat'—and then he grandly presents himself here in his . . . his Sears Roebuck party socks and expects the gay world to dance a jig, right?"

"Who's this nasty man?" Randolph asked Little Kiwi.

"I'm warning you, boy," I said. "I'm burning a short fuse today, thanks to your father's paddle buddy."

"If you don't start being cute," Little Kiwi warned me, "no one will like you."

"Or read your greasy books," Randolph piped in.

"Randolph," I said, mounting the stairs, "today a puffin dies."

With a yelp, Little Kiwi dashed into the bathroom, but I got my foot in the doorway before he could lock himself in, so he ran to the window, stuck the puffin out, and rasped, "Listen, gay America! A crazed fiend is after me, Randolph the Puffin!"

"O puffin," I told him in a Shakespearean manner, "thou hast bought the farm."

"Help! Danger! Fire!"

"*What the Judas heck is going on here?*" shouted Dennis Savage from below as he stamped into the house.

Little Kiwi and I froze. "Now we're going to get it," he whispered.

"I go to support a friend who, despite being celibate for the last three and a half years, is about to die," Dennis Savage went on, as Little Kiwi and I came out onto the walkway. "Have you *any idea* what that's *like*? Do you realize that right now I'm shaking with rage and fear because who knows which of us will be next? And *look* what I *find* when I get here! *Look what I find!*"

He heaved up one of the dining table chairs and threw it across the room.

"I find the two of you cavorting and yelling and making this house the scandal of the walk! What were you doing in the *bathroom*, for heaven's sake? You can't make a ruckus in the regular places?"

He crossed the room and picked up the chair. Suddenly calm, he sat in it, looking suavely up at us as if he had just devised some picturesque new Pines stunt that would soon be all the fashion.

"And," he went on quietly, "I see that umbrella's still with us. Little Kiwi, I told you, that joke staled after a week."

"It staled for me," I said, "after fifteen seconds."

"And the icing on the cake," said Dennis Savage, "is he won't take it out in the rain."

"I don't like getting wet," said Randolph.

I laughed.

"Don't be his audience," said Dennis Savage. He really was upset—not at us, but at the state of health in general. "Don't. Okay? Because he'll just go on doing it."

"I'd go on, anyway," said Little Kiwi, in his own voice.

Dennis Savage shook his head. "I'm just not in a mood for these games. Do you want to see me break down in front of you?"

"No," said Little Kiwi immediately, but then Randolph and I both said, "Yes."

"Very funny," said Dennis Savage. "Did your friend get here?"

"He went to the store for various assundries," said Little Kiwi.

"That's various *and*—"

"Did you meet," Dennis Savage asked me, "the new boy on the block?"

"Little Kiwi's paddle uncle?" I said, coming downstairs. "We met."

"Nice guy, I hear. But he picked a rather unterrific moment to come out in. Great timing they have in Cleveland."

"The whole state's like that," growled Randolph.

"Who told you he's a nice guy?" I asked.

"That time Little Kiwi's parents came to New York," said Dennis Savage, "his father went on and on about Uncle Dave. Especially about their college days. You may think you're joking about that pad-

dle-brother stuff, but from the way he was talking, you'd have the idea
that they were—"

Footsteps.

"Later."

"Had a hell of a time getting back here," said Uncle Dave, pulling
in with the groceries. "Every street looks the same. The guys sure
don't."

"What is that supposed to mean?" I asked.

Dennis Savage quickly introduced himself and busied Uncle Dave
in unloading the haul. I stood aside, silently grumbling. Dave Bast
was a resentable intruder, I felt. But I do believe that a book of com-
ing-out photographs ought to include a view of Uncle Dave's face
when Randolph the Puffin leaned over the edge of the walkway and
asked, "What flavor of ice cream did you get?" Little Kiwi was crouch-
ing so he couldn't be seen on the main floor and Uncle Dave was a
veritable study.

"What's . . . that?" he asked.

"That's Randolph the Puffin," said Dennis Savage, waving it away
as if it were just another element of an ordinary day, soggy corn flakes
or a burned-out light bulb. "Were you planning to cook this as well as
buy it?"

"What flavor?" Randolph repeated.

"Do I talk to that?" Uncle Dave asked Dennis Savage.

"You do if you're gay," I put in. "Because if you're gay you'll have
some taste, however slim or broad, for the camp theatrical. But if
you're straight, you can talk all you want and it'll never hear you."

I spoke mildly, but I guess he saw what was in my eyes, because he
said, also mildly, "Would you like to settle this outside?"

"I'd be glad to," I replied, "you gringo son of a bitch."

Dennis Savage exploded like a fresh mine. "*This*," he almost
screamed at me, "is my guest, okay?" And he told Uncle Dave, "This
is my best friend! So the two of you just cool off! *Now!*"

Little Kiwi, hanging over the walkway railing, looked—as he always did when these things happen—like the first person eliminated

in an all-night Monopoly session. Uncle Dave held his ground but said nothing more. I retired to the deck with *Martin Chuzzlewit*, thinking that if Dickens had seen a gay America instead of the intolerant jackoff straight kind he did see, he might have had a better time here. But then there was no gay then. And, in the first place, Dickens was probably an intolerant jackoff himself . . . and there was Uncle Dave asking if I'd like to Talk It Out.

"Tell you what," I answered. "I'll stay out of your way and you'll stay out of mine. We'll get along."

"That's not good for me," he said.

"Who gives a flying fuck what's good for the likes of you?"

He stared at me as if I had the wrong man.

"You spend twenty years in the closet," I went on, "and you come out here with cruising tips? 'The guys sure don't'?" I stood up, because if you are going to fight, you don't give the enemy an advantage. "I don't know you," I said, "and I don't like you," I added, "and I don't believe in you," I concluded. "So huh?"

That usually does it. But he stood where he was and said, "I know there's a misunderstanding here, and I think we can compensate it."

"Compensate as an intransitive verb without the preposition. Now I've heard everything. What are you, an accountant or something?"

"Yes, as a matter of—"

"You compensate *for* quelque chose. You don't compensate *chose*. Got me, buddy?"

"I can't get why you're so down on me. We hardly met and you're . . . I could tell . . . you were mad about something."

What would Jimbo do at this point? I wondered. Jim would settle down and be amused.

"Was it something I said? Because I apologize. I'm new here, I told you. I'm bound to say the wrong thing, I guess."

I sat down, put *Martin Chuzzlewit* to the side, and regarded him.

"Virgil said you might point me in some directions. You know. Hints on how to . . . I . . ."

"Start with the library. Stonewall classics. William Burroughs, Edmund White, *City of Night*, *The Movie Lover*, *The Boys on the Rock*, *Danny Slocum*. The life. The spirit. The themes."

Typical! I thought, watching him. He doesn't know what the hell I'm talking about.

"I thought I ought to start by visiting . . . the places. The right places. You know."

"No. Do I?"

"I mean, Where do you go to be . . . gay?"

I nodded. "Acceptable question. You could go to a Pasolini movie. You could go to a west side *conversazione*. You could go to the hospital . . ."

"Oh boy, you don't ever give in, do you?"

"Well, who gave you the right to be gay, anyway?" I said. "We don't run this club on open admissions."

"Okay, who does get in?"

"Everybody but straights."

He nodded. "I'm not straight."

It's a cultural thing, Carlo says. It's not whom you bed, it's whom you're kind to, whom you respect, whom you like in some important way. It's who your buddies are.

"I'm not straight," he repeated. "At least, not anymore."

"There's no crossing over," I told him. "What you've been is what you deserve to be. For life."

He looked at me for a moment. "Who let you make the rules, may I ask?"

"I don't make them. I discover them."

"Dave," said Little Kiwi, joining us with the unsavory Bauhaus, tethered and gamboling, "would you come help me walk a dog?"

"Go," I said, figuring that Dennis Savage had cooked this up so he and I could talk.

They headed over the dunes and I went inside.

"Mission accomplished," I said, finding Dennis Savage among the kitchen things, where he was halfheartedly setting up for lunch.

"I want to thank you," he said, "for making a difficult day so much easier."

"Oh yeah? How about thank you for brightening my stay by dragging in that gay Babbitt?"

"Actually, he's a rather eligible dude, all told. He's got money, he's intelligent, he's medically attractive, and, you must admit, he's awfully nice looking." He fussed at a stubborn jar top. "A nice, big fellow."

I shrugged.

"Yes," he said, "I thought you'd noticed."

I took the jar from him. "I'll tell you what I noticed." I opened it. "When that kind gets off the ferry, there goes the neighborhood."

"My hero," he observed, reclaiming the jar. "According to Little Kiwi, this guy really did just get off the boat a week or so ago, so it's too early to tell what he'll be like once he gets his bearings. I remember how rough-hewn you were when you first came out."

"Well, I don't remember you before three or four weeks ago. It's the charitable thing to do."

He spread peanut butter on right triangles of whole wheat toast.

"I hope that's crunchy," I said. "Smooth is for straights."

"Funny his waiting this long to take the step, isn't it?" Dennis Savage mused. "What must have been going through his mind all these years?"

"You surely don't buy this jazz about his not knowing he was gay till he was in his forties, do you? How can you not know what you're attracted to? It's like not knowing that you're wearing pants."

"How soon did you know?" he asked.

"I *never didn't.*"

Silence and peanut butter.

"Have you never heard someone say," he asked finally, "that he wasn't sure what he liked?"

"A euphemistic cop-out for gays who can't confront their fate. Gays who keep looking over their shoulder to see what the straights are thinking of them. You remember Britt Kelso? One of the most effeminate characters going, right?"

"You and he were good friends, as I recall."

"Okay, we were. Till I got sick of his constantly putting down all his friends behind their backs. God knows what he was saying about me."

"I'll tell you sometime, when you're in the mood."

"The day I forgive you for that, they'll make me Pope. Anyway, we kept running into each other, and finally we had dinner. And while telling me about the superb hunk he is currently dating, he blithely lays upon me the scoop that he is also seeing a woman. We're talking about a male who was almost certainly known in high school, to his despair, as Britt the Flit. And after a lifetime of being the absolute bottom, he has become A Real Man. And did he enlarge upon the moral beauty of bisexuality, let me tell you!"

"If that's what he wants."

"He does it to impress himself! When Michael and I gave our joint birthday party, I told Chuck about this and he hit the ceiling. He called it 'gay fascism.' He said Britt was disputing my right of sexual choice."

"Aren't you disputing his?"

Bauhaus crashed into our midst like dirty work at the crossroads and began barking at Dennis Savage. Then Little Kiwi and Uncle Dave trooped in, and Bauhaus jumped up on Little Kiwi.

"What is it, boy? Speak!"

Bauhaus barked twice.

"You do?"

Bauhaus barked once.

"He says he wants to dance on a grape."

"Little Kiwi," said Dennis Savage, "enough is enough, okay?"

"He wants to dance on a grape?" Uncle Dave asked.

"It's his great new vaudeville act," said Little Kiwi, eyeing the walkway. "Later we—"

"Should we eat outside?" said Dennis Savage quickly. "Or is it too hot?"

"Oh, there were such breathtaking men on the beach as we walked there," Uncle Dave said. This sounded so odd, however true, that we all stopped and looked at him. "I mean," he added, "it's quite a place you've got here."

"He's getting the hang of it," said Dennis Savage, setting lunch out.

No. It would be some while yet; he had much to learn. As we ate, he asked the questions one usually hears from the raw recruit—where are the places, who are the people, what are the terms, how do you *know*? Never in my life was it more clear how fully developed gay life had become in Stonewall's mere fifteen years, how much more there was to being gay than to being homosexual. Sexual taste you can be born with; but gay is a host of techniques to be acquired.

It's interesting, too, how differently the system tends in other gay places. San Francisco's gay, for instance, is less elegant and knowing and demanding than New York's, more fraternal and expedient and amiable. In New York, gays tell the recruits you must *become*—if you can. In San Francisco, they say You have *arrived*.

Perhaps Uncle Dave ought to have gone west instead of east, for with his big lumbering physique and shaggy blond mustache he'd already be in, whereas in New York he'd have a lot of nouns to memorize and concepts to assimilate. I'll give him some credit: he was moving fast.

"I don't know," he said as we brought the plates in. "Somehow I was expecting quiche."

"Real men don't cook quiche," Dennis Savage told him. "Real men *order* quiche."

"Real men," said Little Kiwi, "long to watch Bauhaus dance on a grape."

I was about to say something pointed, but Dennis Savage pulled Little Kiwi over to the sink to do the dishes—which unfortunately left me with Uncle Dave. I grabbed *Martin Chuzzlewit* and hotfooted it outside, but he followed me and, before I could sit down, said, "I hold the opinion that one of us owes the other an apology and I don't know who that is, but if you won't say you're sorry, I will. Now, how about that?"

Tell me, boys and girls, who can resist such an overture? I apologized for being short with him and we shook hands. Again *Martin Chuzzlewit* bit the dust, as we talked over breaking into the Circuit, and I then let him in on the Secret Sex practices of Dennis Savages, but the subject overheard us and came roaring out to chide me in what I can only term a viciously inflamed manner, and while he was out of the house Little Kiwi gave Bauhaus a grape to dance on (actually he just rolls over them on his back, whimpering), and then Little Kiwi came out and said, "Hey, everybody look at Bauhaus," and I gave Dennis Savage a few smacks to keep him in shape, and Little Kiwi put *Cats* on the stereo so Bauhaus could dance to something, and Little Kiwi told Dave, "They get fifty bucks for this on Broadway."

And Dave told Little Kiwi that it was amazing how much he looked like Seth when he was in his twenties, and that in fact the boy still looked the way he did when he was a little kid.

"He behaves the same, too," I put in.

And Bauhaus calmed down, and there was one of those pauses, and then Dave asked Dennis Savage if gay life was always like this.

I could see Dennis Savage thinking, Maybe, except when somebody dies—so I quickly suggested we take Dave on a tour of The Pines and the Grove, so he could see all of gay from clones to queens; and we could end up at tea, where the houseboys must be obeyed.

Away we went, Dennis Savage and I recounting events long past, some sage and some silly; and the names of those we knew and only knew of came rolling out. Here was where the last of the great drug fires occurred, there the house where the most spectacular party was given, here the site of the first and only annual Looks Contest, there the house so desirable that the wife gave up the kids in the divorce settlement in order to keep it.

"It must really give you a break to be so close to your history," said Dave. "To be a walk away from all the things you've done." He looked ahead at Dennis Savage and Little Kiwi, walking with their arms around each other. "Is that common, to walk like that?"

"It's more Grove style. The Pines generally tells its tales through eye contact."

He and I had slowed to a stop, and he said, "You know, I'm just beginning to realize how much there is in all this. Yet anyone can do it. I still remember, when Virgil left for the east . . . and he was so open about it. I thought, You just go and do it."

The other two had stopped and turned.

"Is he," Dave went on, "what you'd call . . . well, typical of life in the gay community?"

"Little Kiwi? I wouldn't call him typical of life on earth. How'd he get that name, anyway?"

Dennis Savage and Little Kiwi started back to get us.

"Oh, his sister Anne had a doll named Kiwi. A little man doll. And when Virgil was an infant she started calling him Little Kiwi, and the family took it up. I was the only one who called him by his Lord-given name."

"Why?"

"Because he asked me to. A man's going to grow up sometime, and his name's a part of that, I guess."

"So is his sexuality," I said.

He nodded. "So the little birds leave the nest."

"The big ones, too," I noted.

"Well, but he was the favorite in the family." Little Kiwi had reached us and was staring at Dave. "And it surely tore them up when he lit out of the state."

Little Kiwi put his arms around Dave and Dave riffled his hair.

"It surely tore them up, that's true."

"Well, *really*!" said a disgruntled wimpy older man, edging past us with, I expect, his wife.

"Yes, really," said Dave, in a contemplative manner.

"Oh dear," said the wife. Some people have to have the last word.

Well, we did the Grove, and we did tea, and we did the Pantry, and we did cocktails on the deck, and we did dinner, and during dinner Dave and I went back to a theme we had, shall we say, touched on earlier: that of the timing of self-awareness. How could Dave not have known he was a homosexual all those years? And Dave admitted that he'd had the knowledge all along, but could not accept it till the night he got into bed with a man he wanted sexually.

"What man was that?" asked Little Kiwi.

"Your father," said Dave.

And we were quite, quite still.

"Just remember how confusing puberty can be," he said. "Stimuli of so many kinds working on your senses. Heavy pressures from your gang to do what everyone else does. Your self-confidence trying to get organized. And all through this you're randy as hell. Of course you'd be confused—confused about a lot of things. You take a chance on a girl at a party, kiss her, and instead of getting mad she goes along with it and does nice things to your ego. So of course you think you're in love. That lasts for three days. Then it's some other girl—same thing. Another girl. Then your first crush. It's like flying to another planet— and that lasts three weeks. And you've got a best friend, too, and you know how teenagers get sometimes, swimming together, or rough-housing, and all. So, okay, you think he's got a great body, what's wrong with that? You're conscious of your own body, so why shouldn't you notice his? You get hard thinking about him, but teen-agers are always getting boners. You wake up from a very unusual dream, and he was in it . . . can you be blamed for what you dream? Maybe you killed someone in a dream once—that doesn't make you a murderer, does it?"

"Confusion," I said. "I guess I can see it."

"Besides, you don't want to think you're queer, so you're busy twist-ing everything around for yourself, rationalizing. And since you can't figure out what two men would do in bed, anyway, your dreams aren't all that risky. Meanwhile you're proving you're a man with the available girls. It gets so you can hold mutual bone-off sessions with your best friend and think of it as he-men keeping in shape for the ladies. And finally there comes one time, one event or something, with another guy . . . and I guess that's when you either face up to the truth and stop double-talking yourself, or you decide to live according to the confusion and turn away from the truth." He put his hand on Little Kiwi's head and stroked his hair. "Like father, like son," he mused, as Little Kiwi blushed.

"I'm dying to hear how this comes out," I said, "but since we're also responsible for introducing you to gay, why don't we walk along the beach before it gets too windy to bear and you can finish the story in the famous magic moonlight we have here?"

So we all got into sweaters and hooded sweatshirts—Dennis Savage had to outfit Dave somewhat; we wouldn't let him on the beach out of uniform—and we put Bauhaus on his leash, and off we went to the water's edge where the hard sand is, and there we made Dave turn back to gaze upon the strip of lights that comprises what may be the only gay colony in the history of the world. You say, "What of the Grove?", but the Grove was founded back in the days of the haunted homosexual, of the loving war of queen and hustler, when to be homosexual was to be faggot, queer, bent—Franklin Pangborn or Lucius Beebe, instead of . . . well, for instance, reader: you. The Grove is not gay. The Pines, for all its attitude and casually frantic code of behavior, is gay. And as we regarded it, now in its blasted morale of chaste amusements, of the no-fault cruising of look-but-don't-touch and the survivor mentality that hits those who have simply lived to be thirty-five, we began to tell Dave of its days of glory. Of riding the ferry in a bracing air of anticipation, being able to throw off our covers and be; or of heading for tea, a whole house in force, just to see who our people were, who we are; or of meeting, some weekend, someone's older friend, who would unveil forgotten mysteries of the pre-Stonewall days. Liberty, self-knowledge, anthropology: culture. Our place, in our time. Manhattan is ours, too, in a way—in several ways—but Manhattan we must share. In The Pines, we are the majority.

We all sounded off so thoroughly that we thrilled ourselves, and fell into silence, abashed at our exploits. Even Bauhaus was awed—quiet, anyway. We began to walk, though it was too cold and we should have gone back. And then Dave set in.

"During rush period, when the houses single out certain freshmen and make a play for them, we held weekly meetings, where we would discuss the possibilities. And Seth . . . Virgil's daddy . . . was on top of everyone's list. He was a very . . . attractive young man then. Attractive young man? Do you say that?"

"We say, a beautiful boy," I told him.

"A beautiful boy. Just like Virgil now."

Little Kiwi, still learning to endure these effusions, tightened his grip on Dennis Savage's hand.

"He was an outstanding character, too, on campus, because he went around in tweed suits all the time, and solid ties, and we all thought he was from the east. Like the Great Gatsby."

"Gatsby was from the midwest," I said. "He dazzled the east."

"He dazzled us, anyway. The girls were crazy for him. He really had to fight them off. That was part of his importance to the house, because most of the brothers were in the business school, and they didn't get to know many girls that way. I think they thought Seth might be able to set them up. Just walking around the campus with him you'd meet girls. But there was something else, too. Some of the brothers . . . no. No. It's just that he was very attractive. Beautiful. And everyone responds to that. So he was the first man keyed. And he accepted it, and he fell right in with everything—the brothers, the politics, the code. All the things you take for granted in a fraternity. That was what we called a 'solid man.' At the meetings, the question was always, 'Is he solid?' And Seth was. He was a little reserved, but underneath it he was very sure about things. Sure of himself. And that can be galling to men who aren't all that solid. They're going to go after it, test it, shove it up against a wall and see how solid it really is. The trouble with pledging is the hazing. That's when all the worst guys in the house come out of the woodwork. We tried to make sure we didn't have any worst guys, but somehow they get in. You know—impressive during rushing when they turn on their fireworks, then they get gloomy and solitary."

"Sounds like Dennis Savage's lovers," I would have joked at any other time; but this was a serious night in our lives. We walked along, listening. The wind was bitter, but the house lights cheered us.

"The worst of it is, those guys always take positions of command during hazing. They dream up the programs, administer the disciplines, run the sweat sessions. You can imagine what goes on. And they really went after Seth. It happened in other houses, too. Not to the big handsome guys, but the slight handsome guys. They get victimized. Even tormented. Well, I was Seth's paddle brother, so I could talk to them about it, throw some weight in his corner. They'd ease up on him for two or three days. It'd start in again. And I'd . . . I'd look up from my desk, you know, with your marketing data and your actuarial tables, and the books piled up, and your notes, and the papers of something like a hundred brothers before me. In a T-shirt and shorts, with the fire in the grate. The day was dying down. I'd look up at this . . . beautiful boy in one of his suits, looking so bright and so . . . dismal all at once. And he would ask for my help. And I just wanted to sweep him up and . . . and what? What would I have done after that?"

"My pop was like that?" asked Little Kiwi.

"Didn't he seem like that to you, ever?"

"I always loved him," said Little Kiwi. "I didn't know he was tormented."

"Well, I took care of that, finally. It really created a problem in the house, to interfere with the hazing command. That's not how it works. You're supposed to let them . . ."

"Give attitude," said Dennis Savage.

"Give what?"

"You'll find out."

"Anyway, I got the pledge masters to write what we in my business call letters of assurance to just about everyone in the house. It really put a damper on hell night—not that we had all that terrible a hell night in the first place. Some houses . . . well, you were lucky to get out in one piece."

"The olive race," I murmured.

Dave asked me, "What house did you pledge?"

I shook my head. "We didn't have anything like that. But the Betas and the Dekes . . ."

Dave nodded.

"What olives?" asked Little Kiwi.

"The race ran up the back stairs," I explained. "Five flights. Every pledge in the nude, with an olive in his behind. The loser had to eat the olives."

Even Bauhaus shuddered.

"Each club has its style," I said. "You find the club that suits your style."

"That's what I don't have, right?" said Dave. "The gay club style?"

"Stick with us, kid," I said, "and you'll be wearing leather."

"When my pop came into your room," said Little Kiwi, "was he sad? To ask for your help? Was he afraid?"

"He wasn't sad, but he was afraid. And that's the corn on the cob. Because he came to my room on a night in February, very late. I closed my books and we talked for a while. It had been snowing that day, a real blizzard on. I said he'd better stay over at the house. No point in getting wrecked in the snow."

"How far did he live from the house?" Little Kiwi asked.

"Three blocks. Four. But distance wasn't . . . what was happening then. I wanted to put him in my bed, because he was so vulnerable that minute, and that's why he was afraid—he knew what I was doing. I wanted to get him out of those suits. The ties. He even wore hats. He had a little line of hair that ran down his belly from his navel, and it was as if I could see it right through his clothes. I wanted to trace my finger along it. I wanted to hold his body. I knew that. No rationalizing. I wanted to touch him."

"My pop was afraid?" asked Little Kiwi.

"I believe so. But he didn't seem afraid, really. I turned out the lights and we got undressed . . . talking the whole time, you know. I was cool. I just smiled. And Seth smiled, too. But once I put him in that bed I got my hands on him, and I wasn't confused anymore. I was hard, and he knew it, because we were edged up together, spoon-style. I wanted to squeeze him to death, to have him. But I didn't know how to have him. I wanted to love him. And I told him that. Just those words. Because if I didn't say it, no one would ever know I felt that way, including me. And he turned around to face me, and he had his arms around me. But he wouldn't say anything. I knew what I wanted to hear, but I didn't know how to make him say it. So I felt down for that line of hair, and I stroked it. I said, 'How does that feel?' and I heard him gasp, but he didn't say anything. And, well, we kept on like that. And we started to kiss each other. All over. And we were juicing like crazy. But I might have been dreaming. I might well have been dreaming, I can guess. I've thought about it so often, I honestly don't know what happened by now. Virgil."

He reached for Little Kiwi, and we all stopped walking.

"Seeing you grow up. You're so much like him. Even Anne is like him. Your whole family is like your father. Whenever I look at you, I see him in my room, asking for help."

"I see him decking my allowance and such," said Little Kiwi.

"You should have been there when you were born, Virgil," said Dave. "That boy loved you as he loved nothing else on earth."

We walked in silence for a time.

"Let's start back," Dennis Savage said.

"Is that all the story?" asked Little Kiwi.

"I guess it is," said Dave. "I never got him into bed again. We were still friends, and when he moved into the house the next year we were almost inseparable. We even had the same major, accounting. I guess that doesn't matter. But sometimes we would talk real straight to each other, and once I referred to that night in the blizzard, and Seth denied it ever happened."

"How could he?" asked Dennis Savage.

"Press him," I urged, two decades late.

"He denied it," said Dave. "He looked me in the eye and said no. He seemed a little surprised that I would suggest that we could even . . . and he didn't get stiff on me or back away. He was very calm about it. So we stayed friends. But it had never happened. There was nothing between us except . . . except . . ."

I thought that if that *except* could be explained to the world, George Will would be out of business.

"My pop," said Little Kiwi, moving up to Dave with something on his mind. Dennis Savage and I hung back, allowing Bauhaus to lead us into the driftwood to reflect and comment.

"Aren't you going to rush up and eavesdrop?" Dennis Savage asked me. "Invade our privacy for some putrid story?"

"Putrid is right," I replied. "There is no story. Nothing has happened."

"We learned something, didn't we?"

"We learned that entering into any group will afford one assistants and imposters. Who doesn't know that already? Every club has someone at the door with a list."

A shadow moved at our house as we approached.

"What the hell was that?" asked Dennis Savage.

It moved again. We had left the lights on, and saw with reasonable clarity. Someone was on our porch. Someone waved something in the air.

As we moved up from the water, Dennis Savage tensed, Bauhaus began to bark, Dave looked from one of us to another, and Little Kiwi tore away to run up to the house. I heard him screaming but the wind was wrong and I couldn't hear the words. No matter. I got there soon enough. Bauhaus was leaping about and Little Kiwi had his arms around Carlo, who had been waving at us with a cowboy hat. Carlo threw his arms around us all, and when he got to Dave, he said, "Where'd you come from?" holding him by the shoulders. Dave looked like a character in a Robert Ludlam novel who gets the chance to slip into something by Richard Price.

"Can I get some of that?" said Dave, and Carlo embraced him, too. "Some more," Dave added, taking hold of Carlo as if to kiss his mouth, and Carlo pulled back; but I said, "He's been living in Cleveland," and Carlo grabbed Dave and took him so fervently Little Kiwi asked Dennis Savage if he ought to take Bauhaus for a walk.

"He just *got* walked."

"Who are you?" Carlo asked Dave.

"Carlo's back!" cried Little Kiwi.

"Is this permanent?" asked Dennis Savage, somewhat dangerously.

"We should drink on this," I said. "One gringo custom I've always been comfortable with."

"Who are you?" Carlo asked Dave again. "Why were you in Cleveland?"

"Why were you in South Dakota?" I muttered, heading inside with Dennis Savage to get liquor. We were too full up from dinner to contemplate any serious intake, and decided to ransack the liquor closet for brandy: a toast and a swallow. Carlo's "Who are you?" danced in my head, and as Dennis Savage rummaged I tried to imagine defining who Dave is to Carlo, and who Carlo is to Dave: explaining, in other words—to a man so imbued with the liberty of the sexy brotherhood that he offered to give it up rather than see it dully survive—how another man might be born to it yet try not to need it. Or explaining—to the man who went gringo simply because the world plays by gringo rules—that another man would make the informal challenging of those rules his life's work.

Heck, come to that, could I even explain Carlo to Carlo? I have tried to set him forth in these pages so others may comprehend, but Carlo believes a poem should not mean but be.

"Look at that," said Dennis Savage, coming up for air with a bottle of Grand Marnier, the label so faded it might have been older than we are. "It's funny about New York," he said. "You never see anybody buy this stuff. No one I know drinks it. Yet when you need a bottle there's always one there, way at the back."

"Pour," I said.

Little Kiwi came in wearing Carlo's cowboy hat. "There are two men making out on our deck," he said.

"Could it be love at last?" Dennis Savage asked, setting the glasses on a tray.

"Too early to say," Carlo replied as he brought Dave in by the arm.

"So," said Dennis Savage, passing the tray.

We all looked at Dave; it seemed his toast to offer. "Confusion to our enemies," he proposed.

"My mother would like you," I told him. "That's her favorite toast."

Then we all sat and talked—about Dave's new apartment (on Second and Fifty-sixth), about how best to enjoy one's first New York autumn, about whether or not it's fair to continue calling Virgil by a childhood nickname (it isn't, but we will), and about how long Carlo had returned for. He was evasive, but it was clear this was no mere trip. He was even planning to resecure his old place on East Third Street, a ghastly third-floor walkup he only uses when he's between engagements. It has been sublet so often over the years that the door has given up on keys; when it hears footsteps, it opens.

Some music was played, a late-night pizza snack was served (my famous Tree Tavern recipe), and at length the parties dispersed. Dennis Savage and Little Kiwi went to bed, Carlo, stretched out in Dave's arms for the previous half-hour, fell asleep, and I went up to my room to start this story—because, in the end, something had happened.

I put the lamp on the bed, lay on my stomach, and began to write; and I've taken it down pretty much as it happened. I've registered doubt, earlier in this book, about writing about everyone but myself; but when I put myself into a lead role I feel co-opted, disarmed, uncouth. Writing autobiographically should enhance one's image with dear lies; but a voice inside me warns that clones are invalid, kids are their own tragedy, that a drag queen should not tell but show.

Ontology, huh? That means I need a drink. I slipped downstairs to mix a double vodka—scotch doesn't suit The Pines somehow; it's a metropolitan liquor—and there I found Carlo and Dave still on the couch, asleep. I went into a vacant bedroom, copped a blanket, and covered them. Dave stirred awake.

He yawned. "Is it always so easy as this? To get a man?"

"Oh no. Some never get a man at all. And to come out, move to Manhattan, and get Carlo on a couch . . . that's a feat."

A Delilah is vodka on ice with crushed pepper, a Samson takes lemon peel, and a Samson and Delilah gets both. As I collected the makings of a both, Dave asked, "Why is he called Carlo? He doesn't look Spanish, except his hair and cheekbones."

"A wise old queen named him that in his first year in New York. He said Carlo needed a glamorous name because he was glamorous. Just one name, like all the greats—Charlemagne, Napoleon, Lilo. Something simple. Precise. Charismatic."

"Like your lad himself," said Dave, stroking Carlo's hair. "What *is* his name?"

"Ripley Smith."

Dave smiled. "Couldn't he have been Rip? Wouldn't that be a glamorous name? He looks like a Rip."

I sliced the lemon. Make it a hunk of a slice, for a double. Lot of work tonight, yes? "Be very careful with him," I said, grinding the pepper. "He looks tough, but he ain't."

I lit a candle. As I turned, drink in the right hand and candle in the left, Carlo wheezed and squirmed and hugged Dave in a hunger of death.

"He's exhausted," Dave told me. "He kept falling asleep as we talked."

"He probably traveled directly from Aberdeen, South Dakota to here. He's very impulsive."

"Why the candle?"

"I've a yen to write by candlelight."

"What are you writing?"

"Oh . . . a story about . . . you want anything before I go?"

"I want to hold this man in my arms for the rest of my life."

I nodded. "Romantic, nice. But wait till you get him into bed."

"Is he good?"

"We don't say good. We say hot. And he's not hot—he's sacramental."

I looked in on Dennis Savage and Little Kiwi. The latter, as usual, had thrashed himself into a position half on and off the bed. I righted him, and his eyes shot open. He breathed out, "Come back with Anne." Then he was still.

The house was now dark and abed, and I pulled my window open a bit to inhale the enchanted air and take in the slap of the water. Something had happened after all; yes. I thought thanks were in order: but whom to thank? I've been atheist as long as I've been gay— but I thought that if there was/were/might be a God, it could not be that paranoid Old Testament sheik with the plagues and the tantrums. I looked farther back, to the all-mother, probably less cruel and more forgiving than her male successor. As Carlo says, when you take a problem to your father, he switches you; your mother gives you Cream of Wheat.

So I thought, Hello, let's have some proof. If You exist, show us a lightning flash. You got five.

Nothing.

Maybe that was the wrong test. So I thought, Hello, if You exist, turn on the stereo. You got five.

Nothing.

So I thought, Okay, You don't exist; and the wind swept into my room and blew the fucking candle out.